Also by Michael Blake:

DANCES WITH WOLVES

AIRMAN MORTENSEN

Michael Blake

IVY BOOKS • NEW YORK

Ivy Books
Published by Ballantine Books
Copyright © 1991 by Michael Blake

All rights reserved under International and Pan-American Copyright Conventions. Published in the United States by Ballantine Books, a division of Random House, Inc., New York, and simultaneously in Canada by Random House of Canada Limited, Toronto.

Library of Congress Catalog Card Number: 91–073940

ISBN 0–8041–1150–2

This edition published by arrangement with Seven Wolves Publishing

Manufactured in the United States of America

First Ballantine Books Edition: February 1993

Map by Charles Benefiel

Here's to youth and beauty
Here's to brains and art

Here's to
Sabrina Judge
and
Jocelyn Heaney

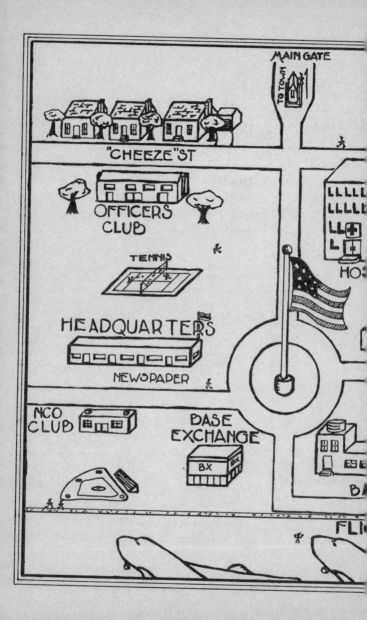

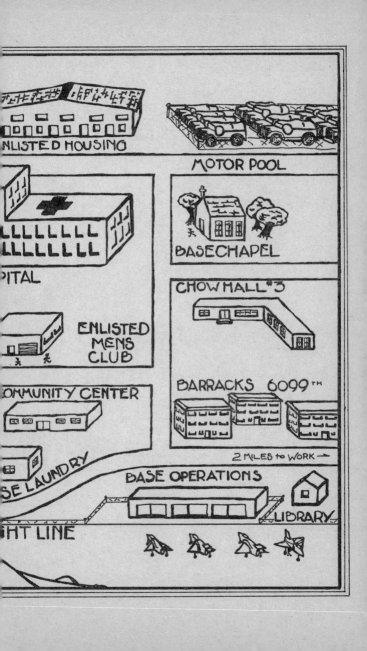

Three Days

☆ 1 ☆

Spring in southern New Mexico is a dirty time. The wind blows all winter and by spring the surface of the earth starts to rise into the air. There are days when it's hard to see from house to house. It's not worth going outside unless there's an emergency. It's just as well to sit inside with everything covered up. The dust still works its way under doors and windowsills, but there's no velocity indoors. It still cakes on the teeth but doesn't sting the face.

On a Friday in 1966 Airman Mortensen was inside. He was sitting on a commode in a U.S. Air Force latrine, smoking cigarettes and farting away his dead time. The latrine had been his constant environment for a month and there was no end in sight.

Airman Mortensen had gotten in trouble. He was going to be court-martialed and while he waited for the board to convene they had stuck him in the latrines. Each morning for the last four weeks, while his friends went off to work as cooks or guards or clerks, Airman Mortensen had stayed behind to clean latrines, two big ones on each floor of the three-story barracks where he lived.

He fucked off as much as he could. The fuck-off time was swelling. He was becoming an expert in the art of making shit cans and urinals and sinks and showers look good without doing much cleaning.

But on this Friday morning it was hard to dream away

the time. The dust storm outside was a bad one and it was impossible to keep anything looking clean.

He dropped the stub of the cigarette between his legs and heard it hiss faintly as it hit the water. The hiss was faint because outside the wind was blowing so hard that it made a shrieking sound in the latrine. It must have been gusting at fifty miles an hour.

There was no way he'd be able to hear the First Sergeant coming down the hall. Usually he could hear the topkick's footfalls in time to get back to work; but with all this noise covering the approach, his chances of getting caught were good. And getting caught would mean latrine duty on Saturday, maybe Sunday too.

It wasn't worth it, so Airman Mortensen got off the commode, opened the stall door and picked up where he left off—steel wooling the fixtures on a bank of sinks. His hands were sore because little pieces of the metal kept breaking off and embedding themselves in his fingertips. But it wasn't too bad. After a month he was as used to the little needles in his hands as he was to the ever-present stink of waste and disinfectant all around him.

He looked up and saw himself in the mirror. He smiled. There were faded outlines on his sleeve where the chevron and two stripes had once been. He'd taken them off himself, slicing through the threads with a razor blade.

It was supposed to be a terrible, humiliating punishment, a branding. But he had a good feeling about the brand. It marked him as a rebel; made him stand out in a standardized society.

As he thought about this, his face clouded. That lieutenant colonel in the Comm Squad was really out to get him. That's what he heard. At some point—nobody would tell him when—there was going to be a court-martial. And he was guilty. He'd disobeyed a direct order from an officer. There was no telling what would happen. He didn't want to think about it.

A strange question jumped into Airman Mortensen's head as he watched his teenage face.

'I wonder if they can tell I'm a virgin,' he thought.

He studied the face carefully but could not decide. At eighteen there was a freshness about it, a freshness that carried a touch of fear. But the fear was masked well, he thought, balanced with a sense of purpose.

Airman Mortensen shook his head at the idea of the virgin question. It had popped into his mind a lot lately and he wished it would go away. He was sick of thinking about it. It was just something to get over, like a cold. Only different.

One of the heavy latrine doors swished open and Airman Mortensen twitched into a working posture as the First Sergeant walked in and stood quietly, letting the door shut behind him like a vacuum. He was flat-footed and erect, his legs slightly apart. His small, intelligent eyes sized up the situation. He looked official in the neatly pressed blue shirt and trousers and tie. He reminded Airman Mortensen of a seasoned manservant.

The First Sergeant cut no slack, but there was a fairness about him which was reassuring. He had taken Airman Mortensen aside when he first started in the latrines and told him to watch his step. The latrine duty was a setup, he said. The disobeyed order was a chickenshit rap and they put him in the latrines hoping that he would snap and do a bigger crime. Airman Mortensen was glad for this information but they were still adversaries. It was only natural that, from the beginning, he would try to fuck off and the First Sergeant would try to catch him at it.

The topkick stepped quietly to a sink and brushed at it with a freckled hand. Then he spoke, his soft voice echoing off the tiled walls.

"You're behind."

"I'm going to be behind all day."

The First Sergeant lowered his voice even more.

"Then I'm going to be on your ass all day, Mortensen."

Airman Mortensen sighed.

"The goddamn dust is everywhere, Sarge. What can I do about that? I can't stop it."

The First Sergeant thought about the dust. For a moment he watched it float in front of his face.

"There's a telephone call for you in the GQ."

"Who is it?"

"How the fuck am I supposed to know?"

"Can I answer it?"

The First Sergeant stared at Airman Mortensen, amazed and disgusted.

"Why do you think I came all the way up here?"

He stepped aside and let the latrine king pass through the door.

☆ **2** ☆

Unlike most of the soldiers, Airman Mortensen had civilian friends. One of them was on the telephone, calling from town. He had found the girl.

Airman Mortensen didn't say anything at first. Then he asked, "What girl?"

"The girl you wanted me to find, butthole. The one from the dance."

"Pat . . . the German girl?"

"Yeah, I found her. And guess what?"

"What?"

"She lives on base. Her dad's an NCO."

"No shit?"

"No shit . . . I got the number."

She was someone he didn't know. A few weeks back they'd danced all night at the Bricklayer's Hall downtown. That didn't happen often at those dances. The girls were usually too nervous to stick with one guy the whole night.

Airman Mortensen had been nervous too. He hadn't said much. She had an accent. He'd asked her about that and she said it was German. She was small and had dark hair. She knew he was in the Air Force. Otherwise, they only talked about the songs after each dance.

But there was a pull between them that everyone noted. Even Airman Mortensen's friends had kidded him about dancing all night with the small, dark girl.

Somehow he lost her when the dance broke up. He searched the kids who were hanging around in the parking lot. He cruised the drive-ins and a couple of walk-in restaurants. But she had disappeared.

In the days that followed, he took the extraordinary step of putting the word out to his civilian friends. He really wanted to find that Pat girl. He really liked her. Now she had been found. And she was on the base, right under his nose.

Airman Mortensen mulled it over in the GQ's office. There were some things to consider. Should he call her now or wait till nighttime? What should he say? Would she remember him? Was the whole idea crazy? He came full circle and decided to phone. The other end rang several times before someone answered. It was her. And it was easier than he could have imagined. She remembered him. She was glad he had called. When he said he'd been looking for her she seemed pleased. When he said he'd like to see her she answered with an echo.

"I'd like to see you too."

When he said, "How about tonight?" there was silence.

Then she said, "Alright."

The latrine king floated through the afternoon. The bane of the shit cans no longer affected him. They seemed suddenly small in his life. He was too busy dreaming of new possibilities. At six o'clock he would be seeing her. By nightfall they might be kissing. Later they might be making out. They might fall in love. All of this was possible.

The First Sergeant checked on him several times that afternoon and each time he found Airman Mortensen busy in ways that seemed genuine. The dust storm tailed off after lunch and by quitting time at four-thirty Airman Mortensen had caught up. Everything was done.

The topkick inspected the cans and pronounced each one passable. He told the airman to knock off. Then he watched the boy in trouble clomp down the hall in his brogans. He watched Airman Mortensen strip off his fatigue shirt and swing it cavalierly over a shoulder. He watched until the airman reached the end of the hall and disappeared down a stairway. He watched because of the whistling. Airman Mortensen had whistled all the way and the First Sergeant couldn't imagine why.

☆ 3 ☆

On Friday night at six o'clock there was little activity on base. The other soldiers were still in the barracks, dousing themselves with scents and powders, hoping that tonight would be the night they would talk to girls. They dreamed of much more but the first hope was for talk.

Airman Mortensen stood alone on the wide sidewalk in front of the enlisted men's club. The early drinkers were inside denting their paychecks but most guys wouldn't start drifting in till seven. Airman Mortensen thought the club was a sad place and rarely went there. But it didn't matter now. His privileges had been suspended. And besides, he was waiting for somebody.

He didn't go for dousing any more than he did for the club, but as he stood on the sidewalk he couldn't help checking his outfit. He wasn't sure about the short-sleeved madras shirt and Levis. Maybe they were too boring. He looked at his feet and saw the heavy Mexican sandals peeking out from his trouser legs. They weren't boring. He always felt good when they were on his feet. They were against the dress code.

Across the tree-lined street he could see the ominous line of ugly buildings where they all lived. He watched his own barracks for a few moments. It was dusk and most of the rooms were lit. He could hear distant shouts of horseplay.

He remembered the words on the telephone and felt encouraged. They were words that promised talk. He

9

would be talking in a little while. Those poor bastards in the barracks were hoping. Ninety-nine percent of them had no chance.

A few minutes after six he saw a light-colored Volkswagen sedan turn onto the street leading to the enlisted men's club. It was moving slowly in his direction and he knew it was her.

As the car got closer he could see more than one girl. There were three.

Airman Mortensen bent to the Volkswagen's open window as it pulled to a stop and stared into the cool face of a girl he had never seen. Her brown eyes were very big but they showed nothing. She gave her cigarette a casual wave and in a deep voice said flatly:

"Hi, I'm Jancy."

Airman Mortensen introduced himself as he glanced at the driver. She was older and looked more open than the girl with the deep voice. She wore her hair the same. It was long and straight and parted on the side. A graceful patch of it swept low across her forehead and was hitched to one side with a barrette. When she smiled, a set of dimples appeared at the corners of her mouth.

Pat was in the back seat, smiling coyly through the coarse, black, untied hair spreading in front of her face. She tipped her head in the driver's direction, toward the girl with the dimples.

"That's Claire," she said.

Airman Mortensen didn't know what to say, so he said, "What're you guys doing?"

"We were just hanging around the house," said the girl with the deep voice. Her big, unblinking eyes remained on Airman Mortensen. "Wanna go over there?"

The latrine king squeezed into the back seat.

The ride didn't last long and being outnumbered, he didn't say much. He just listened to the girls and answered their questions. Claire and Jancy turned out to be sisters. Jancy was fifteen. Claire was seventeen and Pat was sixteen. They were best friends.

Between the lines of conversation, he was able to make a few observations. The sisters were there to see that Pat wouldn't be alone with him in the crucial early stages of their first meeting. Claire's face (which he could study in the rearview mirror without being detected) was wonderfully open, like a friend's. He also observed that the girls' high spirits weren't altogether natural. He was sure they had been drinking.

Airman Mortensen noted too that the VW's turns were taking them to a section of the base which housed officers and their families. He grew more watchful as the little bug swung onto a street which everyone knew was reserved for field-grade officers. The common soldiers called it Cheeze Street. Big Cheezes. It made Airman Mortensen nervous to be traveling down Cheeze Street.

Without warning, Claire whipped the VW into the driveway of a large corner house, screeched to a stop and shut off the engine. It was the one house on base that all six thousand residents knew. More precisely, all six thousand residents knew who *lived* in the house.

The girls piled out as if it was nothing. Airman Mortensen didn't move.

William Brill was young for a colonel, maybe forty-five. He'd made rank quickly. He was going to make general in a matter of weeks. He was suave and dedicated and soulless. He was the base commander and Airman Mortensen, slick-sleeve latrine king, was sitting in his driveway.

He watched Pat and Jancy skip into the house. It was Claire that realized he wasn't getting out. She stuck her carefree face through the driver's-side window. Airman Mortensen watched the dimples form again as she smiled.

"Aren't you coming?"

Airman Mortensen stared at the front door for a moment.

"This is the base commander's house."

"It's okay . . . my parents aren't here." Her smile was growing. "They went to a funeral in Kansas. They're not coming back till Sunday night."

"Oh."

He still didn't want to get out of the car but now there was no excuse to stay.

"We've got beer," she said, pulling the driver's seat forward.

Airman Mortensen stuck a sandal on the pavement and squirmed out. Together they started for the front door. He tried to remain calm.

"We've been drinking beer since about three o'clock," she said.

☆ **4** ☆

There were two more girls inside the house. They were about Jancy's age and very shy.

For the first hour or so he sat in the kitchen, sucking on a tall can of Country Club malt liquor, trying to believe what could not be believed. Five girls and Airman Mortensen, the latrine king, drinking beer in the base commander's house on a Friday night.

While he stayed put, the girls moved around the house like actors in a goofball movie, running in and out of doors spaced along a hallway.

When someone landed in the kitchen they would ask

a question or make a comment but mainly they just zoomed around. Jancy introduced the two new girls to him but Airman Mortensen was already overloaded and forgot the names as soon as they were spoken.

He sat and drank and watched. An Animals record was playing in another room. He tapped out the beat of each song with his foot.

When the malt liquor began to take effect Airman Mortensen's fuck-it threshold lowered. No one would believe this, but what did it matter? He started another sixteen ouncer and began a breeze commentary with himself.

'I am in the base commander's house. I am with five girls. Two of them are the base commander's daughters. I have a thing for their friend and everyone knows it. That's why they are flying around the house like bridesmaid's before the wedding. So what? I am here and that's all. I am fortunate to be here. I'm going to kick out the jams this night. I'm going to get drunk and have a fucking great time for as long as this lasts.'

He felt like a little stroll and moved into the living room. He saw the stereo. Records were stacked all over the floor.

Taking up a large part of one wall was a family portrait. It was a color photograph, carefully posed, blown up and ugly. It was Colonel Brill alright; but he didn't look himself. He was out of uniform and smiling broadly. His wife was at his shoulder. She looked like a nice lady with a lot of secrets. The girls were leaning in on the other side of the photograph, dressed in churchy outfits. Jancy was smiling broadly like her father and Airman Mortensen was struck at how much they resembled each other, especially in the eyes. And their smiles were exactly the same—they both looked fake.

Claire was hanging over Jancy's shoulder and Airman Mortensen studied her image a little longer than the

others. Everything checked out—the plump, round
cheeks, the dimples, the bright, mischievous eyes, the
long, sand-colored hair. She looked real. That was an
accomplishment in a picture like this.

He sifted through the stacks of music and found a
Byrds record he liked. Feeling very comfortable now,
he put the record on the turntable, pushed the volume
up and stretched out on Colonel Brill's carpet. He lay
on his back with his eyes shut and let the music pour
through his ears and into his bloodstream.

Lured by the sound, Jancy appeared in the big living
room. She was aware of his presence but did not speak
or look at the airman sprawled on the ground. Holding
a beer in one hand, she windmilled around to the music, her eyes on the floor.

Pat appeared and the two girls began dancing as part-
ners. Airman Mortensen rolled onto his stomach and
watched them for a few minutes before he too decided
to dance. He kicked his sandals off and began to stomp
around the room like an Indian.

It was a curious sort of involvement for the three
dancers. He didn't try to be at one with the girls. He
didn't take anyone's hand. He didn't lean into someone's face to get off a witty comment. They were all
feeling the music and that was plenty. It made them a
unit.

The record was half over before he opened his eyes
and realized that Claire had joined them. Her eyes were
closed. Her long hair was flying anywhere it wanted.

The four danced through one side of the record without stopping. Airman Mortensen didn't want it to end
but as he flipped the disc over he saw Pat and Jancy
wander into the kitchen for more beer. Pat gave him a
split-second look, one of those glances that promised
something more. Somehow the glance rubbed him
wrong. He didn't like it.

He looked at Claire and the image of her held him. She was standing alone, suspended in the middle of the room. Her head was bowed. Her eyes were still closed. She was waiting for the music to move her again. Her commitment was something to see and Airman Mortensen watched her for as long as he dared.

At last he lowered the needle. It made contact with the record and music boomed through the speakers. She didn't move right away. She let the music build. Gradually, it put her legs and feet in motion. Then her arms began to move.

When she was up to speed Airman Mortensen began to move too. They danced through several songs, apart but together, united in waves of sound as they spun around Colonel Brill's living room.

Pat and Jancy came back. They laughed and talked as they danced. When he heard their voices Airman Mortensen was distracted. But he was not interrupted. Neither was Claire. They were dancing.

At last the beer wore everyone down. Jancy's face started to get chalky. She stopped dancing and began to weave. Then she said something to her sister and Claire led her off to the bathroom.

The two other girls had disappeared long ago and it was just Pat and Airman Mortensen now. They danced a little longer but it was halfhearted and when the record ended they drifted back into the kitchen.

Pat was hungry.

Airman Mortensen was confused. So much had happened since six o'clock. Finding a girl he'd met at a dance suddenly seemed to be a part of the past. But she was there, jamming her hand into a box of vanilla wafers. He leaned against the drainboard. He reached for the box of vanilla wafers, his hand fumbling with hers.

Fingers found fingers and in a blink he was trying to dump the box gracefully on the drainboard as they embraced. His face was buried in her neck but it was disturbingly strange. They were hugging each other hard but there seemed no reason for it. Nothing had passed between them.

As Pat pressed against him Airman Mortensen looked over her shoulder and saw Claire coming toward the kitchen. She saw him and blushed. After a moment's hesitation she said cheerfully, "I'm coming in."

Pat and Airman Mortensen broke away from each other as she swept past them to the sinks.

The three of them chatted in the kitchen for a few minutes. Claire laughed at her sister's dilemma. This always happened when she started drinking.

The older sister shook her head doubtfully.

"Jancy always drinks too much," she sighed, "and she's only fifteen."

The kitchen was quiet.

Pat yawned and tottered away from the refrigerator.

"I'm going to bed," she said. She didn't look at Airman Mortensen. She didn't say anything to him. But she gave his hand a distinct brush with her own as she left.

A grandfather clock started to strike somewhere in the still house. Not knowing what to do, Airman Mortensen silently counted the bongs.

A headache was starting to dig around behind one of his eyes and he was feeling uneasy. His heart was confused about the German girl. He wasn't so sure now about standing around in Colonel Brill's kitchen. And he didn't know what to make of Claire. She looked sad as she ran a sponge along the drainboard.

He wanted to go and he wanted to stay. But without some kind of sign he could do neither.

The clock bonged for the tenth time and stopped.

Claire had her back to him. She was rinsing the sponge.

"Do you sleep in the barracks?" she asked from no-where.

"Yes."

"Maybe it would be easier if you just slept here to-night. I'm still a little drunk."

She tossed the sponge behind the faucet and faced him with an ease that seemed forced around the edges.

"Are you?"

"Am I . . . ?"

"Are you drunk?"

"Oh . . . yeah . . . a little."

"Then you can sleep here."

"Whatever's easier."

She was yawning. "That would be easier for me."

There was something shy about the way she stuck out her hand.

"Well, I'm glad we met," she said.

Airman Mortensen shook her hand.

"Me too."

She yawned again. "Pat's just off the hall . . . about halfway down on the right."

Airman Mortensen looked down the darkened hall. "Okay," he said vacantly.

"Goodnight."

"Goodnight," he replied and watched her leave. She still looked sad.

Then he was alone in Colonel Brill's kitchen.

☆ 5 ☆

It was too dark to find the light switches and he thought if he tried groping for one he'd knock over an heirloom. So Airman Mortensen walked down the hall with careful, baby steps.

He paused at the first open door and a moment later Pat's voice came out of the back bedroom.

"I'm in here."

He walked into the dark, found the edge of the bed and sat on it.

"Are you asleep?" he asked politely.

"Sort of . . . are you going to stay here?"

"Yeah. Claire was tired . . . she went to bed."

The covers shifted as Pat scooted over to make room.

Airman Mortensen started taking off his clothes, letting them pile up next to the bed. He undressed fearlessly, not thinking once about his virginity. He thought only of putting his arms around a naked body and kissing in the dark. The prospect of flesh on flesh obliterated all other considerations.

She stuck her tongue in his mouth so quickly that he was thrown off balance. But shortly he met hers with his own, willing to be carried along wherever she wanted to go.

They kissed hard for a few moments. Then he pressed a hand on one of her breasts. They were both trapped under a bra and when he fumbled to release them she pushed her head into his chest.

"No," she murmured.

He stopped, wondering what he should do. When she felt his indecision she started kissing him again and the opening round of the tryst was repeated for another few minutes.

Airman Mortensen had a hard-on. He'd had it from the beginning and she'd felt it from the beginning. She'd allowed it to play around between her legs as they rolled under the covers.

But now, as his fingers inched along her stomach, edging toward her underpants, she stopped his hand with one of her own.

Airman Mortensen didn't say anything when this happened. It had happened before of course and when it did he rarely said anything. Sometimes he would say, "What's the matter?" But he didn't tonight, mainly because he was no longer so certain of his affection for this girl. He couldn't figure why but something was missing.

In a small voice she said, "I want to get used to you first."

"Okay," he said.

They talked about Claire and Jancy for awhile. Jancy was wild. Claire could get a little wild but mostly she was levelheaded.

They talked about him. Apparently the girls had done some research. They already knew he was from California when they picked him up in front of the enlisted men's club. They knew that sometimes he played music downtown. She intimated that being from California made him a fairly hot item.

He knew all about the hot item thing. Girls from New Mexico liked guys from California. It was presumed that guys from California were hip.

But listening to all this did not make Airman Mortensen feel very hip. He thought that if he was hip he would be losing his virginity right now. 'Shit,' he said to himself, 'I would have lost it a long time ago.'

In the end though he let his disappointment pass. The touching and kissing felt good. He reminded himself that this was a first night and despite whatever was missing, there might be more nights to come. Maybe they would find what was missing on one of those nights and just keep going.

He reminded himself of this several times as they French-kissed and dry-humped through most of an hour. At last it was just too exhausting and they tried for sleep.

Airman Mortensen lay awake for awhile, letting his hard-on die away as he monitored the rise and fall of her shoulders. He thought of many things as he lay in the dark but one recurring sentence kept marching into his head:

'This isn't right; it's not right.'

Deep down he knew why it wasn't right but could not admit it, even to his secret self. The answer lay dormant all that night and well into the next.

☆ **6** ☆

The German girl was in a deep sleep. Airman Mortensen wished he could be sleeping too. His mouth was cottony with last night's cigarettes; and a crack in the bedroom curtain was letting the sun through to torment his swollen eyes.

While she slept he sat up and tried to blink away the fuzz in his head. He did this carefully, hoping she wouldn't wake. He did not want to talk to her, least of all now in the awkward light of morning.

It was one of those unspectacular but damnable hangovers, the kind that lingers like a low-grade infection. As he wriggled into his pants he knew he would be a step behind all day. More than once he staggered, having to hop on one foot as he pulled up the jeans. The hops made a thudding sound on the bedroom floor and Airman Mortensen grimaced. But she was a good sleeper. She didn't stir.

He shut the door softly and made his way down the hall. He paused at a gaudy mirror and tried to straighten the crazy sleep creases in his hair. While he was patting at his head he heard the distant sound of people talking.

The sisters were sitting in the kitchen, facing each other across the breakfast table.

Claire was spreading jam on a piece of toast while Jancy clung morosely to a cup of coffee. They were both wearing old, faded bathrobes that hung loosely on their bodies and the familiarity of these old robes helped put Airman Mortensen at ease as he stood in front of them.

"Good morning," Claire smiled, passing the slice of jam-covered bread to her sister. "Did you have a good sleep?"

"I slept okay."

"Want some toast?"

Jancy said nothing. She was looking at him with her secretive eyes. Her face was very pale, sickly. Airman Mortensen wanted her to respond, so he directed his reply to her.

"I think I'll have a beer," he said, half turning to the fridge. "Anybody else?"

Jancy's big eyes stayed fixed on him as she spoke.

"You fucking bastard," she said, biting off a corner of her toast, "I bet you didn't sleep at all."

Airman Mortensen glanced at Claire and saw her laugh behind a hand.

"Whatever you're thinking is wrong," he answered. Then he looked at Claire again.

"Can I have some coffee?"

For ten minutes they sat at the table talking about nothing. This was much better than lying in bed with Pat talking about something. The coffee was clearing his head and it gave him a good feeling to start the day outside the company of men.

But when he got up to pour himself another cup he saw the kitchen clock and his heart crashed. The kitchen clock read nine-forty.

"Is that clock right?" He was hoping that the clock was somehow wrong.

Claire looked at the little watch on her wrist.

"Yes."

"I gotta go."

"Do you need a ride?"

Airman Mortensen checked her bathrobe.

"You're not dressed."

"That doesn't matter. I'll just drive you. I won't have to get out."

It took five minutes to get back to the barracks but in that time Airman Mortensen said a lot. He told her about his trouble, about the chickenshit charge and how it came to be and how he was now the latrine king.

She had a few questions but mostly she listened, her eyebrows rising in shock from time to time.

When Airman Mortensen confessed the part about being latrine king, her eyes got small. She looked ready to beat someone up.

"That's awful," she said through clenched teeth.

As they rolled into the parking lot fronting the barracks he told her about having to report to the First Sergeant every Saturday morning. He had to report by nine and this was the first time he'd been late. There was going to be punishment.

She stopped in front of the walkway and let the bug idle. She sat in her bathrobe, gazing at the barracks, listening to the last of it. When he was finished, she whispered, "Those bastards."

Airman Mortensen watched the barracks with her.

"Well, they don't like me. I'm always fighting them. I guess I wouldn't like me either."

Claire's eyes dropped briefly into her lap.

"I like you," she said quietly.

Then she looked up at him, her green eyes filled with empathy.

"I hope you don't have to work too long."

Airman Mortensen shrugged bravely.

"Me too," he said with a laugh. He was trying to cheer her up. She looked so sad.

He saw her smile as her eyes dropped once more into her lap and for lack of anything else to do, he put his hand on the car's shifter and wiggled it a little.

Her hand fell on his. It fell without motive or forethought. At the moment it fell Claire herself could not have said why it did. It was just something that happened.

Airman Mortensen stared through the windshield and Claire watched the center of the VW's steering wheel. For a few seconds there was nothing but the noise of the car's idling engine.

Her eyes were still on the steering wheel as she spoke, soft and uncertain.

"We'll all be at the house."

"The number's in the directory?"

"Yes."

"Okay."

Airman Mortensen got out. When he bent to the window her face was happy again.

"Bye."

"Bye."

The bug shot forward. He stood on the sidewalk and watched it go. She was looking at him in the rearview mirror. Then she waved and Airman Mortensen, hoping he would be seen clearly, jerked his hand up and, in a frantic fleeting motion, waved back.

☆ **7** ☆

When Mississippi Newt was out of uniform he was in uniform, another sort of uniform.

He always wore the same things: a lime-green phosphorescent trench coat, a white T-shirt, slacks, pointed black shoes and wraparound sunglasses. He was too skinny to be alive. His face looked like a skull. A skull wearing sunglasses.

Airman Mortensen ran into Mississippi Newt on the stairway going up to the second floor.

"Furss be lookin' fo' yo' ass, Moat."

"When was this?"

"Man, I see him fi' fuckin' minutes ago, man . . . you gon' wurk yo' ass taday Slic . . . dat Furss, he look piss."

A grin covered Newt's face. His head bobbed up and down like a toy bird that drinks out of a glass.

"Heh, heh, heh," he laughed, the hehs in time with the bobbing head. "Yo' ass is grass taday, Slic."

"Fuck you, Newt."

The black soldier bristled. His lip curled as he stepped in front of Airman Mortensen. He stuck a hand deep into his pants pocket and leaned into the slick sleeve's face.

"Don't tawk that shit ta me, you gray mutherfucka." His voice rose higher and higher as his hand dug around in the pocket. "I . . . I . . . I . . . cut yo' white, muthafuckin' ass."

Newt was always threatening to cut somebody. So far as anyone knew he had cut no one. But that didn't mean he wouldn't. Newt was crazy.

Airman Mortensen rolled his eyes.

"I got a lot on my mind, Newt. I don't have time for your bullshit."

He pushed past him and took the stairs two at a time to the second floor landing. Newt's cackle was lifting behind him, bouncing off the stairwell walls like weird music.

"You don't have time cuz you gon' haffa be a nigga taday, you gray muthafucka. You gon' be a nigga all this day, Slic . . . heh . . . heh . . . heh . . ."

But Airman Mortensen wasn't listening. He rammed through the door and saw Bernie Testa. It looked like Bernie had just finished in the latrine. He was plodding unhappily down the hall with a shaving kit in his hand. As usual his fresh, white boxer shorts were hanging high above his belly button. A T-shirt was tucked meticulously under the waistband. The flip-flops on his feet made a sorrowful, rubber click-clack as he walked.

Bernie was small. His long, sad face always looked as though it had received or was about to receive bad news. This expression made him vulnerable and led to a lot of teasing. Most of the guys routinely called him "Testicle" instead of Testa. Bernie hated the nickname but was powerless to do anything about it. On hearing the nickname he would often hang his head and say nothing, hoping it would not be repeated. It was worse when he made a big deal out of it.

On rare occasions he would throw out his jaw, summon his most authoritative voice and say, "Cut it out . . ." But this technique usually backfired and Bernie would find himself being teased about the sound of his voice or the size of his jaw or the height of his shorts.

Adding to Bernie's woes was a gullibility that was legend around the barracks. Though Bernie had acquired a certain wariness, his reputation was well established and guys were constantly trying to trick him. Henry and Bennett had once told him that a blonde "with the biggest tits you have ever seen" was waiting for him in the parking lot. She was asking for him by name. Bernie instantly denied this foolishness but Henry and Bennett swore up and down it was true. After fifteen minutes of swearing up and down, Bernie began to crack and at last he changed into his good pants. Then he combed his hair, put on his new sports coat and went down to the parking lot.

No one was there.

Bernie found Henry and Bennett barricaded in their room. Through the door he could hear hysterical laughter.

First he kicked at the door. Then he got a mop wringer and began to smash it against the door. Henry and Bennett stopped laughing and told him to stop but Bernie kept swinging the wringer.

Finally they came out. Bernie wanted to fight them. If it had gone any further they would have knocked him silly but by that time enough people had been drawn to the commotion. Airman Mortensen helped subdue Bernie. They stayed up late, having a heart to heart, and eventually everything blew over. But people still tried to trick him whenever there was an opportunity.

Bernie was Airman Mortensen's roommate and the latrine king had real affection for the little Italian, the sort of affection some people have for the runt of

the litter. He never hurt other people and he had
manners. But Bernie tried too hard in everything he
attempted and sometimes his futility irritated even Airman Mortensen.

On balance, however, he liked his roommate.

"Bernie."

Surprised at the sound of his own name, Bernie
jumped. When he saw Airman Mortensen coming toward him, his big eyes got bigger and a hand went to
the massive cross that hung around his neck like a fishing line sinker. A hand usually went there when he was
under stress.

"Oh geez . . . why weren't you here? The First Sergeant is lookin' for ya . . . he's all steamed up."

"I know he is."

"He's really mad."

"I know," Airman Mortensen griped, "what did he
say?"

Bernie looked away, his eyes falling to the floor as
he concentrated. His fingers were wrapped tight around
the crucifix. He always took forever to reply. If someone asked Bernie the time, he was likely to study the
hands of his watch carefully before answering.

He stroked the sharp point of his clean-shaven chin.

"I don't know if I can remember exactly what he
said."

"That doesn't matter, Bernie . . . What did he say
roughly?"

The Italian's sad eyes were now as large as plates and
the idea of being shot at sunrise flashed in Airman Mortensen's head.

"He said for you to come to see him . . . in his
office."

"Okay," said Airman Mortensen, starting for the
stairs leading to the ground floor.

"If you need help let me know," Bernie called after him.

Airman Mortensen glanced over his shoulder at the ludicrous figure standing helplessly in his skivvies.

"I will, Bernie . . . thanks."

"Let me know what happens."

"I will."

The First Sergeant leaned back slightly in his desk chair and made a little tent with the freckled hands.

"Where have you been?" he asked mildly.

Airman Mortensen was tempted. He almost said it. He almost said, "Colonel Brill's house. I spent the night there." But as he watched the pinpoints of the topkick's eyes, he decided it wasn't worth it. That would just open another family-sized can of worms. And in the end he knew it would be Airman Mortensen who would have to eat the can of worms, a bite at a time most likely.

"I got hung up. I'm sorry I'm late."

There was a long silence. The First Sergeant's eyes seemed to get smaller as he stared at his catch. He was weighing something.

At last the First Sergeant placed both hands on the arm of his chair and pushed himself up from his seat. Saying nothing, he walked out of the office. Airman Mortensen followed.

They went only as far as the roomy, first-floor utility closet. The First Sergeant silently inventoried the buckets and mops and buffers and cardboard boxes. The cardboard boxes were filled with Lysol and toilet scrapers and deodorant cakes and steel wool and paper towels—the tools of Airman Mortensen's trade.

"Well . . . ," he said, pausing for subtle effect, "let's wax the halls."

Airman Mortensen's jaw tightened at the word

"halls." Halls meant all three floors. Each hallway was the length of a football field. It would take at least an hour to lay wax on each one, another half hour to buff.

The latrine king stepped into the closet and started to drag out a five-gallon tub of liquid wax. But as he struggled with the heavy bucket, the First Sergeant spoke again.

"You know what?"

He was looking along the baseboard of the hall.

"I'm seeing a hell of a buildup. We better strip first. And get some blades and catch the edges."

Then he laid a hand on Airman Mortensen's shoulder and said, "Let's have a good job, huh?"

With that he ambled slowly back to his office.

Airman Mortensen saw himself trotting up behind the First Sergeant. He saw a claw hammer tight in his hand. He saw himself wind up and swing with all his might. He saw the hammer bury itself in the back of the top-kick's head. He saw it go in claw first.

☆ 8 ☆

Airman Mortensen didn't go to work right away. He sat in the closet, on one of the stripper tubs, and tried to calm his homicidal ideas with a cigarette. He started to think about the impossible task he faced.

First he'd have to lay down stripper with a mop. While the stripper was eating into the old wax he'd be working the hallways' edges with the razor blades. Then he'd have to put a scrubbing pad on the buffer and move down the length of the hall bringing the old layers up.

Then he'd have to mop up the residue, rinsing and wringing the filth from the floor every few minutes. He'd have to wait for the floor to dry before he laid wax. Then he'd have to wait for the wax to dry before he buffed.

One hall would take hours. Three were an eternity. Without the edges, he might have a chance. But he'd have to do the edges by hand. There was no chance.

Two soldiers walked past the closet. They were in civilian clothes and Airman Mortensen realized something that made him feel worse.

It was Saturday.

Most everybody had weekends off. That meant guys would be going in and out all day, tromping back and forth on every hall. They would all be pissed, waiting for him to finish each section before they could get in or out of their cubicles. A lot of them would track up the floor anyway. On top of it all he would have to be a cop. On top of everything else there would be yelling.

"Fuck the goddamn Air Force." He stuck his head into the hall and barked it out. "Fuck the goddamn Air Force."

Airman Mortensen spit on the end of his butt and flipped it into the corner of the grimy closet, leaving it for some other poor bastard to clean up a year from now. He imagined the First Sergeant finding it when he was gone. It would have his own name on it, along with a message. The message would say, "Fuck you, Sarge."

Finally, Airman Mortensen went to work. It took longer then he'd estimated but he worked hard and, after several hours, the first floor was done. He didn't have much trouble with the other soldiers. They could all see that he was in a rage and, for the most part, they stayed clear of the slick sleeve. He made a lot of noise while he worked, taking his anger out on the equipment and slamming the monstrous buffer against the sides of the wall. No one messed with him.

During these first hours he thought of the night that had just passed. The idea of being in Colonel Brill's house—walking on his carpets, leaning on his drain-board and actually sleeping in a bed that was personally owned by the base commander brought little smiles to his face.

He took comfort in the thought that he alone among thousands of enlisted men knew the inside of Colonel Brill's house. He caught himself grinning as he me-chanically guided the mop down the hall. It was a small thing really and no one would believe it, but the thought of being in that house one minute and this hall the next helped the time pass. It was funny.

Something more important happened while he was scraping the edges. Working on hands and knees, he had covered half of one side when he decided to break for a smoke.

As he sat smoking, his back against the cinder-block wall, his lower body soaking in stripper, Claire's face popped into his head.

He was happy to see it. He liked the roundness of it. He liked the light, soft hair and the cheery, devilish smile. The face was always smiling. It was wonderfully warm, like the faces women used for selling soap and stoves on television. When her smile popped into Air-man Mortensen's head it was directed solely at him.

Her face kept him going. In the four hours it took to finish the first floor, she made at least a dozen visits. Not wanting to cheapen these appearances, he held them back, summoning the face only when he needed it most. But several times it came unannounced. Those were the best times of all.

In the final phases of the first-floor operation, the First Sergeant walked up and stood at his side. Airman

Mortensen cut off the buffer and watched as the top-kick's practiced eyes critiqued his effort.

"Good job," he said at last.

Then he backtracked to the office.

Airman Mortensen switched the buffer back on and thought to himself.

'He's never said that before. Maybe he feels guilty. Good. Maybe he'll let me off. Naw, he won't do that. He's feeling guilty. Good! I hope he fuckin' dies of guilt.'

☆ **9** ☆

Airman Mortensen hauled the buffer up the second-floor stairs. It was heavy and he had to take a step at a time. He went back down for the tubs of stripper and wax, hauling them up separately, also because of the weight. By the time he'd made two more trips (for the mops and buckets and wringers) his state of mind had gone from gray to black.

The night at Colonel Brill's house seemed far away. A cruel joke. A deceptive dream from which he'd waked. Claire's face stopped coming. He didn't want to think about it anymore.

The whole thing was a fake.

The scuffed and dirty checkerboard floor wasn't fake. Neither were the sickly, cream-colored walls of cinder block. Or the globes of yellow light, spaced at uniform intervals overhead.

The smell that came off everything wasn't fake. It was the smell of all that was lifeless. Natural aromas,

even something as repugnant as a fart, were quickly
suffocated by the overwhelming odor of institution.

He dumped a pool of stripper on the floor and as he
spread it around with the mop, Airman Mortensen began to think that being a latrine king was the only reality of his life. He worked his way down the floor,
each stroke more furious than the last. This was his
reality and Airman Mortensen hated it with the single-
mindedness of a maniac.

There was nothing he could do to change the darkness of his thinking. He had to do this work. He had to
live in this place. Then he thought, 'I could kill' and
suddenly he wanted to kill. There was no one around,
but Airman Mortensen's urge to kill was a mad dog
lunging against a cheap leash. He looked at the mop in
his hands and wished it would come alive so he could
destroy it. He lifted it off the floor, trying to will it
alive.

Then he heard footsteps.

The neat, meek personage of Bernie Testa, airman
second class, was walking toward him.

The glare that came to meet Bernie was terrible. He
turned away and for a moment or two pretended interest
in the work being done on the floor.

Airman Mortensen's voice was dead.

"What do you want?"

The face was so awful that Bernie could only manage
a brief look at it. He focused on the mop bucket.

"I just wanted to see how you were doing."

"Well you can see, can't ya?"

Airman Mortensen gave Bernie's J.C. Penney outfit
a contemptuous scowl.

"How was the wedding?" he sneered.

Bernie still didn't want to look at the disturbed face
but now he was confused. He had to look. He didn't
know anything about a wedding.

"What wedding?" he asked curiously.

"Jesus fuckin' Christ, Bernie . . . look how you're dressed."

Bernie looked down his shirtfront. He checked his fly. Then he gazed up at Airman Mortensen with a baffled expression.

"What's wrong?" he said, checking his trousers again.

Airman Mortensen leaned on the mop, made a cradle with one of his hands and put his forehead in it. The steam was going out of him.

"Nothing's wrong, Bernie. Forget it. Everything's fine. Go shave or something."

Airman Mortensen started swinging the mop again. The little Italian kept his distance but he didn't move.

"You're not in a very good mood," he said, watching the movement of the mop.

Airman Mortensen stopped in midswing and felt the urge to kill returning, an urge that Bernie was unable to fathom. They stared at each other. Out on the flight line a B-52 was roaring down the runway. When the plane's engines got farther away, Bernie spoke up.

"Aren'cha gonna tell me what happened?"

Airman Mortensen now saw himself as Hardy trying to get through to Laurel.

"Can't you see what happened?" he said, waving a free hand in the air.

Bernie looked up and down the hall.

"You're doin' the floor."

"Floors. I'm doin' all three floors."

"You have to strip too?"

"I have to strip too."

"Geez," Bernie whispered to himself.

Wishing he was alone, Airman Mortensen turned his back and started the mop once more. But Bernie continued to hang around.

"You'll never get finished today," Bernie observed. "You'll have to work tomorrow."

"That's right."

Airman Mortensen swung the mop viciously, slamming it back and forth against the baseboards a dozen times before he had to stop and rinse.

Bernie was still standing by.

"I'll help you," he said resolutely.

"Why would you want to do that?"

Airman Mortensen wrung the mop savagely and started up again. Bernie was following on his heels, trying to compose an answer.

" 'Cause you're getting a raw deal and you're my friend. You're my only friend. I don't know why you hate me so much."

Airman Mortensen stopped. He glanced back at the great expanse of hallway yet to be done. Then he looked into his roommate's eyes.

"You'll be in a world of shit if the First catches you helping me."

Bernie didn't take his eyes away. He didn't blink.

"Fuck him," the little Italian said. "Fuck the First."

Working together, they finished the second hall in half the time it would have taken Airman Mortensen to do it alone. They weaseled a few beers from some drunken airmen rolling dice in one of the rooms and after downing one of the beers, Airman Mortensen's black mood was replaced by something more like himself.

When the buffer wasn't going they talked and he had to admit Bernie's company made the biggest difference of all. It made a big difference for Bernie too, even though he detested the work. Left to himself, he would undoubtedly be lying fully clothed on his bunk, his hands behind his head, staring at the ceiling for most of the afternoon. Instead, he was engaged in lively conversation with a well-known troublemaker.

Bernie's favorite topic was his mother. He confessed that he'd been babied too much. In some ways he held this against his mother, the constant fussing that had smothered him. Airman Mortensen knew all about it of course. He knew that Bernie tensed up when he got into this aspect of the years with his mother.

But when it came to food Bernie's eyes would shine with ecstasy and it was "My ma . . ." this and "My ma . . ." that as he ticked off the cavalcade of Italian specialties Mother Testa was able to produce.

Airman Mortensen had heard the delicacies ticked off more than once but he didn't mind hearing them reiterated. They put Bernie in a wonderful humor. His eyes would flutter and he would actually rub his stomach as he ran down the list of pastas and sauces and meats. The stuff in the chow hall was ninety-nine percent revolting and the thought of all that delicious, homemade food set Airman Mortensen's mouth to watering.

As usual, the topic was closed with an invitation.

"When all this is over you gotta come to Connecticut. You gotta come to my house. We'll be treated like kings, I swear to God. My ma'll put out a meal . . . she'll put out a meal that'll make you come in your pants . . . I swear to God . . . no kidding."

"Well, if you're gonna come in your pants," Airman Mortensen would reply, "I guess I'll have to go."

"Damn straight you will," Bernie would command. Puffed up with thoughts of food and power, he'd give the razor blade a little extra elbow grease as they worked their way down the edge of the hall.

Sometimes Bernie would inquire about Airman Mortensen's ma and the reply was usually marked by its length. It was very short.

"She's great," the latrine king would say. "Best mom in the world."

It was true. She was great. She took great pride in her son. She encouraged and supported him as few mothers do.

Airman Mortensen could not remember being kissed or hugged. He knew it must have happened. But when he tried to think of a particular instance, he could not remember one. A perfunctory peck on the cheek perhaps but that was not something for remembering.

It was a missing link between them, the lack of touch, and though he didn't see the connection, this lack of touch made Airman Mortensen a needy person. He didn't think of himself as needy but he was.

So he rarely talked about his mom except to say she was "great." Any more detail would have taken him into territory which would make him more vulnerable than he already was. He didn't want to get into that. He couldn't afford it. He was fighting on too many fronts already.

As all soldiers do, they bitched about the service. The constant griping was a form of therapy.

Rumors about getting orders were always flying around. Everyone dreamed of another duty station, the theory being that anyplace else would be better than this place. But getting orders was a tricky proposition. Bernie was a good example. He dreamed of going to Germany, where the girls were "big and bosomy." He dreamed of being eaten whole by a big Teutonic girl. Japan had a certain appeal too. It was very foreign, a good place to live down a reputation. And of course the oriental women pretty much did as they were asked.

But there was always the chance that the orders would read Greenland. There was nothing in Greenland but liquor and television and a lot of time indoors. Or North

Dakota. Bernie said if he got orders for North Dakota he might as well check out altogether.

Airman Mortensen was going nowhere. The court-martial had frozen him and the predicament he faced was the squadron's most talked-about scenario. With men living in such close proximity, there were few secrets and everyone knew the particulars of his case.

He had come to the base as a radio operator, fresh out of basic training and tech school. His place of work had been a one-room, cinder-block house filled with banks of equipment. The only window to the outside was a plastic peephole, six inches by six inches, cut in the front door.

For three months Airman Mortensen had reported for work at midnight. Until eight o'clock the next morning he had sat alone in the block house, listening to the hum of the transmitters, trying to fill the time between hourly radio checks.

"Cinderella, this is Gopher, over . . ."

"Gopher, this is Cinderella, you're loud and clear, out."

That was all. In an eight-hour shift he answered the call from California with a one-sentence reply eight times. It was the full extent of Airman Mortensen's job.

In the fifty-nine minutes between radio checks he read books, dreamt of other realities and tried to stay awake. No one came to the bunker during his shifts and no one called. At eight o'clock in the morning his relief arrived and Airman Mortensen took a two-mile taxi ride back to the barracks, where he tried to sleep a few hours in the noisy daytime.

There was one other aspect of Airman Mortensen's job, and that was training. All soldiers were required to take periodic tests to increase proficiency at their jobs. Passing these tests supposedly upgraded a person's skill and knowledge. Successful testing was also a vital cog in the promotion process. Those who didn't pass didn't get promoted. The testing process was considered important to everyone.

There was no one to train Airman Mortensen, not from midnight to eight. But he was sized up as a smart lad from the beginning. His supervisor gave him a stack of bound tech manuals and a folder of sample tests.

"Drill yourself on this," the sergeant said. "If you've got any questions come see me. You won't have trouble."

Night after night Airman Mortensen sat in the cinderblock house and night after night the manuals and the sample tests sat untouched in a metal filing cabinet.

His plan was brilliantly simple. He would fail the test on purpose. The higher-ups would look into it and find that he was incompetent at his job. A powwow of some kind would be held and at this meeting it would be determined what sort of work Airman Mortensen was suited for.

After three months of "training," he took the test on a cold winter day when the trees were bare and everyone was wearing gloves. Finding a secluded seat at the back of the gray classroom, he stared down at six pages of questions and an answer sheet. He smiled confidently. Then he slipped the questions under the answer sheet and doodled on a piece of scrap paper until the allotted time had almost expired. With five minutes to go, he playfully penciled in the multiple-choice answers (a,b,c,d,e) without looking at a single question.

Airman Mortensen's plan, so simple and brilliant, was a bust. When the test came back he was called on the carpet and asked to explain how an intelligent airman could have achieved an idiot's test score.

The soon-to-be latrine king realized instantly that he had miscalculated. Thinking fast, he tacked in what seemed the safest direction.

"I don't know," he countered. "I guess I just don't understand it. I've never been very good at technical stuff."

No one really believed this but it wouldn't have mattered anyway. Airman Mortensen's test score had come to the attention of the Comm Squad's commander, a Lieutenant Colonel Tollefson. As an Air Force officer, he followed everything to the letter. Any deviation from rules, regulations, or official thinking made him nervous and when Lieutenant Colonel Tollefson saw the test score he started making phone calls.

He'd never seen such a low test score. It was a blemish on the squadron's record and threw a monkeywrench into the Lieutenant Colonel's ongoing goal of making the squadron tops in testing. It was screwing up the percentage. It might even affect his carefully orchestrated, nip-and-tuck drive for promotion to full colonel. For all these reasons Airman Mortensen's test score could not be tolerated and Lieutenant Colonel Tollefson made erasure of the blemish a top priority.

They needed to get at him and a day or two after the score came in Airman Mortensen was switched to the day shift. Lieutenant Colonel Tollefson personally assigned two staff sergeants to take turns training the flunky. Airman Mortensen's sleep patterns improved but in between hourly radio checks he found himself being grilled with unflagging zeal by a tag team of Air Force career men.

The trainers were incredibly thorough. Having been assigned by Tollefson himself put them both on the hot seat. If this shitbird didn't pass his goddamn test they would be in trouble too. They were relentless.

For the first couple weeks Airman Mortensen tried to play the dunce. But that only made his trainers more desperate and more relentless. With no other way out Airman Mortensen gradually began to absorb the material he was being force fed. The absorption process gained momentum and as time ground on, the trainers began to relax a little. The cinder-block school settled into a smooth, educational rhythm.

When the second test was a week away the exhausted trainers, worried that their student might be getting over-stuffed, reduced the grilling strategy.

This gave Airman Mortensen needed time to consider a strategy.

If he failed the test, his two mentors would find a way to kill him. If he passed the test, he would die a slow, spiritual death in the cinder-block house out in the sagebrush. It was like trying to choose between hanging or the electric chair.

On the Friday afternoon he and the two sergeants walked into Lieutenant Colonel Tollefson's office, Airman Mortensen still had no idea what he was going to do.

The sergeants had told him that the meeting with Tollefson was pure formality. The "old man" would ask him if he was ready to take the test. Airman Mortensen would say yes. Tollefson would ask a couple of easy questions pertaining to radio operation. Airman Mortensen would answer the questions correctly. The lieutenant colonel would shake the student's hand, wish him luck and they would leave.

There were three ominous chairs waiting in front of the Comm Squad commander's desk. The sergeants and Airman Mortensen saluted their chief and were asked to sit. The sergeants reported briefly on their pupil's satisfactory progress. Airman Mortensen could see they were jittery. Great stains of perspiration were spreading like oil spills around the armpits of their uniforms.

The meeting was interrupted by a phone call. Airman Mortensen watched the heavy folds of skin on the lieu-

tenant colonel's face ripple up and down as he spoke a
few curt sentences into the receiver.

Then everything went into slow motion.

Airman Mortensen's heart began to thump loudly.
Tollefson hung up, placed his arms on the desk and
started to speak. Airman Mortensen suppressed a grab
at his chest. His heart was turning somersaults.

"Well, Airman," the lieutenant colonel said point-
edly, "are you ready to take the test?"

Airman Mortensen's mouth opened.

"No, sir."

A silent shock wave shook the office. Blood was
draining from the faces of the two sergeants. Airman Mortensen thought briefly that they might faint.
Tollefson's face was flushing purple.

"What?"

"I'm not ready, sir. I'll never be ready. I don't want
to be a radio operator; I never did. I'm no good to the
Air Force as a radio operator. With all respect, sir, I
should be doing something else."

Airman Mortensen didn't know where these words
came from. They just spilled out of his mouth.

There was another shocked silence. Then, Lieutenant
Colonel Tollefson looked at one of the sergeants and
said:

"Get him out of here."

The following Monday morning Airman Mortensen
was dressing for work when two men knocked on his
door. It was the First Sergeant and a second lieutenant
from the Comm Squad. He recognized the second louie
as one of Tollefson's assistants.

Reading from a written directive, the second lieutenant
told him he was relieved of duty, that he had temporarily
been reduced in rank, that he was to await word of his
pending court-martial, and that until further notice he would
report directly to the First Sergeant for work detail.

At that moment Airman Mortensen was transformed into slick sleeve, the latrine king.

* * *

In the course of working the second-floor hallway, he and Bernie had reviewed the events that led to his downfall. They were putting a shine on the finished floor when the big buffing pad slipped off. Bernie stood thinking as Airman Mortensen tilted the machine on its side and readjusted the pad.

"What will they do at the court-martial?" the roommate wondered. "I mean, it's already pretty bad."

"I don't know."

Airman Mortensen glanced up.

"You think I did wrong, don'cha?"

"No," Bernie said quickly, "I don't think that."

"You think I'm crazy?"

"Naw," Bernie whined, screwing up his face.

They stopped talking. Airman Mortensen righted the buffer and walked the cord to a spot where it could be plugged in. The little Italian followed.

"I just think you're maybe too stubborn."

"Well, you're probably right about that," Airman Mortensen sighed.

He knew it was true. As he guided the buffer from side to side he checked off random entries in a very long list. Quitting college after one semester because it was bogus. Hitchhiking to Idaho with no money because it might be interesting. Still a virgin because he had this idea that it mattered who you did it with. Joining the Air Force because he couldn't land a job or didn't want to. Resisting every step of the way through basic training. Saying "no sir" to Tollefson when "yes sir" would have done the trick.

He was stubborn. He was stubborn growing up and
he was stubborn now. He could have taken his time with
the buffer. He could be doing a stand-out job. But he
didn't believe in the job so he was doing less than his
best. He refused to give in and at that moment it occurred to the latrine king that his life had been a three-
part litany. Resist, fight, lose. Resist, fight, lose. The
same song over and over and over.

He realized why he had sighed when Bernie brought up
his stubbornness. He had sighed because there was no way
to change. Resist, fight, lose. He was stuck to it.

☆ **10** ☆

By six o'clock they had reached the third floor. It
was dark outside. Inside there was heavy traffic. Most
of the hundred airmen who lived on the third floor were
getting ready for Saturday night and did not take kindly
to Airman Mortensen and Bernie clogging up the hallway with half a ton of cleaning gear.

Some of the third-floor people, noticing that the work
was just starting, hurried up, hoping to get out before
there was stripper all over the floor. Those who were
too sick or hung over or broke to go out were already
in foul moods. Several of them warned the latrine king
and his helper not to take all night.

For the most part Airman Mortensen and Bernie ignored the others. They'd come a long way and they
were going to finish.

They were starting to pour stripper when a voice rang
out behind them.

"Hey, Mortensen."

It was Don Wallace. He was heading in their direction, navigating past their equipment with the delicacy of a dandy.

Airman Mortensen and Bernie exchanged groans.

Wallace was a pain in the ass. His hair was thick and wiry and red. His skin was pink and pitted. When he smiled there was more gum than teeth. He was from Georgia and bragged constantly about Southern girls. His favorite phrase was: "Boys, I cain't hep it . . . I am just a hog for pussy. I was born a hog for pussy and will die a hog for pussy."

The gummy grin was in full flower.

"Looks like we got a coupla boys just crazy for work. Y'all oughta be out chasin' down some pussy."

Airman Mortensen started mopping.

"We leave that to studs like you, Wallace."

The Georgia playboy grinned even wider, exposing the particles of food trapped between his large yellow teeth.

"Well said, slick sleeve . . . follow big Don's lead and you can't go wrong."

Bernie had been thinking all the while. Now he was ready to speak.

"How come you're in uniform?"

"Aw, I'm pullin' GQ. Ain't that the shits on a Saturday night?"

Airman Mortensen was sick of him already.

"Well why isn't that big, Georgia nose in a fuck book? What're you doin' up here?"

Wallace's eyebrows shot up. He leveled a finger at the latrine king. "You'd better watch it, hoss . . ." Then he got coy, the grin getting wide again. "Or I won't tell you what I am doing up here."

Airman Mortensen waited.

At last Wallace relented. "You got a phone call."

"Right now?"

"Yup."

Airman Mortensen was starting down the hall. "Well, why didn't you say so?" he snorted.

"She sounds like a pretty young thing," Wallace shouted. Then he mimicked the caller's voice with a thick, southern accent. "May I speak to Airman Mortensen, please?"

All the way down the stairs he hoped it would be her.

"Hello?"

"Hi . . ."

"Claire?"

"Yes."

"Hi."

"I was thinking about you. How's it going?" Then she added, "Pat wants to know too."

'Pat's not calling me,' Airman Mortensen thought.

"It's not so good," he said.

"I'm sorry. Are you going to be able to come?"

"I don't know. I've still got a whole floor to do. What time is it?"

"Six-thirty."

"I probably won't get out of here till nine or ten."

"That's okay."

"It won't be too late?"

"No."

Airman Mortensen wanted to say more but he couldn't think, so he said:

"I'll call you when I'm done."

"I hope it goes fast for your sake."

"Me too."

There was silence.

"I better get back," he said.

"Okay."

"I'll call."

"Okay."

"Bye."
"Bye."

☆ **11** ☆

Hearing her voice brought hope back and Airman Mortensen flew up the steps. The words he'd heard on the telephone meant nothing to him. The sounds of the words mattered like nothing else. He was going to see her face again.

As he raced along, Airman Mortensen pumped himself for the enemy, the work that stood between himself and that face. By the time he reached the third-floor landing he was certain that a new, all-time speed record was going to be set in knocking off the last hallway. Nothing could possibly stop him.

Bernie was standing absolutely still at the far end of the hall as the broad back that Airman Mortensen knew so well advanced along the hallway, homing in on his roommate. It was the First Sergeant, showing off his uncanny knack for showing up just when everything was going good. Knowing there was going to be a confrontation, Airman Mortensen quickened his step. He wanted to be in on it.

In his usual way the topkick didn't say anything at first. His eyes roamed the floor and the equipment while the latrine king and his helper waited. Bernie glanced desperately at Airman Mortensen. The slick sleeve shook him off briskly, "Stay cool," he said with the quick snap of his head, "stay cool and don't worry."

At last the First Sergeant let his eyes land on the little Italian.

"What are you doing here, Testa?"

Already whipped, Bernie could barely manage a mumble.

"I'm helping, sir."

The First Sergeant looked to Airman Mortensen, then back at Bernie.

"You must like to work . . . working on a Saturday night."

Bernie was so scared his eyes were watering.

"No, sir."

"Then tell me what you're doing here."

"I just wanted to help," Bernie croaked. "He's my roomy, I . . ."

Airman Mortensen interrupted, "C'mon, Sarge, he's trying to give his buddy a helping hand. That's what we're supposed to do in the Air Force. We're 'sposed to help our buddies."

The First Sergeant said nothing but Airman Mortensen wasn't intimidated. He kept going.

"I told him not to. I told him you'd get pissed but he wouldn't listen to me. What was I supposed to do . . . punch the little guy for trying to be a buddy?"

The First Sergeant stared at Airman Mortensen for a full ten seconds and the latrine king stared back. Then the topkick turned away. He ran his eyes along the hallway's baseboards.

"This floor's in pretty good shape," he said, not looking at either of them. "Forget the stripping. Just lay the wax and hit it with the buffer . . . then call it a day."

He started down the hall.

Bernie looked confused. In a panic, he called after the First.

"Can I help him now, sir?"

The First Sergeant stopped and turned around. Airman Mortensen rolled his eyes.

"Or do I . . . ," Bernie continued, "should I stop?"

The First Sergeant turned a deeper shade of red but in the end he said nothing and went on his way. Bernie and Airman Mortensen watched until he started down the stairs.

"What should I do?" Bernie asked Airman Mortensen.

"He doesn't give a shit, Bernie; you can do anything you want."

Airman Mortensen capped the bucket of stripper and began slopping wax on the floor.

"I'll tell you what I'm gonna do," he grunted. "I'm gonna wax this fuckin' hallway and get the fuck outta here."

The latrine king didn't want to say anything about the girl on the phone but there was no getting Bernie off the subject. A girl on the phone was major news and he wanted the story.

While they waited for the wax to dry, Airman Mortensen sketched out the last twenty-four hours of his life. Bernie listened in disbelief to the finding of Pat and the making of the date.

When Airman Mortensen told about arriving in Colonel Brill's driveway the little Italian's jaw dropped and for the rest of the story his mouth hung wide open. At the times when Airman Mortensen paused, Bernie would whisper, "Geez." He said "Geez" half a dozen times.

Once the wax was dry, Airman Mortensen wasted no time in driving his buffer down the long hallway. As the machine swept back and forth Bernie kept its thirty feet of cord out of the way. He was thinking hard while he held the cord, trying to digest the enormity of what he had heard. At last he was ready to try some questions.

"It sounds like you like the other girl . . . what's her name again?"

"Claire."

"Yeah . . . it seems like you like her."

"What makes you think that?"

"Just the way you're talking. Maybe she's more your type."

"Maybe . . . I don't know what my type is."

"It just seems like you like her."

"You're right."

The big pad slipped off once more and Airman Mortensen swore as he dropped down to wrestle it back on. Bernie tilted the machine on its side and pondered a number of scenarios until he hit one that was terrifying.

"God . . . ," he started.

The voice of terror attracted Airman Mortensen's full attention.

"What would . . . what would happen if he found you in his house?"

"What?" Airman Mortensen was getting peeved again.

"What would Colonel Brill do if he found you over there?"

"Shit, I don't know. You think he'd shoot me or something?"

Bernie dropped his eyes and put a hand to his chin, thinking it over. Then he looked up.

"He wouldn't do that, would he?"

"Jesus H. Christ, Bernie. Of course he wouldn't shoot me."

"Nawww," Bernie smiled, shaking his head, "of course not. I don't know what gets into me sometimes."

"You can say that again," Airman Mortensen said,

taking the buffer's steering arm in both hands. "You're
a goddamn nut case, if you ask me."

☆ **12** ☆

But as his sandals carried him noiselessly along the
clean sidewalks crisscrossing the base, he thought about
it. At one point he actually pictured a muzzle flash
coming from the gun in Colonel Brill's hand. Turning
down Cheeze Street, Airman Mortensen made a mental
note to check on the colonel's scheduled return from
the funeral in Kansas.

It was a quiet Saturday night in the officers' section
and he was thankful that no one was on the street. Even
so, he watched the houses from the corner of his eye,
half expecting a door to be thrown open at any moment.
A stern-faced officer would then appear and call out:

"You, Airman."

When he saw the empty driveway in front of Colonel
Brill's house he grew more anxious. The tan VW was
gone. He wished he'd called ahead as planned instead
of coming straight over.

But he could hear music throbbing inside the house.
And it wasn't a sing along with Mitch Miller. Neil
Young's guitar lead was carrying all the way to the sidewalk and that gave him enough assurance to make the
front door. He gave it a modest rap and stood back,
waiting out the seconds. No one answered. He knocked
again, harder this time. Still nothing.

Too much time was passing on Colonel Brill's porch.
A car drove slowly past and for a moment Airman Mor-

tensen thought about going back to the barracks. He could call from a pay phone.

Instead, he sidestepped across the lawn and peered through the living room's partly drawn curtains. Records were scattered on the carpet. The stereo's power light was glowing red. The turntable was spinning and he could see the needle arm rocking up and down.

Airman Mortensen returned to the front door and hammered on it. A few seconds later the door opened slightly and Jancy's expressionless face appeared in the crack.

The face didn't move but the low voice said, "Hi," and the door opened wider as she stepped back to let him in.

"I'm watching a movie," she said and started to walk back into the house.

There'd been no greeting, no offering, no nothing. Disoriented, Airman Mortensen stood stupidly in the foyer. Then he followed, his eyes focused on the long brown hair bouncing back and forth to her boyish gait.

Jancy led him to a new room, the den. She plopped down on a deep, high-backed couch, stretched her legs on a coffee table and stared across the room at a television screen. The sound was off but the picture wasn't. Godzilla was wrecking Tokyo.

Airman Mortensen stood awkwardly as Jancy picked up a highball glass and took a sip. Then she looked up at him.

"Want a drink? There's plenty."

She motioned to a cabinet with her glass. One of the doors was ajar, exposing a small forest of liquor bottles.

Airman Mortensen selected tequila. While he poured some into a glass of his own he asked Jancy the obvious question.

"Where's everybody?"

"They went to get pizza," she answered, not taking her eyes off Godzilla. The monster was tangled up in a bunch of high-tension wires.

Airman Mortensen sat on the couch with his drink and they watched the movie in silence. The Buffalo Springfield soundtrack coming from the living room fit the film remarkably well. The tequila also fit well and after several solid belts Airman Mortensen began to relax. He stretched out and slipped his sandals off, letting them fall carelessly over the edge of the coffee table.

"It's good with the sound off," he commented.

"Yeah," she said.

When Raymond Burr started talking to some scientists Jancy jumped up and clinked through the bottles in the liquor cabinet until she found some rum. She brought the bottle back to the coffee table, poured out a drink and returned her big-eyed gaze to the screen.

Airman Mortensen couldn't read her at all. She didn't seem drunk but it was hard to tell. Maybe she was plowed. Or maybe she didn't care for his company. Maybe she was shy. She was only fifteen. Or it might be that she was preoccupied with some problem known only to herself.

Luckily, the tequila had begun to chase this kind of thinking out of his mind. He was in the colonel's house again, relaxing on the couch in his den, watching his TV, drinking his liquor. The barracks were flying further away with each ticking second. And he was becoming absorbed in the movie. Japanese soldiers with white helmets were firing rockets at Godzilla.

"Claire likes you."

When he looked at her, Jancy's eyes were still on the screen. Suddenly she lifted her glass. But before she placed it to her lips she gave him a sideways glance and for the first time, Airman Mortensen saw a twinkle of mischief in her eye.

"I can tell," she said.

"Oh yeah?" he teased. "What did she say about me?"

Jancy looked at him like he was the dumbest person on earth.

"She didn't say anything. I'm her sister . . . I can tell."

She turned back to the screen. Airman Mortensen didn't say anything because he didn't know what to think. And he was afraid to think for fear his thinking would be wrong.

The Japanese Air Force was preparing to drop an A-bomb on Godzilla when he heard the faint noise of a car. The noise stopped. Doors slammed in a rapid one, two and Airman Mortensen felt his heart jump.

He thought he had no expectations. He only wanted to see a face that made him feel good; that's what he told himself. But when he heard the girls' voices coming into the kitchen his heart jumped again and he had to get off the couch.

☆ **13** ☆

Compared to tendencies toward violence or creativity or suicide, the tendency for good manners is trivial. Yet the mechanisms of politeness are as intricate as any others.

The simple act of opening a door for someone might be traced to a deep-seated fear of rejection or a chronic need for making the right impression. The "You're welcome" after a "Thank you" might come from constant childhood drilling or it might come from something so simple as a lack of imagination.

Wherever Airman Mortensen's manners might have come from, they were much on his mind as he made the short walk from the den to the kitchen. Each step was fraught with difficulty. He didn't want to sleep with Pat another night. He didn't want to kiss her again. He had nothing to say. He wished she was not there. If she wasn't there he would be spared the chore of having to appear and speak. There was a good chance she would see and hear the nothingness he truly felt.

But the manners made it impossible to ignore her, so Airman Mortensen sucked it up as he walked into the kitchen. His polite eyes found hers and held them long enough to send out a word.

"Hello."

"Hi," she said, the whites around her dark pupils flashing on and off as she turned quickly to the refrigerator and opened the door.

Airman Mortensen glanced across the kitchen and found Claire standing under the light hanging over the dining table. She was looking at him with a sweet, half smile.

"Hi."

"Hi."

There was something in her face that told him she wanted to say more but she too turned away. She placed the fingers of one hand on the edge of the pizza box and stared down at the restaurant logo.

Pat was looking for something in the refrigerator and, in the dogged spirit of the well mannered, Airman Mortensen did the opposite of what he wanted. He hung over the door, trying to seem interested.

"How ya doin'?" he asked.

She answered him with a curt shrug of her shoulders and spoke into the refrigerator.

"I don't see any Parmesan cheese."

The pizza box was taped shut. Claire was clawing at it with a fingernail.

"It should be in there," she called back.

Airman Mortensen laughed a little.

"What do you need cheese for?" he said to Pat's back. "You've got a fucking pizza."

Pat's head tilted to one side. One eye glared through the hair hanging along her face.

"I like lots of cheese."

She was looking in the refrigerator again.

"That's okay with me," he said, trying to make peace.

But Pat was still fuming. "That's just the way I am," she added.

Across the kitchen Claire shrieked, "Oh God, I can't believe these people . . ."

She was holding the pizza up with two fingers, as if it were something found in the bottom of the dirty laundry hamper.

"They didn't cut it."

In the hysterical fashion of a teenager Pat jumped to her friend's side and stared at the pizza pie like a passerby viewing an accident victim.

"Oh God," the German girl exclaimed. "How gross! Where's Jancy?"

Airman Mortensen had come around for a look at the botched pizza. "She's in the den," he said.

Pat sped out of the kitchen to fetch Jancy.

For what seemed a very long time Airman Mortensen stood under the light hanging over the table and stared blankly at the uncut pizza.

It was a strange and beautiful phenomenon—two people side by side, transfixed by a pizza. Each one was staring at the disc of dough and cheese because there was nothing to the image. A bar of gold would have been just as meaningless because at this moment the two were aware of each other's presence and nothing else.

Airman Mortensen detected a slight turning of her head. He turned his and looked into her eyes. They were quiet and beautiful.

She moved her lips.

"What should we do?" she asked softly.

Airman Mortensen tried to form a response but could not. The live face, a few inches from his, was even better than the imagined one he had dreamed of all afternoon.

Pat and Jancy were coming into the kitchen. Airman Mortensen's eyes drifted back to the pizza lying in its box.

"I don't know," he answered.

Jancy gave the pizza a suspicious look as she skirted the dining table and pulled out a chair. She sat slump-shouldered, holding her rum bottle like a pirate. Claire was digging through one of the kitchen drawers and Pat was whispering something into her ear but Jancy was staring up at Airman Mortensen. Smoke from a ciga-rette was rising in front of her big eyes.

"Got a pair of scissors?" he asked, one eye squinting provocatively.

Jancy didn't answer. She turned in the chair, pulled open a drawer in the cupboard behind her, produced a gleaming pair of shears and, in a slow, dramatic way, placed them on the table.

For a few seconds Airman Mortensen smiled at the lethal object lying next to the pizza. He reached down slowly and picked up the scissors. Lifting them to his line of sight, he gave the blade several psychotic clicks.

By now Claire was standing at his side, holding a bread knife upright in one hand.

Airman Mortensen noted the bread knife and, still playing the psychotic, looked deep into her eyes.

"Are we going to saw this pizza," he intoned, glancing skeptically at the knife, "or are we going to cut it?"

"Cut it," Pat giggled, a hand going to her mouth.

"Cut it," Jancy said hollowly.

Airman Mortensen looked at Claire. She was trying to keep from smiling as her eyes narrowed.

"Cut it," she whispered.

They all crowded close to the food.

With a surgical flourish, Airman Mortensen clicked the blades again, lifted the pizza an inch or two off the carton and slipped the scissors into position.

"Now, what we'll do," he began, "is that we'll each take a turn and no one has to cut out a wedge or any of that bullshit. As for me, I'm going to cut out a big, juicy square . . . watch."

He started the scissors through the pizza and in very little time had cut two sides of the intended square. Suddenly the scissors stopped. He had noticed a large piece of topping, the largest on the pizza. It was sitting outside his territory.

He pointed at the unidentifiable glob resting on the blanket of cheese.

"What kind of meat is that?"

The three girls leaned a little closer to the pizza. Claire poked at the glob with a finger.

"It's sausage," she announced.

Airman Mortensen lowered his head and sniffed the mound of ground pork.

"That's a good-sized piece of meat," he said with obvious envy.

Jancy caught his drift instantly.

"You can't have it . . . it's outside your slice."

Airman Mortensen fixed her with a leer.

"Maybe I'll change my . . . route."

Pat had been listening all the while and was now confident enough to put in her own two cents.

"You can't cheat," she said, mimicking Jancy's warning tone.

Claire's arms were folded under her breasts. She'd been thinking.

"Well, who does get the sausage," she said sensibly. "We haven't decided the order of cutting."

"I do," said Jancy.

"Why you?" her sister complained.

"I was here first."

"You were watching TV."

"I should go next," said Pat. "I'm the guest."

Jancy gave the German girl a rough poke on the arm. "No way, you little bitch."

"I go next," Claire cut in. "I'm in charge of the house and I'm the oldest and I paid for it."

"You used Dad's money," Jancy shot back. "That doesn't count." She lifted the bottle for another swig. The rum was still going into her mouth when Pat smacked her arm in retaliation.

"Godammit," Jancy blubbered. A trickle of rum ran out of her mouth and a few drops fell onto her shirtfront.

"Jancy!" Claire yelled. "That's my shirt."

"So what?"

"You're staining it."

About the time Pat hit Jancy, Airman Mortensen saw his opportunity and took a wild detour. He was scissoring furiously and had almost succeeded in circling the large lump of sausage when Pat noticed what he was doing.

Her scream froze the sisters but a split second later all three girls dove for the pizza just as Airman Mortensen tried to carry off his prize. The grabbing lifted the whole pizza and for a few lightning moments it hung suspended in midair. Then Airman Mortensen ripped half of it from the girls' grasp and bolted out of the kitchen.

With the great hunk of pizza wadded between his hands, he sprinted down the hallway. The girls' screams were close behind him and there was no time to really think. He didn't want the whole pizza. He only wanted the prime hunk of sausage, and just now it lay buried beneath the folds of dough he was clutching.

He thought of shooting into a bathroom and slamming the door but before he'd completed the idea, someone's hand raked his shoulder and Airman Mortensen, instinctively veering through the first available doorway, found himself back in the den.

He vaulted over the couch and fumbled with the pizza as the girls piled up in the doorway. But he was laughing so hard at the thought of wolfing down the tidbit they coveted that one of the folds flopped over his hand before he could stop it. Airman Mortensen watched in horror as the disputed ball of pork tumbled onto the carpet.

He went after the sausage and the girls went after him.

The mass of bodies rolled around the floor of the den, a tangle of arms and legs and shrieks. His own wild laughter had paralyzed Airman Mortensen. He couldn't stop thinking of the moment when he would pop the meat in his mouth.

The girls' faces were red as cherries. Each one leered into his as they struggled. And out of each set of gritted teeth came the same command.

''Give it.''

''Give it.''

''Give it.''

Airman Mortensen laughed even harder but he would

not give up the sausage, even when Claire and Jancy
teamed up to pry his fingers open. His hand was slick
with pizza grease and no one could take a firm hold.

Someone pinched him in the butt and Airman Mortensen yelped. At the same time he squirmed away from
the pain, he made his move. Working the meat up to
his fingertips, the latrine king drew the sausage within
range of his mouth.

But in the crucial instant of transfer Claire made a
perfect swipe at his hand and the worn-out hunk of
sausage was suddenly airborne. It flew up in a slow,
graceful arc, bounced through the doorway and landed
neatly in the center of the hall carpet, right between
Booter and Sky King, the Brill family cats.

Sky King turned and ran but Booter immediately
pounced on the meat, taking it down in one gulp.

Pat and Jancy had followed the sausage's flight and
were halfway to the hall when they saw the cat swallow.
The two girls ran screaming after Booter as he bounded
into a back bedroom, his tail high in alarm.

Breathless, Airman Mortensen and Claire stayed
where they were, sprawled together on the floor of the
den. Airman Mortensen couldn't see her face but he
could feel the pressure of her thigh against his foot and
as he lay half on his back he willed the pressure to stay.

Claire didn't move and he hoped that she was conscious of his foot's passive pressure. He hoped that she
wanted it there. The latrine king hoped this with all his
heart.

She bowed her head slightly and, as Airman Mortensen watched the rise and fall of her breathing, he
thought, 'I hope that right now she is thinking of me
and nothing else.'

☆ 14 ☆

The four of them lounged in the den for a few minutes, winding down from the pizza excitement and recounting great moments of the high jinks which had just taken place.

Jancy retrieved her rum bottle from the kitchen and silently poured drinks into juice glasses. Pat took a sip of the dark liquor and gave Airman Mortensen a come-on look which made him feel so uncomfortable that he walked over to the TV and pretended interest in finding a show to watch.

While he was flipping channels Claire declared her aversion to rum and brought up the issue of low beer reserves. Everyone agreed that more beer was a good idea and, because the girls had no way to get it, Airman Mortensen volunteered to make the run.

He would need a car of course and Claire instantly offered hers. When she said, "You can take my car," Airman Mortensen's romantic imagination detected something beyond the utility of finding more beer. He imagined that she didn't care about beer at all but that she wanted him to be close to her in any way possible, even if it was just driving her car.

Airman Mortensen cowboyed a little as he cut along the base's smooth streets. But not too much. There were other things he liked better.

He liked having his butt in the spot where hers usually was; having his hands on her wheel and her shifter; having his foot bounce back and forth from her brake to her accelerator. That feeling was better than cow-boying.

Because he didn't want to screw anything up he turned the radio down as he cruised out of the main gate. When he passed the white-gloved guards with the stupid silver helmets on their heads he realized that since he was officially confined to the base he was no longer legal. Then he realized that he would be a minor scor-ing beer. That was another crime. He would have to find a tap. He'd done it lots of times but it too was against the law. He would be carrying the beer back to the base. That was probably some sort of crime too. He would be handing the beer over to three underage girls. No doubt about that one.

But Airman Mortensen wasn't bothered by any of this. Normally, he stayed clear of crime but on this particular night he was feeling a curious and exhilarat-ing power—the kind of power a sometime pool player feels when his cue gets hot. He felt bulletproof.

Instead of going into town and looking up someone who could be trusted, he pulled in at a busy, well-lit liquor store a quarter mile from the front gate. Then he leaned brazenly against one of the store's window ledges, waiting for a likely subject.

When three single guys got out of a late-model Chevy, he stopped the driver, squinted through the pesky smoke coming from the cigarette between his lips and stuck a ten-dollar bill he'd folded down the middle in the man's hand.

"Buy me some beer, huh?"

The surprised driver stared at him. Airman Morten-sen didn't blink.

"What kind?"

"Country Club . . . three six-packs . . . keep what's left, that's cool."

The bulletproof, slick-sleeve latrine king waited for

his tap at the liquor store entrance. When the driver walked out, his arms loaded with beer, Airman Mortensen relieved him of the contraband in full view of the two clerks inside.

The guard with the stupid silver helmet snapped to attention and saluted when he saw the blue officer's sticker on the VW's bumper. Airman Mortensen was tempted to hoist the open beer sitting between his legs but opted for a sensible, two-fingered boy scout salute and sailed on for Cheeze Street.

In Colonel Brill's driveway he cut the engine, fired up another Pall Mall and tried to get a handle on the wonderful thing that was running around loose in his heart, the thing that made him bulletproof. But as he sat in the dark, listening to the engine cool, analysis escaped him. There was a face and there was a name. Nothing else.

✯ 15 ✯

Knocking seemed ridiculous now. He twisted the knob on the front door and carried the three six-packs into Colonel Brill's house as if he'd been coming in and out for years.

There was no one in the kitchen and for reasons he didn't understand, Airman Mortensen was suddenly on edge. He dumped his beer on the kitchen table and listened.

There was gunfire coming from the den. Someone was watching the TV. He thought he could hear female voices but they were faint and he couldn't be sure.

He listened in the other direction and heard a steady, mechanical chugging. It sounded like a washer. It seemed weird—a washer going this late on a Saturday night.

At any other time Airman Mortensen would have investigated these sounds but for the moment he was not interested in TVs or washers or even the beer he'd brought back. He didn't want to see Pat or Jancy. His heart had put him into a trance. He was stretched out on a table, heavily drugged, floating in a happy fog of images—the five letters of her name, the shape of her breasts, the sound she made when she coughed. Every image and every thought, no matter how mundane, made him delirious. There was room for nothing else and Airman Mortensen was so excited he had to bite his lip to keep from losing what little control he had left. His romantic imagination was running everything now.

He tried to calm himself by putting the beer in the refrigerator. Slowly, a can at a time, he lined them all up on one shelf. Airman Mortensen was thinking how impressive they looked, so many tall cans standing together, when the voice came to him.

Though he'd been completely alone and wasn't expecting it, the voice didn't startle him. If anything, it had the opposite effect. It was a familiar hand, coming to rest softly on his shoulder.

"You got it."

He brought his head up slowly and saw her face. It was peeking out from a doorway, a happy, fresh face radiating nothing but good. Several seconds went by before he made his playful reply.

"Didn't you think I was gonna get it?"

"No . . . I mean yes." A flush passed over the face in the doorway.

"You thought I was going to fuck it up, didn't you?"

"Nooooooo . . . ," she whined. The long sandy hair rippled from side to side as she shook her head. She pouted a moment longer, then looked up bashfully, her clear green eyes shining with hope.

"Do I get one?"

Airman Mortensen sighed theatrically.

"I don't know what you've done to deserve one."

"I'm doing the laundry."

"Doing the laundry?"

"Somebody's got to do it."

"It's Saturday night for God's sake."

Claire stood full in the doorway, slumping like a woeful Cinderella. She locked two fingers together and scraped a toe across the floor.

"I'm in charge of the house," she said, her voice breaking. "I thought if I did the laundry someone might be pleased." She was doing her best to stay in character but the beautiful smile kept threatening to break through.

Airman Mortensen took a beer out of the refrigerator and walked it over. Grasping the can's lip with two fingers, he held it in front of her face.

"I might be making a mistake," he said sternly, "but you may have one."

She took it from him and gazed into his face.

"You're always so kind to me . . . I don't know what to say."

If he were starring in a bad movie Airman Mortensen would have settled it then and there. He would have put his face close to hers, slipped his arms along her ribs and pulled her close. Then he would have kissed her. But Airman Mortensen was just Airman Mortensen. All he could do was smile, as he marveled at her face.

"Are you really doing the laundry?" he asked.

"Yes," she laughed. "I guess it was a stupid thing to do. But I'm almost done. Come on."

Airman Mortensen got a beer of his own and followed her into the laundry room. The dryer had been making the weird chugging sound. Claire pronounced the load fit for folding and Airman Mortensen gallantly insisted on helping.

"I'll do the towels," he said, knowing it would be impossible to screw up towels.

"I was doing this when Kennedy was shot," she mused. "Do you remember what you were doing?"

"Oh yeah, I remember." Airman Mortensen was ditching his algebra class on the day Kennedy was shot. More specifically, he was making out in a car with a religiously inclined girl when someone brought the news to the school parking lot. He omitted that information. "I was sitting in a car," he said.

They talked about Kennedy's murder for awhile. Both thought it unlikely that Oswald acted alone. They moved on to guns. Neither one could understand the country's fascination with firearms. From there they slipped into a long discussion of movies. Movies led to food and food led to elementary school.

Long after the folding was done they hung around the laundry room, breezing from one topic to another, sometimes forming their comments with studied passion, sometimes lapsing into play. Through it all there wasn't much room for silence. They were finding out about each other and, with so much held in common, it was hard to stop talking.

Airman Mortensen was well into his second beer and had just revealed the circumstances of his first real kiss, a whole afternoon of fifth-grade kissing at a Saturday matinee, when Jancy appeared in the laundry room doorway.

Her eyes were heavy-lidded and she was having trouble standing.

"You're drunk," Claire said.

"Yeah," the younger sister replied. "I'm going to sleep."

"Where's Pat?" Claire asked, taking a step toward her sister.

"She already crashed. She's drunk too. Well . . ."

Jancy stared at them for a few seconds as she swayed in the doorway. Then she half lifted a hand, said, "Goodnight," did a shaky about-face and lurched into the kitchen. One of her thighs crunched against the breakfast table but she righted herself and staggered down the hall to her bedroom.

Claire's response was automatic and Airman Mortensen watched as she followed her little sister down the hall. Then he got another Country Club and went into the living room. He felt like listening to some music.

The lighting in the living room perplexed him. There was an overhead burning, plus a couple of lamps. He hated overheads, especially late at night, but thought twice about turning it off. He didn't want her to come back and think he was trying to set a mood. Then he thought, 'Well, maybe I am . . . but . . . well . . . so what?' He liked the room better once the overhead was off, so much so that he extinguished one of the two remaining lamps. Then he settled under the soft glow of the last light, which was sitting next to the stereo, and began to rummage through the albums on the floor.

He was trying to decide between Muddy Waters and the Blues Magoos when Claire came back. She paused in the doorway, not looking at him, working something over in her mind. Airman Mortensen sensed the sadness he had seen in her from time to time.

She turned away and disappeared, returning seconds later with a beer of her own. Wordlessly she sat on the floor next to Airman Mortensen, popped the can and took a long drink. She wiped the corner of her mouth and smiled at him.

"How's Jancy?" he asked.

"She's asleep."

"Did she get sick?"

"No . . . can I have one of your cigarettes?"

"They're Pall Malls."

"What does that matter?"

"They're really strong . . . I call 'em red lung suckers."

She picked up the pack and turned it in her hand. Then she shook out a long, white cigarette and examined it.

"I'll try one anyway," she grinned. She stuck the cigarette in her mouth and Airman Mortensen lit it for her.

"What's with Jancy, anyway?"

"I don't know," Claire sighed. "She's old for her age but she's too young to do things. She's bored a lot I think."

"So is everybody," Airman Mortensen commented.

Claire sighed again. This time her whole body went up and down with the deep breath.

"The world is all fucked up."

"You can say that again," he laughed.

"The world is all fucked up."

Airman Mortensen lit a Pall Mall for himself and held the match, watching it burn.

"You know what I think?" he said wistfully. "I think it's gonna get a lot more fucked up before it gets better."

"I think you're right . . . it's too bad."

They drank simultaneously from their beers and were quiet. Airman Mortensen toyed with the record pile.

"Do you have any Dylan?"

Claire smiled at her hands and shook her head.

"God, that's funny," she said.

"What?"

She stood on her knees and started to search the records with a purpose.

"I was just thinking I'd like to hear some Dylan. Dylan's the best."

"I know," he agreed. "When you compare anybody else to him there's no comparison. If it wasn't for Dylan I'd be insane."

"Me too."

☆ 16 ☆

Colonel Brill's house wasn't much when you got down to it.

Defense Department dollars had built the place to a set of dimensions befitting the habitat of a base commander. These dimensions were somewhat larger than other homes on the installation and included a few, spartan extras. Instead of a carport, for instance, the Brill home featured a two-automobile garage. The spacious laundry room was another example of an extra. So was the den.

Colonel Brill was only the current resident. There had been a long line of previous commandants and when Colonel Brill got transferred again, as he inevitably would, a new base commander would move into the big house on Cheeze Street.

Each family had its own characteristics of course, but it would have been impossible to erect a structure every couple of years to suit the tastes and needs of new occupants. Because of this, the building's design, aside from previously mentioned dimensions and extras, was

conceived to function like a blank scrabble piece or a
child's coloring book.

It was a roof and walls and flooring, made comfortable with paint and furniture and carpeting, colored
rather randomly with various nicknacks the Brill family
had acquired in their years of military globe-trotting.

All in all it was a forgettable place. But there are
times when a certain room, no matter how nondescript,
might, on a certain night, take on a special aura. It
might even become the setting for a private and precious piece of human history. The Brill family living
room became just this sort of place in the wee hours of
a long-ago spring morning in New Mexico.

Claire and Airman Mortensen listened to both sides
of *Bringing It All Back Home* with intense concentration. After hearing a long song like "It's Alright Ma,
I'm Only Bleeding" Airman Mortensen would lift the
needle off the player and they would talk for as long as
they wanted about the wonderful ideas behind the lines.
Then they would start the record again.

When they listened to something beautiful like "Love
Minus Zero" there was nothing to discuss. Airman
Mortensen would squirm to his knees and walk stump-
like toward the record player saying, "God, let's hear
that again, huh?" and Claire, lying in place on her side,
would exclaim dreamily "Yes!"

The clock drove deeper into morning but they didn't
notice. The living room had become a timeless place,
a cube floating in space, and after listening to a whole
record it seemed that no time had passed at all.

Airman Mortensen grabbed up the *Turn, Turn, Turn*
record and exhibited the cover.

"Byrdorama?"

Claire was sitting now. She pressed both hands together and held them expectantly in front of her chest.

"Oh yes!"

The first crash of Roger McGuinn's guitar brought Airman Mortensen to his feet. Claire jumped up too and suddenly they were dancing.

"Gotta turn it up," Airman Mortensen shouted happily and, without breaking stride, he sidehopped to the volume knob and gave it a crank.

They danced as they had before, only harder and wilder. They weren't just celebrating the music now. They were celebrating this night. They were celebrating being together.

The dancing was very free and it's doubtful that either before or after, Colonel Brill's living room saw the likes of such dancing.

At the end of each song Airman Mortensen stood where the music stopped, bent at the waist, his hands on his knees, gasping for breath.

Claire took little walks around the room, brushing her hair back with both hands, her eyes on the ceiling and closed most of the time.

After four songs Airman Mortensen developed a tremendous sideache and had to stop. He lay flat on his back and shut his eyes against the pain as he dug a hand into his gut.

Claire kept asking if he was okay and Airman Mortensen kept saying it was just a sideache and would go away in a couple of minutes, which it did.

When he opened his eyes she was walking back into the room with a fresh Country Club. He propped himself on an elbow and took the beer.

"It's okay now . . . thanks."

"Are you sure?" she asked, sitting Indian style in front of him.

"Oh yeah, it was just a sideache. I don't know if I can go anymore though."

"Me neither."

"But that was great . . . I never dance like that."

"Me neither."

She took the beer out of his hand and sipped at the place where his mouth had been.

Airman Mortensen was suddenly aware that it was just the two of them. 'There is nothing but us,' he thought. All at once he wanted to tell her what he felt. He wanted to touch her. But he couldn't.

The slick-sleeve latrine king looked around the room in a quiet panic.

"I wonder what time it is?" he asked lamely.

At the instant he said this Airman Mortensen could have kicked himself a mile. He watched helplessly as her head dropped.

"I don't know," she said softly.

Her lips had tightened and he could see her eyes shifting nervously over a tiny patch of carpet at her feet. It was not a sight he could bear and Airman Mortensen triumphed over whatever fears were lurking inside him with a single decisive motion.

He reached out and took her hand.

One of Claire's fingers moved between his when he did this.

Her eyes were still on the carpet but they weren't moving anymore.

"I think about you," she said sweetly, placing both hands around his. "I've been thinking about you the whole time . . . I can't help it."

Airman Mortensen sat up. He was sitting Indian style too. They were knee to knee. It was absolutely still in the house; yet he could hear nothing. He bowed his head and covered his face with his free hand.

"I can't believe this," he said.

"What?" she whispered.

"I see your face in my head all the time. I see your name. It's there all the time."

"I do too."

He heard her sniffle and tilted his head to get a look at her face. The tears that had filled her eyes were running slowly down her cheeks. Airman Mortensen's throat tightened. His nose started to stuff up.

"Is it bad?" he asked, only half joking.

She glanced at him shyly, smiling in spite of her tears. Then she dropped her head and sniffled again.

"This has never happened to me," she confided, her breath coming hard, "not like this. It's so wonderful, it's scary."

Airman Mortensen had been fighting it since his throat began to tighten. But now he was losing the battle. The wetness in his own eyes was out of control and when one tear fell along his face more began to follow. It was like pain to speak but he did.

"It is wonderful, isn't it?"

"Yes," she sniffled, "I guess I must be in love."

"I guess I must be too."

They looked up at the same time and, after all the holding back, it was a great relief to see each other's faces. Airman Mortensen sniffed hard and wiped at his cheek.

"I'll tell you what," he said, his composure coming back in a rush, "I'd hate to think how I'd be if you didn't love me."

Claire rolled her eyes and laughed.

"Oh God, I'd be dead."

They fell silent again, averting their eyes. Airman Mortensen didn't know what to do. He heard the clock bong twice and looked at Claire and saw her lips. He saw the full sculpture of them for the first time. They were exquisite. He moved his head forward and, in so doing, tripped a mysterious mechanism that put Claire's head into motion too.

Their mouths came together in a gentle press and Airman Mortensen tasted her breath. It tasted fresh as turned earth and though he had kissed girls befoie, the latrine king had never tasted anything like this. It was heavenly.

The kiss didn't last long but the thrill of its tenderness could not have been matched by a thousand kisses.

They pulled slowly away and sat cheek to cheek and knee to knee, so quiet that they could hear each other's breathing.

"Let's dance," Airman Mortensen whispered.

Neither one spoke as they got up. Claire waited in the center of the room while Airman Mortensen searched out a slow song on the Byrds record. He placed the needle between the tracks and went to the girl in the center of the room.

Still they did not speak. They came together like an ageless couple. The touch and the smell of each other, even the pressure of their bodies, so new and exciting, seemed somehow familiar.

They shuffled across Colonel Brill's carpeting with no pawing or groping or grinding. There was no worrying about what the other might be thinking. There were no trips, no crunched toes, no "oops, sorrys."

Claire rested her face against his neck. Airman Mortensen laid his on her shoulder, filling his nose with the smell of her sweater and the skin beneath it. He didn't feel her face or thighs or breasts as separate entities. Everything was one. One person with a name. Claire Brill. He could feel her heart beating against his.

When the song was over they stood motionless, one draped over the other, waiting for the record to track through the next song. Guitars crashed but they didn't dance.

"It's so late," she whispered, holding onto him.

"Yeah."

He loosed his arms, led her to the stereo and turned off the music.

Under the glow of the remaining lamp they stood
forehead to forehead, unable to move. The house was
so still and once again Airman Mortensen didn't know
what to do. The patch of her forehead where it pressed
against his was overwhelming.

"I can't sleep with Pat."

She slid her hands up to his shoulder blades.

"I hope not," she whispered.

"I didn't want to sleep with her last night. I think I
wanted to sleep with you. I only want to sleep with
you."

Claire sucked in her breath and gasped. She brushed
his lips with hers and hung her head on his shoulder.

"We can't tonight."

"But I can't sleep with her. I can only sleep with you
now."

"I know, I know," she breathed.

Her face crimped in thought.

"I'll make up a bed in the den."

"Okay."

They sleepwalked arm in arm down the hall. Claire's
face was bent to the floor.

"I think I love you," she said.

"I love you too," he answered.

Airman Mortensen stopped and she looked up at him.
Her eyes were glistening.

They kissed long and slow, so slow that the kiss
seemed to last forever. Then they walked on, down the
hall to the den.

✩ 17 ✩

After they pulled out the Hide-a-Bed Claire insisted on leaving to find fresh sheets. Airman Mortensen stood at the foot of the converted sofa and tried to think. So much had happened in such a short time. His mind couldn't keep up with so many developments.

Sleeping with Pat. Getting drunk in Colonel Brill's house. Claire . . . Claire, Claire. Every sentence of his thought held her name. It was too much and he convulsed at the thought of what would happen next. For a second or two the idea of being far away seemed appealing.

Then she came back, hugging a set of sheets to her breast, and it was all simple again.

Their arms crept around one another and the sheets fell to the floor. They kissed with more fervor than before. Claire pulled her mouth back from his.

"Hey," she whispered.

He looked into her happy eyes.

"What?"

"You've got to help me," she said, stooping to retrieve the fallen sheets.

Airman Mortensen watched her back. "I don't know about sleeping here," he said.

"What's wrong?" she asked, coming off the floor.

"Nothing's wrong . . . I'm just thinking . . . what will Pat think?"

"I don't know."

"You guys are friends. She's gonna find out."

Claire dropped her head.

"Yeah, she'll have to find out." Her lips twisted as she thought about it. "I'll just tell her."

"Maybe I should go back," he suggested. "Maybe that would make it easier for everybody."

Claire probed one of his belt loops with a finger as she thought it over. He could see the creases of doubt on her face. When she brought her eyes up they were shining like a child's.

"But I want to see you when I wake up."

Airman Mortensen melted.

"You'll see me," he said reassuringly.

It took a minute or two to throw out the sheets and tuck in the edges. He sat on the edge of the bed and took off his shirt. She kissed him quickly, whispered "Goodnight" and hurried out of the room. Airman Mortensen was alone once more in Colonel Brill's house.

The bed was a little short, his heels hung over the thin mattress, but all in all Airman Mortensen felt on top of the world. His life had changed tonight. There was no doubt about it.

He turned on his side and pulled his legs up, bringing his heels back onto the mattress. He tucked his hands under his chin and floated. He wanted to dream about Claire all night long and wake to her face first thing in the morning. So long as he had her lovely face in his head nothing else really mattered.

Airman Mortensen did dream about his girl, beautiful dreams starring the face of Claire Brill. As the morning hours inched along, the handy, roll-out bed in the den became a palace of dreams. And Airman Mortensen got his wish—her face was everywhere. The dreams were very vivid, so vivid at times that in his half sleep the latrine king could not tell if he was awake or not. At last she actually climbed into the bed, sliding under the

covers to nestle at his side. Airman Mortensen's arms
groped for her body and he heard himself purr out the
words:

"Claire . . . ohhh . . . Claire."

"What?"

The voice sounded real.

"Huh?" Airman Mortensen stammered.

"Claire . . . you said Claire!"

He came awake and as the dream receded into reality
he thought he saw Pat sitting up in the bed. Airman
Mortensen tried to rise up but he could only blink
dumbly at the girl who was glaring down at him.

"Claire," she hissed. "You said Claire."

The covers shot up and in the fuzzy night light he
saw her plant her feet on the floor, bounce off the bed
and stomp out of the room. He could see the bra strap
flat across her back, the bikini look of her underpants,
the coarse black hair.

It was Pat.

Airman Mortensen rolled onto his back and stared at
the ceiling, watching strange jets of light jump in his
eyes.

"This is fucked," he whispered to himself. "This is
really fucked."

☆ **18** ☆

The first thing Airman Mortensen saw when he woke
was Claire. She was wrapped in the old blue bathrobe.
The smile on her face was intact. She slid onto the bed
and settled close to the latrine king.

"I love you," he murmured. Then he yawned as she settled her head against his neck. They held each other.

Her voice sounded tinny. "Did you sleep well?"

"I don't know . . . I thought about you all night."

"Ohhh," she moaned, "I did too."

"You thought about you?"

"Nooo, I thought about you."

Her head came up and they pressed their mouths together in a kiss. Then he whispered against her lips.

"Something happened . . . something really weird."

"What?" She pulled away a little.

"Well . . . Pat came in here. She got in the bed."

"She did?"

"Yeah . . . ," Airman Mortensen sighed. "And I think I fucked up . . . royally . . . I thought she was you. I said your name a couple of times before I knew it was her."

"Oh God."

"I didn't know, ya know . . . I thought it was you."

Claire took an extra breath and blew it out.

"What did she do?"

"She left."

"Was she mad?"

"Yeah."

Claire thought for a moment.

"What is it?" he asked.

"She won't come out."

"Out of where?"

"Out of her room."

"Oh God," Airman Mortensen grumbled, dropping his head into his hands, "I really screwed up."

"Well . . ."

"I didn't know . . . it was dark."

"I'll get Jancy to talk to her. She won't talk to me."

Airman Mortensen tried to find something to say as he toyed with the sheet's hem.

"I hope this doesn't wreck your friendship."

"It probably already has," Claire sighed.

Airman Mortensen stared gloomily at his lap.

"Oh, don't worry," she said, rubbing one of his knees, "she'll get over it. I would've had to tell her about us anyway."

"Yeah, I 'spose."

She slipped off the bed and smiled at him uncomfortably.

"There's coffee in the kitchen . . ."

Airman Mortensen nodded.

"You can stay in bed if you want . . . I'll be back."

The latrine king lay under the covers for a few minutes but couldn't go back to sleep. He got dressed, neatened the bed and wandered down to the kitchen. For a few more minutes he sat alone at the table smoking a Pall Mall and gulping the coffee. Then he wandered back toward the bedrooms to find out what was going on.

Jancy was just slipping through the guest room doorway. Claire was watching from a discreet distance down the hall. Airman Mortensen could tell by her posture that she was worried.

There were voices inside the guest room. Airman Mortensen recognized the German girl's tone, rising higher as it bled through the door and seeped into the hallway and he knew it was time for him to go. The whole house was focused on the German girl's grief. And he was the cause of it.

When he tiptoed down to Claire he saw that she was crying too. He told her he was going. She said it was a good idea. When he turned to leave she pinched at his shirt, tugged him back and buried her face in his chest.

"I love you," she sniffed.

Airman Mortensen patted the smooth brown hair on the back of her head.

"I'm sorry you have to go through this," he said. But she didn't seem to hear him.

"I love you," she said again.

☆ **19** ☆

Airman Mortensen was so beat by the time he got back to the barracks that he took off his sandals to mount the second flight of stairs, thinking their removal would somehow lighten his load.

Sunday was the quietest time on base. A tiny percentage of troops got up for services at the forlorn little chapel down by the hospital. But these men were generally quiet anyway.

The main hell-raisers were asleep in their metal-frame beds on Sunday morning, recovering from the ravages of alcohol and the stress of trying to maneuver girls. There were usually a few guys lounging in front of the dayroom TV, watching sports.

But it was too early even for that. The games back East hadn't started and as Airman Mortensen plodded down the deserted hallway he actually felt good to be back in the barracks. After all that had happened it was a relief to be alone again in a place that, no matter how much it might be detested, was home.

There was a sudden muffled cheering from one of the rooms just ahead of him. Airman Mortensen pressed an ear against the door and heard voices inside, many voices. He knocked and the voices stopped. A moment passed. No one answered. He knocked harder.

"Whosit?"

"Mortensen."

"Wha' you wan'?"

Airman Mortensen laughed. "I want to come in mother-fucker . . . why do you think I'm knockin'?"

The door opened partway. A cloud of cigarette smoke floated into the hall. Then a black head poked through the cloud, bobbing first one way, then the other, looking for signs of trouble. It was Lee DeHart. A silk stocking was stretched tightly on his head. The whites of his narrow eyes were yellow. A cigarette jumped up and down between his lips as he spoke.

"Wha' you doin', Mort?"

"I'm comin' into your room . . . unless you're prejudiced."

The black man looked up and down the hall once more. Then he receded into the smoke and Airman Mortensen followed.

Before the military he had known no Negroes. There might have been one or two in high school but he'd never spoken to them. It wasn't until a few months ago, in basic training, that he talked to his first Negro.

Not unless Mae was counted. Mae was the maid his mother had employed off and on for many years. But it was hard to think of Mae as a Negro. She had been part of the family. She ran the household.

If Airman Mortensen had reached back in his memory he would have been hard pressed to remember anything beyond the features and voice of the aggressive black woman who had lived in his childhood. He could not have remembered where she lived because he had never been to her home. Or if she had a husband or children. If she ever cried or where she went on vacation or what she liked to watch on television. What kind of friends she had. None of this information had ever presented itself. It never seemed necessary. The kitchens of his boyhood were just the kitchens, the bedrooms just the bedrooms. And Mae was just the maid.

But these black men weren't just anything. They were wild and colorful and sometimes scary. But they were easy too. From the day he stepped off the bus in Texas, the day his drill instructor proclaimed that his soul might be God's but "for the next six weeks your ass is mine," Airman Mortensen had found himself able to slip in and out of the black men's lives with hardly a ripple.

This he did in spite of the reticence on the part of both black and white. The ways might be subtle, but in 1966 the military was still deeply segregated. Although there were exceptions the races generally preferred to room together and were not discouraged from doing so. And practicing racists had little trouble keeping their distance from one another at home and on the job.

Many barriers had dropped, however. The men showered in the same stalls, shaved in the same sinks, shit in the same toilets. They ate together, drank together, sometimes gambled together and in the hivelike atmosphere of the barracks, couldn't help being privy to many intimate details of one another's lives: the deaths of relatives, trouble in the work-place, the "Dear John" letters that broke hearts, the trading of styles and expressions, the stories of past lives lived in every corner of the country.

Airman Mortensen had an innate curiosity about people and perhaps it was this trait more than any other that made it easy for him to cohabit with people of different colors. Whatever it was, he got along, especially with the black men who lived on his floor, the men he was watching now.

Lee's room had been turned into a card parlor and

from the looks of it the game had gone on all night. They were gathered around a desk in the center of the messy cubicle. The players were slumped in chairs, their black skin contrasting wildly with the white skivvies and T-shirts. Empty bottles of sloe gin and local wine and low-grade vodka were stashed under their chairs.

There were half a dozen men in the room, four of whom were still lounging around the table trying to conjure a few more winning hands. Airman Mortensen knew them and they knew him, but except for Michael G. Taylor, no one acknowledged his coming with more than a glance.

Michael G. Taylor was tall and pleasant and, at seventeen, young for his age. Being thought of as a man among men was his constant desire but he was far too self-conscious and inexperienced to pass muster as anything but a boy. He was wary of the whites but trusted Airman Mortensen more than he did most grays.

"Whatch you doin', Slick . . . creepin' around this time a mornin'?"

MGT asked this with a chummy leer that showed off a set of large and beautifully formed teeth.

Lee DeHart had sunk back into a study of his latest hand but, as always, he was listening. His words, so distinctive in their melody, were about Airman Mortensen but intended for MGT.

"Where you think he been, boy? . . . he been out tryin' to get him a taste."

Lee's eyes fluttered and Newt, who had been hanging over DeHart's shoulder, put a hand over his mouth and laughed, his bony shoulders vibrating underneath the green, phosphorescent trench coat.

Keeping his eyes on the cards, Lee laughed too, a deep chuckle rumbling up from the bottom of his throat.

MGT cast about desperately. The other men in the

room had caught the contagion of Newt's laughter. Even Carl was smiling.

"Who you callin' boy?" MGT challenged. His lips curled as he stepped toward Lee. His arms hung steadily at his sides. His hands compressed themselves into balls.

Lee never looked up. He casually rearranged his cards. The inevitable cigarette bobbed in his mouth again.

"I'm callin' you a boy . . . boy . . . you askin' Mort 'bout all dis shit when you ain't never had no tas' yoself."

"You a lying mothafucka," MGT squawked.

"Now don' be callin' me no liar," Lee warned, calmly tilting back in his chair. His heavy-lidded eyes glanced at the dealer. "Gimme two cards, nigger."

Michael G. Taylor stood his ground helplessly, suddenly indecisive. For a moment his mouth formed words that refused to come alive. Then he thrust his head out belligerently and squawked again.

"I've eat more pussy'n you ever seen, Lee DeHart, and if you say I ain't you a darn liar."

Solemnly, deliberately, Lee picked up each of his new cards.

"You ain't," he said.

MGT lifted his fists slightly. His jaw flapped as if in a fit.

"You can' call me no boy, mothafucka . . . you see how much a boy I is you get off your black ass. C'mon, c'mon." MGT feinted and jabbed. One of his long-fingered hands brushed Lee's shoulder. "C'mon."

Lee's ears went flat against the sides of his head. He slammed down his cards and shoved his chair back.

MGT's fists went higher. He backed up a couple of steps, scared stiff. But before he could blink twice

Newt's nose was an inch or two from his and the high voice was hissing.

"You dumb muthafucka, don' start no shit." Newt's hand was deep in a trench coat pocket, fumbling for the legendary knife. "U get usef cut, you dumb muthafucka. U wan' get cut now? I . . . I . . . I cut U . . . mutha . . . fucka."

Michael G. Taylor's jaw went slack. His eyeballs rolled in their sockets. Newt was threatening him, Lee DeHart was dodging around behind the Mississippian, waving a finger as he said all manner of nasty things, and everyone in the room was suddenly hollering at once. MGT was baffled by the uproar. He'd only wanted to assert himself. He didn't want to fight Lee DeHart.

Airman Mortensen squeezed between Newt and MGT.

"Fuck this, MGT, you don't need this shit."

Carl appeared at Airman Mortensen's side.

"C'mon, Michael, let's get some air," he said.

Together they herded the young man through the door and into the hall. All at once, everything was quiet.

Biting his lower lip, MGT paced back and forth, his eyes boring into the checkerboard linoleum at his feet.

Carl and Airman Mortensen watched MGT stop and slap the yellowish flat of his hand against the cinderblock wall.

"That muthafucka's always ridin' my ass . . . he *always* ridin' it. I'm gone beat 'is head in . . . I swear."

But there was no fight in him now, only hurt. Wearily, he laid his forehead against the block wall and, knowing he was on the verge of tears, Carl and Airman Mortensen shyly averted their eyes.

The black men were always at each other. In the months he had known them Airman Mortensen had seen many of these squabbles break out. Sometimes the yelling was as terrible as the high-pitched squeal of fighting

horses. Sometimes men had to be held to keep from
having at each other. Though he wasn't there, Airman
Mortensen had it on good authority that Newt had once
pulled his knife. But apparently Newt had waved it
around just to prove that he actually had a knife. In his
brief experience Airman Mortensen had never seen the
black men come to blows. He had become used to their
raucous word battles and for a young white man who
had never known Negroes it was almost like entertainment, like a show to be enjoyed.

MGT was a little different. He really felt for MGT.
They rode him mercilessly. And the more MGT tried
to front himself as a man the more they rode him.

Carl laid a hand on the boy's shoulder and spoke
soothingly into his ear.

"Hey, Michael . . . calm down, man."

"MG . . . ," Airman Mortensen put in, "it's no big
deal."

MGT turned his head enough to look at them with
one, glistening eye.

"He picks on me, man."

"Fuck it," Carl said quietly.

"Say what?"

"Fuck it."

MGT looked to Airman Mortensen for sympathy.

"I'm with him," Airman Mortensen smiled.

The hurt boy came off the wall, wiping his eyes with
a forearm.

"You jus' gray muthafuckas . . . both y'all jus'
gray."

Carl and Airman Mortensen looked at each other.

"Yeah," they said simultaneously.

The three soldiers shared grunts of laughter. Then
there was a silence, during which MGT looked long-
ingly in the direction of his room. He ground the heels
of his big hands into his face.

"I'm gonna go sleep," he announced, sounding very tired.

"You should," Carl said. "You've been up all night, you ain't worth shit."

"Who ain't shit?" MGT answered, starting down the hall. "Y'all ain't shit neither . . . and neither one y'all's been up all night." These last words came with a glimmer of his regular cockiness. He shuffled a few more steps down the hall and peeked over his shoulder, his boyish eyes bright once again.

"Y'all ain't shit."

His strut got stronger with each step and by the time he reached the door to his room Michael G. Taylor was bopping. One of the big, yellowed palms closed over the doorknob and he glanced back at them once more, his face full of teeth.

"No suh," he chuckled happily, "y'all ain't shit."

At this point Airman Mortensen wasn't really listening. For the last few seconds he'd been thinking about Carl, intrigued by his freshness. No matter the time of day or night Carl always seemed fresh. He'd been up most of the night but not a hair was out of place. The lines in his face had gone no deeper. The diamond-patterned sweater vest didn't show a single piece of lint, much less a stain. The slacks still held a crease. The leather on his loafers' toes were beginning to give out, but what there was of polish remained unscuffed. The small teeth, set in the small mouth, still gleamed despite the pack and a half of camels he smoked every day.

"You comin' back in? You wanna play a few hands?"

"I don't think so," Airman Mortensen replied.

"Well . . . ," Carl pursed his lips in the sweet little grin that was his trademark. "I'll see you."

"See you later."

Airman Mortensen watched Carl's back as he slipped

into the room full of cigarette smoke and gently closed
the door behind him.

'How strange,' Airman Mortensen thought.

No one was better liked than Carl. He treated everyone with respect and softspoken courtesy. He never had
problems in the office where he clerked, was rarely
boisterous, even when drunk, and consistently minded
his own business.

Carl and Lee DeHart were so different, such an unlikely pair to be roommates. But they were more than
roommates. They behaved like brothers and no soldier
who knew them could argue otherwise.

Carl was a charter member of Lee DeHart's loose
knit gang, the gang that shuttled constantly between the
base and the small, black ghetto downtown. Carl was
always with them, effortlessly sharing their talk and music and booze and even their women. When they went
downtown to "ride the bull" (a huge black woman with
a lumberjack's appetite for sex) Carl went with them.
He "rode the bull" too.

No one talked much about Carl's membership in the
DeHart gang but everyone, including Airman Mortensen, thought it strange. In dress and speech and build
and color, Carl was the epitome of his race.

He was white as a slice of Wonder Bread.

✩ 20 ✩

Airman Mortensen tried to sleep but the world was
too much with him. He lay between the sheets of his
narrow bunk and felt his body vibrate with fatigue.

Every cell begged for rest. While his body tossed and
turned, Airman Mortensen's mind pulsated with a wild
array of pictures and words.

For a time he tried to fight off the images and commentary that paraded behind his closed eyes. But he
was his own captive audience and the show going on in
his head refused to stop. Not knowing whether he was
asleep or awake, the latrine king let the diorama spin
past at full speed.

He saw the hiker's body for the first time in years,
saw men in heavy jackets struggling up the Merced River's bank with the corpse. The picture of that foggy,
spring morning in Yosemite rolled on and Airman Mortensen shuddered at the thought of losing his own ten-
uous hold on a rock wall. He saw his boot scratching
at a sliver of ledge that would not hold him. He saw
himself falling down the face of an outcropping, gathering speed as he plunged hundreds of feet toward the
river below.

Another scene, a slow drive-by on Highway 101 just
north of La Jolla. The sheet-covered bodies, six or seven
of them, lying on gurneys in a ragged row at the edge
of the road. Some bodies were noticeably smaller than
the others.

His mother gasped and held her head in her hands
but otherwise no one said a word about the accident
scene as the old Buick cruised up the coast to Grandad's
house in Laguna. But everyone was shook, even his
father, and he remembered the faceless dead. They visited him all the rest of the day. They visited him as he
stood on his grandfather's grass, hosing the sand from
his little knit trunks after an afternoon of play at the
beach. They visited him now, so many years later.

'Always with me . . . always with me.'

Grandfather held court for the grownups from a big,
thronelike chair at the end of a long room. He fueled

his colorful stories with Old Stag bourbon and White
Owl cigars.

Smoking Salems . . . Salems stolen from Mom's cigarette drawer in the Ocean Beach house. Running down
the alley to meet friends. Opening the fresh pack, the
neat, white filters standing in formation like treasure.
Smoking one after another. Not inhaling.

The Strand Theatre down by the beach. Going there
on Saturday afternoons. Gorging on candy: Milk Duds,
Good 'N' Plenty, Dots. Folded popcorn boxes sailing
through the projector's silver light, headed for Tarzan
swinging across the screen. Sitting in the dark with Kay
Kiner, an arm around her small, square shoulders.
Kissing her smooth lips. Getting kissed back.

Walking into Mom and Dad's bedroom in the house
on Point Loma. Mom face down, spread-eagled on the
bed, naked. Her feet cocked at uncomfortable angles.
She looks dead. She's not dead. Something happened.
I don't know. I know but I don't. Dad, in one quick
motion, throwing a bed sheet over her. "Don't come
in here . . . don't come in here."

Dreaming in the bedroom downstairs. What was the
dream? Can't remember. What was it? Something in
the bed. Something under me. Something wet. Did I
piss in the bed? No way. Sitting up in the dark, turning
on the soft lamp to see, staring down at the wet stuff
on the sheet. What is it? Touching the stuff. It's slick,
greasy. Where did it come from? Did it come from me?
God . . . it did. It came from me. It must be . . . it
must be . . . Strange. A mystery . . . a miracle . . .
yes . . . a miracle.

Patty . . . quiet Patty on her paint pony. Patty with
the long, dark hair and the pale, blue eyes like stone.
Meeting her under the pepper tree, crawling under the
branches that touch the ground to where she waits, sitting against the trunk. Not saying much. Her not saying

anything. Not remembering a single word from her mouth. Offering her neck, brushing her hair away. Offering her lips, so big, so warm in the stillness of noon. Wanting my hand on them. Those breasts, so round and large, the flesh like no other flesh. No further. Impossible to go further. Paralyzed. Paralyzed by wonder. Patty saying nothing. Pale, blue eyes like stone.

Pooka the black dog, always in the road. A truck in the morning, a panel truck coming fast. No horn, no screeching tires. Pooka running in a crazy circle, brain smashed, legs all rubber. Pooka dead in the road. The truck never stopped. The truck never stopped. Jimmy on his knees in the street, next to Pooka, pushing at a lifeless paw.

Jimmy and the dinner chicken. "I can do it . . . I can do it . . . I'll do it." Bringing the axe down, the chicken squirming in his hand. No one can look. A glancing blow that only half chops through the neck. The hen at a goofy gallop around the yard, head flopping at its side, blood squirting out of the hole in its neck. Everyone screaming. A dark comedy. A gross movie.

So many movies. Jumping the fence at the drive-in. Coming through in the trunk. Worried about laughing too much. Worried about carbon monoxide. Sitting in the back seat with Kathy Orwell. Making out. Making out. Steamed windows. Fumbling for snaps, eyelets, straps. Exhausted.

Exhausted on Mona Driscoll's couch. Between her legs. Pumping. Pumping for hours. Denim scratching soft skin raw. Pumping. How much longer? Mona's ass, great in blue jeans. Always in blue jeans. Never saw it.

Never saw anybody. Never saw Mary who couldn't kiss. Never saw Suzanne who loved the basketball player who was first. Suzy James, skinny and beautiful, holding my hand. Suzy James . . . went to the hospital and never came back. Never saw them. Wonder what some- one looks like. All that effort. Never saw them. Maybe never ever. All that time. All those faces.

Claire's face. That's better . . . yeah . . . better. Soft hair. Dimples. Smile. Shining eyes. Shining at me. I'm in her eyes. She loves me . . . I guess. Does she? She says she does. I love her. Yeah . . . yeah . . . I do. What will happen?

What's that smell? What's that smell all over her face?

A second before he opened his eyes Airman Morten- sen realized that he was smelling something real. It was bringing him back, the gagging-sweet, alcoholic odor of brand-name cologne. He heard a light clanking of metal and blinked. His bloodshot eyes began to focus.

Bernie was standing in front of the wall locker. He had dressed down to V-neck T-shirt, white GI shorts, dark socks and black, low-cut shoes. He looked ridic- ulously old. The little Italian was slipping his Sunday slacks on a hanger, taking care to keep the crease in line. Airman Mortensen saw him pick off a piece of lint and hold it in front of his egg-shaped eyes.

"Find a dingleberry, Bernie?"

"Huh?"

"Did you find a dingleberry on your pants?" Airman Mortensen sat partway up and grabbed for the madras shirt hanging on his bedpost. The smokes were in there.

Bernie was confused. "What're you talking about? What dingleberry?"

"Forget it," Airman Mortensen said, striking a match. "How was church?"

Bernie fingered the big crucifix on his neck. "Okay," he said.

"What'd the priest have to say?"

"Aww . . . ," Bernie sighed unhappily. He sat in a chair next to Airman Mortensen's bed and put his hands together. "Nothin' much . . . marriage."

"Well that's pretty good . . . ," Airman Mortensen took a big hit off his Pall Mall. "You like the idea of marriage."

"Yeah . . . well . . . maybe . . . ," Bernie smiled shyly. "I'd much rather get laid."

Airman Mortensen laughed. "We'd all rather get laid."

"Yeah," Bernie said, nodding his head.

"Is it time for chow?"

Bernie gazed at the face of his wristwatch for what seemed eternity.

"Four minutes."

"You wanna eat?"

"Sure."

Airman Mortensen pushed back the last of his covers and started pulling on his Levis. He was buttoning up when he noticed that Bernie had yet to move. The big, Italian eyes were staring at him, waiting for him.

"What?"

Bernie grinned meekly. "Did you get laid?"

"Aww, Bernie . . ."

"C'mon, you gotta tell me."

"Like shit."

"C'mon, I'm your roomie."

"Big fuckin' deal."

"You gotta tell me somethin' for chrissakes."

Airman Mortensen considered. There was a lot to tell and not to tell. Bernie would need to have certain things clarified.

"It's too complicated . . . I'm starved, I wanna eat."

"Just tell me if you got laid."

"Why is that so important?" Airman Mortensen was getting hot.

"It just is," Bernie said, swinging his head back and forth like a child.

"Okay," Airman Mortensen relented, "the answer is no . . . I did *not* get 'laid.' "

"Shit," Bernie moaned, slapping a bare knee with his palm. He got up fast from the chair, stalked angrily back to the wall locker and started to select his lunch clothes.

"What's it to you?" Airman Mortensen asked, genuinely curious. "What's the big deal?"

"No big deal," Bernie said huffily, rifling through his hanging shirts. "You're my buddy, that's all. I wanna see you do good."

Airman Mortensen pulled a sandal strap over his heel and wondered briefly how long his roommate would be in deciding what to wear to the stinking chow hall.

"Well, if it's any consolation . . . I think I might get laid. It's not exactly the point, but I might get laid, okay?"

Bernie's head swiveled back like an owl's. His eyes were just as big.

"Yeah?"

"That's what it looks like . . . I'm not sure."

Joy flooded over Bernie's face. "God . . . that's great!"

"Just get dressed would'ya . . . just wear anything for Christ sakes."

☆ 21 ☆

Next to holidays, Sunday chow was generally considered the best. Plastic flowers were produced to grace each table in the cavernous hall and chances were good that the meat would be a little more appetizing than usual. Steak was served once or twice a month, invariably on a Sunday, and few men in Airman Mortensen's squadron walked the several hundred yards to Chow Hall Number Three without imagining its giant grill covered with sizzling steaks.

Most always these dreams of steak were shattered. Most meals featured mundane entrees of cereal-based meatloaf, shit-on-a-shingle (chipped beef on toast), roast beef aged beyond edibility and rubbery, chemically gorged chicken imported from dubious poultry farms in the Deep South.

It was true that some of the soldiers had grown up with worse. These men happily lapped up each meal, no matter how suspicious, but the vast majority of eaters, beset with chronic horniness, job disenchantment, barracks boredom and unbearably long enlistments, moved down the serving line like sticks of dynamite ready to blow. They looked at the food with an animosity exceeded only by hate for those who prepared it—the hapless cooks.

The real cooks stayed in the hidden recesses of the chow hall, leaving the job of serving to lower-grade airmen. These men stood behind the line in grubby whites, joylessly dishing out slop to customers whose one common denominator was ingratitude.

Not a week went by that someone's pent-up frustration didn't boil over into a shouting match. And it wasn't uncommon for fights to break out over the size or quality of a portion. On steak day in particular the likelihood of a fistfight was high. Soldiers who forever dreamed of steak wanted good ones.

Airman Mortensen had seen punches thrown across the serving line and on one occasion an airman had actually broken the glass-lined barrier, scrambling over the cafeteria-style tubs of food in an attempt to get his hands on the throat of an arrogant cook.

The thought of strangling someone crossed Airman Mortensen's mind as he sat with Bernie at the height of Sunday lunch. He was sourly contemplating the pink slab of pork, coated with yellow grease, that lay in the middle of his plate. Sawing through it with a dull knife, he bent back the folds for a better look. To his discerning eye it was too pink.

Glancing at the tables nearby he saw that other soldiers were talking and eating in the normal, high-volume fashion. Several plates were already clean and many more were being mopped up. By all accounts it was a successful lunch but Airman Mortensen looked again at his pink chop and found himself unconvinced.

Bernie was going to town with his meat, tilting his head slightly to fork in the last oversized hunk. He grabbed a napkin as grease and pork juice dribbled from the corner of his mouth. As he dabbed, the Italian noticed the latrine king's hesitation.

"What'sa matter?"

Airman Mortensen looked down at his plate and pushed the meat with a fork.

"I don't think this shit is cooked."

"Take it back," Bernie said. He picked up his pork bone and began to work it over as if it were an ear of corn.

Airman Mortensen stared at the crowded serving line, thinking it over.

"Naw, fuck it." He shoved the hated pork chop off his plate.

"You don't want it?"

Bernie stabbed the rejected chop with a knife and hoisted it to his own plate. There he made a visual inspection of Airman Mortensen's exploratory cut. Then

he dipped his large, Roman nose close to the meat and
sniffed.

"It's okay."

"Hey . . . be my guest."

While Bernie plowed through the second pork chop
Airman Mortensen ate half of his salad and two dishes
of vanilla pudding. Claire zipped in and out of his mind,
sometimes as a smiling face, sometimes as a soft, feeling hand, sometimes as a voice that said, "I love you."
In little, fleeting moments he was sure he could smell
her. It was wonderful having her in a place like this,
amidst hundreds of noisy men and rattling silverware
and chair legs scraping back and forth on the dirty floor.
Her memory was a hidden charm that worked whenever
he rubbed it.

"Hey, Mort."

Vic Pinkowski was standing at the tableside, an empty
tray in both hands, his sad, brown eyes gazing out of a
face mottled with pockmarks.

"Hey, Vic."

"Some of us guys are gonna go throw the ball around
. . . wanna join us?"

Airman Mortensen still felt leaden from the long night
at Colonel Brill's.

"I don't have a glove."

"That don't matter . . . the squadron's got a whole
duffel bag of shit. I already checked it out. C'mon . . .
we're just gonna hit ground balls and flies . . . just a
little workout."

"Now?"

"Yeah."

"Where you gonna be?"

"At the little park over by the flight line. You got
sneakers?"

"Yeah."

"Well c'mon then, you lazy fuck."

"Okay. I gotta change and make a call."

"Don't flake out on me."

"I'll be there."

Airman Mortensen watched for a few seconds as Vic weaved through the crowded hall with his tray. He didn't have much of a body, especially for athletics. It was dumpy, almost misshapen, and the tendency to flab would become permanent in a few years.

But Vic had motivation, an instinct to perform, that transcended his unlikely physique. On a basketball court he consistently outwitted the best Negro players with quick first steps, sly passes and committed drives to the hoop.

His quick first step helped around the infield too. He could dig out hard smashes to the hole and, through sheer tenacity, he was able to turn the double play. Clutch hitting was his specialty.

This was all done despite a heavy smoking habit and a penchant for drinking beer as if it were springwater. Vic was always the first to break a running sweat and his exertions turned the acne-scarred face red as a party bulb. He was an unattractive fatso from New Jersey with bluish pimples on his chest and chronic athlete's foot. No one minded having Vic drop by for beers and smoking and bullshit but his roommates never lasted too long because no one really wanted to live with Vic.

When it came time to compete, however, Vic was fearless. He played hard against the grain of his defects, hard enough to inspire teammates to do better. Like Carl, he was mild-mannered and minded his own business. Airman Mortensen respected him. You could count on Vic Pinkowski.

As he plodded back to the barracks the latrine king noticed that the day had turned brilliant. The air was at a perfect temperature, the sky was clear and there was the barest suggestion of a breeze. He also noticed that green shoots had begun to burst out along the branches of the bare trees. Maybe the idea of running around the ball field wasn't so bad.

Feeling better, he glanced down at Bernie.

"Let's have one of those cookies."

Moments before, Bernie had made what for him was an extremely bold move. He had swiped two chocolate chip cookies as they left the chow hall. Taking food from the hall was forbidden but no one paid attention to the unenforceable rule. Bernie was one of the few who took it seriously and right now he was keenly aware that the cookies stuffed in his jacket pocket were "hot."

The Italian looked about uneasily.

"Let's wait till we get back."

"Will you give me a fuckin' cookie?" Airman Mortensen snapped.

He grabbed at the jacket pocket but Bernie shied away with a grin.

"I'm not gettin' busted, man."

"Gimme one of those cookies."

"Naw, let's wait. We just ate, for chrissakes."

"You're serious aren'cha? You're sweating bricks over taking a couple of stupid cookies out of the chow hall."

"So what if I am? They're my cookies. You didn't take 'em."

"You're a fuckin' case, Bernie . . . I never saw such a chickenshit."

☆ 22 ☆

The latrine king took his time getting to the ball field.

He dressed slowly, asking Bernie more than once to come with him. But, saying he felt tired, the Italian lay on his bunk, stretched out in shorts and a T-shirt, determined to nap through the afternoon.

Airman Mortensen dilly-dallied in the hallways and stairwells, shooting the breeze with several of the guys. He knew it was a stall. What he really wanted was the telephone inside the GQ's office. He wanted to call. It was a little pain that grew worse with the passing of each hour. A million years seemed to have passed since he saw her last. A girl in an old, blue bathrobe. The tug from behind his shirt. The "I love you," not once but twice. The soft lips. The smell. The silky hair. The pretty eyes. All of these things had grown dim. It made him uneasy.

He stared through the glass outside the office. No one was around. The telephone was sitting prominently on the desk. What if the colonel was home? He didn't want to hear that voice. Maybe the girls were cleaning up the house. Maybe Claire and Pat were talking. A voice in his head said, 'Give it some time . . . don't call . . . give it some time, you idiot. Don't worry . . . don't call.' Airman Mortensen obeyed the voice. He turned away and walked into the glistening New Mexico afternoon.

Poor Vic. He was standing next to the backstop. The

bag of equipment was leaning against the chain-link cage. He was completely alone.

"Where is everybody?" Airman Mortensen asked.

"Shit . . . I don't know." Vic sucked at the last of his cigarette and flipped it into the dirt. "I told all kinds of guys . . . they said they were comin'. I don't fuckin' know."

Airman Mortensen surveyed the empty ballpark. Untrimmed crabgrass fringed the infield. Unfilled divots were posted at the bases like tiny waterholes. The outfield lawn was dry and brown. Clumps of flat and deadly goathead weeds were growing here and there.

"Maybe everyone figures it's too early for softball," he said, trying to make sense of the busted afternoon.

Vic was staring out at the field too. He slumped against the cage, his fingers clinging disconsolately to the chain-link. "Fuck, I don't know."

Airman Mortensen glanced at the bulging duffel bag. "Well what the hell . . . there's two of us . . . let's throw the ball awhile. I don't give a shit."

They played catch for ten or fifteen minutes. Then Vic grabbed a bat and hit fly balls to Airman Mortensen. Then they switched and Airman Mortensen hit fly balls to Vic. But there wasn't much spirit in the playing. It was too lonely.

They were close to quitting when three carloads of guys from an air police squadron pulled into the parking lot for a game. The sky cops were short on bats and it was quickly calculated that the addition of Vic and Airman Mortensen would bring the two teams close to full strength. There would be a game after all.

It was one of those surprising times, a time when something sour turns sweet.

A brand new softball, hard as a brick, came out of its box and the players really hammered it in the first few innings, producing a lot of runs for both sides. But each team made defensive adjustments, the new ball gradually softened and by its middle innings the game had settled into a true contest.

Vic was at shortstop and he played spectacularly, coming up with a ball on half a dozen hard grounders that seemed certain to make it out of the infield.

He shined at the plate too. In his third at bat, with the bases loaded, the tubby airman second class pulled a pitch over the opposing left fielder's head. To top it off, Vic himself came all the way around to score, sliding home in a tremendous cloud of dust.

Not an inning went by that Vic didn't receive some sort of congratulations from his newfound teammates. He tossed them off with a shrug of the shoulders but Airman Mortensen saw unmistakable sparks of pride in the sad brown eyes.

The latrine king roamed center field for the same team. He loved the open space of the outfield and galloped back and forth over the dusty grass making all the routine plays as well as a few dazzlers. The best of these was an over-the-shoulder, fully extended, one-hand grab of an awesome drive which he made at a dead run. It was the third out of the inning and several excited teammates jogged out to meet him, shaking his hand and slapping his back with their gloves.

As a batter he made good contact on every trip to the plate. He would have hit safely in every at bat had it not been for a diving grab of his line drive in the fifth inning. That play also ended the inning, depriving his team of a chance to break things wide open. But it didn't really matter. It only added to the suspense.

The game was such fun that no one wanted to stop. They were like schoolboys who could play right through dinner without a second thought. But the light was going and, after eight full innings, it was decided to play only one more, even though both teams were tied.

With one away Vic beat out an infield hit. Then he got a good jump and made it to second on a fielder's choice. He danced around the bag, clapping his hands and shouting encouragement as Airman Mortensen stepped into the batter's box. The latrine king had been switch-hitting all afternoon and took his last at bat from the left side. The first pitch was a beauty and he hit a scorcher down the line. The first baseman made a valiant dive but the ball was blazing. It caromed off the tip of his glove and jumped into right field.

Airman Mortensen took a short turn at first and saw Vic steaming around third base. Then he saw the throw from right. It seemed a little high as it sailed over his head. It sailed over the catcher's head too and Airman Mortensen jumped ecstatically as Vic, carried in by the cheers of his teammates, thundered across home plate.

The next batter ground into a double play and Airman Mortensen's team trotted onto the field for the last time, leading by the thin margin of the run Vic had scored.

The opposition's first batter popped out to third but the next one knocked a clean single into left field. Another single to the left followed and there were men on first and second. The next batter lifted an easy fly ball to Airman Mortensen and there were two away.

But then the enemy's lightest hitter fooled everyone by laying a perfect bunt down the third-base line. Bases loaded, two down, bottom of the ninth.

The other team's best hitter, a huge moose of a first baseman, made several vicious practice cuts and stepped into the box. He'd torn the ball to pieces all day and now he was glaring murderously at the mound. What everyone dreaded happened on the first pitch. The moose unloaded with all his might and the ball exploded off his bat. The left fielder and Airman Mortensen reflexively broke back as the ball shot toward left center, rising like a rocket.

But suddenly Vic Pinkowski was rising too, somehow lifting his dumpy frame into space. At the last instant of his impossible rise Vic's glove jabbed higher into the air and met the ball. The pop of the impact sounded like a rifle shot and the collision of man and ball visibly jostled Vic as he hung in space. He jackknifed and tumbled back to earth in a heap. There he lay, spread-eagled on the ground, his glove hand high above his head. The softball showed clearly in the webbing.

It was just an anonymous, neglected ball field in New Mexico; no media, no fans, no money riding on the outcome. But to every man who had played the game, Vic's fantastic, eleventh-hour catch provided the perfect climax to a perfect game. Winning and losing had ceased to matter as competitors from both sides wandered around the field shaking hands.

To a man they stuck around, eager to rehash the thrill of so many highlights while someone made a beer run.

Airman Mortensen was particularly happy for Vic Pinkowski. The flab and zits and heavy Jersey accent were entirely forgotten as he humbly fielded compliment after compliment.

After three or four beers his voice got loud but the star of the game never tooted his own horn. When his name came up Vic answered with a simple "Thanks" or "Yeah, I had a pretty good game." But he couldn't contain a little-boy smile from time to time, a smile that seemed to make Vic glow all over. When he saw the smile Airman Mortensen's own heart warmed. He'd never seen Vic so happy.

But there were other things to think about and as the men lit their cigarettes in the dark around the ball field Airman Mortensen withdrew to the fringes. It seemed so long now, so much like a dream. The only way of holding the dream was to think of her without interruption. But doubt was rising along the walls of his thought.

Maybe she thought it was a dream too. Maybe she was reconsidering. Maybe the hassle with Pat had cast a pall over everything.

Feeling suddenly antsy, he leaned against the fender of an air policeman's new Mustang and shook out another Pall Mall. The smoking didn't do much to calm him. His heart was flopping again, this time with alarm. He wanted to get back to the barracks. He wanted to be in a place where she could find him. 'If she wants to find me at all,' he thought. He knew it was a stupid and foolish thought but he had it just the same.

Vic had downed a six-pack and was too wobbly to take a turn with the duffel bag as they walked back in the dark. Shouldering the awkward bag by himself irritated Airman Mortensen. He was dead on his feet but his mind was alive with thoughts of the girl inside the big house on Cheeze Street. What was happening over there? What was happening. 'Goddamn this fucking bag,' he thought.

"You okay?" Vic blubbered.

"Yeah, I'm okay."

"Okay."

But Airman Mortensen's darkening mood was evident, even to Vic. He could see it through his stupor and as the ominous lights of the barracks came into view the airman second class tried to end the day on a bright note.

"You know what?"

"What?" Airman Mortensen kept his eyes on the barracks. He no longer wanted to look at Vic.

"We oughta go out for the squadron team . . . you and me."

"Yeah," Airman Mortensen said blankly.

"We oughta go out . . . you and me . . . together."

But Airman Mortensen didn't say anything more and

Vic, sensing that he should keep his distance now, staggered along the street without saying another word.

☆ **23** ☆

The Georgia playboy was pulling GQ again. He was leaning back in the big chair, his lumpy nose hidden behind the cover of a girlie magazine, and Airman Mortensen was frustrated by the sight of him. Don Wallace was the last person on earth he wanted to talk to.

"Wallace."

"Yo."

'Better be civil,' Airman Mortensen thought.

"You pullin' GQ again?"

"Woodruff gave me twenty bucks to take it . . . hard, cold caish hoss."

"Cash is cash."

"You got it," Wallace said. He laid the skin mag on the desk and stretched both arms high over his head. "Caish is caish." Yawning, he noticed the duffel bag. "Been playin' ball?"

"Yeah."

"I been thinkin' about it maself . . . I cain hit like a son of a bitch. Don't know as I'd have the time though."

Wallace picked up the magazine and started flipping the pages. "What can I do for you?"

"Any calls?"

"Not much tonight . . . been pretty quiet."

Airman Mortensen thought, 'You stupid, fucking cracker, I'd like to drag you behind a pickup for a mile.' But he said, "I mean for me."

"Seems to me someone did call," Wallace said vaguely. He stroked his chin like a bad actor.

"Who?"

"Don't believe the party left a name."

"Male or female?"

"Female I believe."

"What'd she say?"

"Let's see now . . . what did she say . . . nothin' nasty . . . dang it."

That was enough. His face flushing, Airman Mortensen placed both hands firmly on the desk and leaned menacingly close to Wallace's face.

"Just tell me what she said. I don't need your fucking bullshit right now, Wallace."

The playboy bristled. "Oh yeah?"

"I'll fuck you up, I swear to God."

"Oh yeah?"

"Yeah . . . and I'll do it while you're sleeping."

The pupils in Airman Mortensen's eyes were like pins. His homicidal urge was real.

"Alright, alright. Jesus, Mortensen, you always got the rag on."

"What did she say?"

"She said she'd call back tomorrow."

"No name, huh?"

"No name hoss . . . but her voice was pretty enough to get me interested." Wallace wiggled his eyebrows lecherously.

Lifting the duffel bag, Airman Mortensen sidled out of the office with a parting shot.

"Believe me, Wallace, she's not your type."

The Georgian got out of his chair to call after the latrine king. "Hell, man, when you're a hog for pussy any type'll do . . . and I am a hog for pussy, y'hear . . . p-u-s-s-y."

* * *

The barracks seemed strangely subdued. There was usually plenty of commotion on a Sunday night. Most always the soldiers were piling back into town from weekend trips or bustling about with little chores for the coming week. And some guys couldn't resist a last card game or beer bust in hopes that Monday would never come.

But tonight there was nothing. It was odd to walk the length of the hall without seeing a single soul. Airman Mortensen paused at the door to his room and listened. Water was running in one of the latrines. It was the only sound of life and for a moment he had thoughts of investigating.

Instead, he twisted the knob and went inside.

Instantly, he knew something was wrong. The room was filled with a stifling odor. And something was in Bernie's bed. The blankets were all humped up and something or somebody was moving underneath them, rocking back and forth in a slow, sick motion.

"Bernie?"

"Uhhh," the Italian groaned.

"What's going on?"

There was no immediate reply and Airman Mortensen stepped to the side of his roommate's bed, where the light was better. Bernie was under the blankets, swaying on all fours like a doped cow. His pillow was covered with a yellowish goop that had the look of creamed corn.

"I threw up," he said feebly.

"Oh God . . . in bed?"

"I was asleep."

"Jesus, Bernie . . ."

Suddenly Bernie made a low guttural bellow, the covers flew up and he tumbled out, nearly falling onto the floor. He groped for the door and pulled it open.

"What? . . . what'sa matter?" Airman Mortensen stammered.

But Bernie lurched into the hall without answering. A knot was twisting in Airman Mortensen's stomach but he forced himself to walk to the door and look out.

Bernie was bent forward, careening crazily for the nearest latrine, his bare feet flapping on the hallway floor like swim fins.

As he watched, Airman Mortensen's mouth parted in disbelief and horror. Before his eyes, a wet brown stain was forming on the bottom of Bernie's shorts. He'd never seen someone's bowels go out of control.

Airman Mortensen stood in the doorway and thought. Whatever had gotten hold of Bernie was virulent, some strange, powerful bug that would likely mow through the barracks like a flash fire. It wasn't the season for this sort of thing but he reminded himself that with so many men packed together it could happen anytime. It had happened before with various strains of flu.

The prospect of getting sick sent a shiver of doom through him. 'God, I can't get sick.'

Just as suddenly he realized it didn't matter. Whatever had Bernie, if it was as toxic as it looked, already had him. Whatever had Bernie . . . it was awful to laugh but he couldn't help himself. Poor Bernie . . . vomiting in his sleep, shitting in his pants.

'I better go see,' he thought.

The first stall door was the only one closed. He tapped lightly with a knuckle.

"Bernie? You okay?"

"Ohhh . . . I'm shittin' my guts . . . God."

Airman Mortensen tried to reply but couldn't. Laughter was bubbling up in his mouth. He stepped back and turned his head away. The urge to giggle was near to overwhelming.

"Is there anything I can do?"

"Noooooo . . . ," the woozy voice moaned, "go away."

"Okay . . . I'll come back and check on you."

"Ohhhhh . . . go away."

"You sure?"

"Yeah, yeah . . . just leave me alone . . . ohhhhh . . ."

Something had to be done about the room. Its air was already rank with the smell of Bernie's vomit and tonight would be too chilly for open windows.

He decided to strip the bed. Miraculously, the green wool blanket was untouched. He spread it on the floor, gingerly pulled off the sheets and picked up the hideous pillow between two fingers. Then he dumped the whole mess on the open blanket and tied it into a bundle.

Sheet exchange wasn't until Tuesday and whatever extras there might be were locked up tight in a first-floor storeroom. So, looking like a beardless Santa in olive drab fatigues, he hiked the load a half mile to the base laundry. It was probable that the laundry would be closed on Sunday night but 'what the hell,' he thought, 'you never know.'

The blazing lights gave him heart and when Airman Mortensen looked through one of the converted hangar's grated windows he saw a whole shift of white-uniformed soldiers manning the machines.

"Thank God," he whispered to himself.

He stood outside, banging on a locked door for five minutes before a dour staff sergeant answered.

Airman Mortensen said, "Hi," and quickly stepped inside, knowing that once in, it would be harder for them to turn him away. Still shouldering the messy load, he told his story to the disinterested staff sergeant. He had to shout over the noise of the laundry equipment.

The sergeant stared at him glumly, then said, "C'mon," and led him deeper into the laundry. After following a long, twisted trail through the steamy plant, they finally located the staff sergeant's boss, Tech Sergeant Ramos. Again Airman Mortensen shouted out his story and again it was listened to with disinterest. In the end he was advised to speak with Senior Master Sergeant Krisle, who had left on an unknown errand but would return.

Forty-five minutes later, after sandwiching several Pall Malls around a machine-vended Scooter Pie, Airman Mortensen emerged from the break room and discovered that Senior Master Sergeant Krisle had been on the premises the whole time. Five minutes ago he had spilled something on his uniform and had run home to change. He would be back.

Hearing this, Airman Mortensen muttered, "Likely fuckin' story," and drug his vomit-coated load into the parking lot, there to await the arrival of Sergeant Krisle, who mercifully returned in half an hour. There was a distinctly desperate tone in the third telling of his story. But Sergeant Krisle seemed to listen without irritation.

When Airman Mortensen finished, the sergeant pulled out a wadded handkerchief and evacuated each nostril of his rather large nose, digging deep into each pit before stuffing the damp rag back into his newly changed pants.

"You been waiting long?"

"Yes, I have."

"Normally, I couldn't do this," Sergeant Krisle intoned, "but . . . uhh . . . well . . . I'm gonna let you talk to the lieutenant about this."

Airman Mortensen lugged his sack to what he hoped was its last destination, a small office at the rear of the laundry.

Lieutenant Eccoles, a close-eyed, sharp-faced officer fresh out of college, was in. But the timing could have been better. A pizza pie had arrived and Lieutenant Eccoles had just opened the flat box. In fact, he had a

half a wedge of the pizza crammed in his mouth when
Airman Mortensen appeared in the office doorway and
gave him a snappy salute.

Obviously perturbed by Airman Mortensen's correct
show of respect, the lieutenant clumsily pulled the slice
from his mouth to return the salute. To make matters
worse he grazed his forehead with pizza grease and had
to fumble for a napkin in full view of the anonymous
trooper.

"Who are you?" he asked gruffly.

Airman Mortensen could see dough and cheese rolling in his mouth like mortar in a mixer.

"Airman Mortensen, sir. Senior Master Sergeant
Krisle said I should see you."

"I'm eating."

"It'll only take a minute, sir, I'm sorry to interrupt
('You lazy, fucking loser')—I've been waiting a long
time."

Lieutenant Eccoles waved his hand brusquely and
Airman Mortensen launched into his story. By now his
tale was well edited but before he'd gone more than a
paragraph, Lieutenant Eccoles started flipping the pages
of a large, loose-leaf binder on his desk. Satisfied with
what the binder told him, the lieutenant shifted impa-
tiently in his chair for the remainder of the story.

"What squadron are you in, airman?"

"6099th, sir."

Lieutenant Eccoles scanned his binder. He had begun
to nibble at the partially eaten wedge.

"You people exchange bedding on Tuesdays."

"I know, sir."

"Well, come back on Tuesday."

Airman Mortensen wanted to pull a gun and order
the lieutenant to stuff the pizza up his ass, piece by
piece.

"Bernie Testa is a good airman," he pleaded. "He's

very sick. He can't sleep in this stuff.'' Airman Mortensen jiggled the load for emphasis. ''No one could sleep in this, sir.''

Lieutenant Eccoles suddenly looked interested.

''What's the name?''

''Mortensen, sir.''

''No, no . . . the other one.''

''Testa, sir . . . Airman Second Class Testa.''

''Bernie Testa? . . . little Italian guy from Connecticut?''

''Yes, sir, that's him.''

''Huh . . . he used to work for me, we're both from Bridgeport . . . huh . . . Bernie Testa. He's sick, huh?''

''Yes, sir. It's coming out of both ends, sir.''

''Alright, alright,'' Eccoles snapped, quickly waving off any more detail.

A black airman was passing by the office.

''Washington!'' Eccoles shouted.

The black airman stopped in his tracks.

''Get this man a set of sheets.'' He glanced at Airman Mortensen's smelly bag. ''Anything else?''

''Pillow, case and blanket, sir.''

''Pillow, case and blanket,'' Eccoles repeated, taking a vicious bite of pizza.

A salute and a ''thank you'' and Airman Mortensen was gone, following after Airman Washington. They traveled the length of the laundry, coming at last to a great storeroom of bedding. They talked as they went and when Airman Washington heard the story of what his brother airman had been through he shook his head and sighed.

''Shit, man, you shoulda asked me right off . . . I woulda slipped you some sheets . . . shit, man.''

''Well, I got 'em,'' Airman Mortensen yawned, tucking the fresh bedding under his free arm. ''What do I do with this?'' He jiggled the load again.

"Just drop it on your way out, man."

"Thanks, I appreciate it."

"No sweat."

Airman Washington held out a hand and Airman Mortensen gave him the traditional, thumb-entwined black shake.

"You say your bro's got it comin' outta both ends?" Washington questioned.

"Yeah."

Washington's eyes narrowed. "Where'd he eat?"

"Chow Hall Three."

"Ohhhhhhh, shit."

"Yeah, but I ate there too. I'm fine."

"Y'all eat the same shit?"

"Yeah. Well . . . wait a second. No . . . we didn't. I didn't eat the pork chop."

"That could be it."

"Yeah," Airman Mortensen said vacantly. Airman Washington's theory made sense alright.

Washington smiled broadly and wagged his index finger.

"That's what it is, man . . . fuckin' chops."

☆ **24** ☆

Airman Mortensen rolled Airman Washington's theory around in his mind all the way back to the barracks and by the time he reached the door to his room had decided it could be nothing else. He'd been right about that lousy meat from the start.

Bernie was curled fetally on the bare mattress. He'd

been barfing into a bucket at the side of the bed and when he raised up on one arm Airman Mortensen was shocked by the pasty, ghoulish color of his skin. His eyes looked like they'd been driven several inches deeper into his skull.

"What happened to my bed?" he asked weakly.

"I got you some sheets and a new pillow . . . get up . . . can you get up?"

"I think so."

Bernie struggled to a sitting position but it didn't last long. The motion was more than his queasy stomach could handle and a few seconds later he was hanging out of bed, retching into the bucket. The latrine king had to turn away to keep from gagging. Thankfully, there wasn't much left to expel. Bernie pulled himself back on to the bed and curled into a ball, trying to remain as still as possible.

"Bernie?" he whispered, draping a fresh blanket over his roommate.

"Yeah . . ." Bernie wasn't bothering to open his eyes.

"Is anyone else sick?"

"I don't know . . . yeah . . . I think so . . ."

"Is there anything I can do?"

"I just wanna sleep," Bernie mumbled. He pulled the blanket high on his head.

The odor of the vomit was distinct again and Airman Mortensen thought of pushing the bucket deep under Bernie's bed. But that idea was only good if Bernie stopped upchucking. Playing it safe, he opened a window next to his bed and let some of the crisp night air float into the room.

It wasn't very late but the latrine king felt tired. He stripped down to his white boxers, picked up his shaving kit and headed for the bathroom to splash a little water on his face and brush his teeth.

Nothing could have prepared him for the scene that greeted his arrival in the latrine. At least a dozen men had crowded into the big bathroom—men whom Airman Mortensen knew by face and name, men who walked and talked normally, men with distinctive characteristics that set them apart. But on this night they were not the men he knew. They were a pack of green-skinned, plague-stricken goons, operating with no control of their stomachs or bowels.

Every stall was occupied by pork chop eaters. Outside, other pork chop eaters were waiting, dancing in agony from one foot to another as they pleaded with those inside to get out. Some of these waiting men had opted for the sinks and Airman Mortensen spotted MGT among them. He was squatting on the floor, his hands clutching the edge of the basin, trying to conserve energy for the next wave of nausea. The wave had already caught the men on either side of him. Both were heaving violently.

In desperation, a few sick soldiers had crawled into the shower stalls. Among the men sprawled in the murky chambers were Carl and Lee DeHart.

Airman Mortensen's own stomach began to turn. Pissing out the window would be better than returning to the latrine that night. As he was leaving, Vic blew through the door, staggered to the last empty sink and let go with a high-pressure, fire-hose blast.

The latrine king was brushing his teeth at a water fountain out in the hall when he noticed Newt sweeping past, his green, phosphorescent trench coat billowing behind him like a full-length cape.

"Hey, Newt."

"Yo, Moat."

"You okay, huh?"

"Sheet yes . . . I don' eat no por' . . . dat por' be

rancid shit . . . dat por' a muthafucka . . . Newt don'
eat dat shit, no suh . . . heh, heh, heh.''

Airman Mortensen tried to sleep but the pictures of
the latrine and the suffering there hung in his mind. The
more he thought about it the more he was outraged.
Someone had screwed up with that meat. It was probably bad when the Air Force bought it. But of course
the Air Force would find a way to duck its responsibil-
ity. There would be some kind of investigation. A second lieutenant would be sent to conduct a probe of
Chow Hall Three but, in the end, he would find nothing. The cooks would cover for each other; supply and
procurement would cover for each other. The investigating lieutenant would be most vulnerable but he would
undoubtedly find a way to cover for himself. The inci-
dent and its investigation would quickly recede in memory, on its way to being forgotten altogether. Pork chops
would miss a turn or two on the menu but otherwise
nothing would change.

It was the military way. There could be no advance-
ment without blemish-free records. One smudge would
wreck the delicate and standardized cycle of promotion
and, though much hot air was blown about on behalf
of the ''common'' soldier, his needs were the last to be
served. It was the same in peace as it was in war; officers and high-ranking noncoms threw the common
soldier overboard at the first hint of trouble.

As he lay in the dark, Airman Mortensen realized
that his body had tightened. He wanted to punch somebody. His hands had rolled into fists, fists that wanted
to hit but could not. What if he found the officer or the
noncom who had let the meat pass? What if he found
the cook whose shortcut had produced so much suffering? So what if he kicked the guilty party into mush?
Nothing would change. Some unacknowledged form of
poetic justice might be won but no one would really

benefit. As the avenging warrior his own reward would be crucifixion. And every soldier on base, the whole armed forces for that matter, would stand by and watch, watch without a word as the avenger was led off in chains to an anonymous prison, never to be heard from again.

Airman Mortensen began to feel small. He was one person in a cubicle, confined behind the invisible walls of a military installation a mile or two from a backwater town in New Mexico. One tiny person with numbers for a name. Out of thousands. Lying here in one bed out of thousands. And a slick sleeve at that. Because there was nothing he could do, there was nothing he could feel.

With a conscious effort, he made his body relax. He was lucky and that was all—lucky he hadn't eaten a pork chop that day.

✩ 25 ✩

The latrine traffic stayed heavy all night and Airman Mortensen finally fell asleep to the sound of toilets, flushing with the relentless cadence of waves banging at a coastline.

He woke with none of the outrage he felt the night before. He knew only that an impossible and odious task was imminent and he took his time getting ready for work.

Bernie was weak and still experiencing ripples of nausea but, like most of the other airmen, he decided to take a crack at getting through his regular workday.

Sometime before dawn he had dragged himself to emergency sick call. There he produced a stool sample, the first of hundreds for the unprepared and thoroughly irritated hospital staff. Any problem of this magnitude was received by medical personnel in the same way a nest of wasps receives an arrow.

Airman Mortensen sat on the edge of his bed figuring the hospital people had reported the increase in sick call and that the wheels of a bogus investigation were already in motion.

"They were pissed, huh?"

"Oh God." Bernie paused as he straightened the knot in his tie. "That's not the word for it. I guess I was like one of the first guys to get there and the guy in charge of stools says, 'You're the sixth guy I've seen in the last half hour . . . where did you eat?' And I says, 'Chow Hall Three' and this guy fuckin' comes apart . . . starts kickin' chairs around . . . stuff like that."

Airman Mortensen laughed and took a drag on the day's first Pall Mall. "Yeah, I can see that," he laughed.

Bernie slipped an arm in the sleeve of his blue uniform jacket. "Boy, you've got the worst job in the world today . . . I'm tellin' ya . . ."

"Yeah," Airman Mortensen sighed, "you can see I'm fallin' all over myself to get started."

"Well, see ya later . . . I might be back."

"Yeah."

Numbly, Airman Mortensen slipped into the set of fatigues he had worn for a week. Then he sat shoeless on his bunk and smoked another cigarette, not caring where the First Sergeant might be at the moment. He could no longer bear the tension of resistance. Every day of his latrine king reign he had resisted. But he gained nothing. After a night of round-the-clock puking and diarrhea, his domain had sunk even lower. The

work facing him now could not be approached with a
light heart and he wouldn't be able to go thirty minutes
with gritted teeth. That would send him over the edge
for sure.

The only way to go was as an eyeless, boneless,
chickenless egg. As an eyeless, boneless, chickenless
egg he could scrub the toilet bowls and swab the urinals. As a complete zero he would be able to mop the
floors and make the sinks white again.

To achieve and maintain this state would require a
cessation of certain types of thought, a shutting of his
mind to the one subject that gave him hope. In a way
he wished Claire could somehow cease to exist altogether. If that were the case he wouldn't even be
tempted to think of her.

As he pushed the girl in the blue bathrobe further
away he allowed himself a few last thoughts. Among
them was the bittersweet notion that they were doomed
anyway. "Look at me," he said to himself, staring at
his own dreary image in the floor-length mirror behind
the door. "Me and her? No way. Not in a million years
you dumb piece of shit . . . you . . . are . . . fucked."

Usually he started on the third floor and worked
down, a routine designed to create a slight, directional
goal for the day. But this morning goals no longer mattered and he started on the second floor commodes because they were closest.

He mopped around the toilets first, pausing for crusty
spots which he handled with a scrub brush. The defense
of nonthought was going well. He hummed "Row, Row,
Row Your Boat" dozens of times, then "Who's Afraid
of the Big Bad Wolf" dozens more. When his throat
got tired he did "London Bridge Is Falling Down" in
his head. He counted the inch-square tiles on the floor
of each stall and the wall of louvered windows at the
far end of the latrine. He multiplied these by the num-

ber of stalls and latrines in the barracks. Then he estimated the number of barracks on base and multiplied
again.

He worked in the slow, steady manner of the brain
dead and on several occasions he thought, without any
feeling, 'I am dead.' Once he said it out loud. "I am
dead." The echo of these words was still bouncing off
the walls when the door made its whoosh sound and
the First Sergeant's even steps clicked across the latrine
floor. Airman Mortensen was on his knees in front of
a toilet. Normally he would have gotten to his feet.
Today he didn't. He continued to run a green toilet
brush around the bowl's rim.

From behind him the familiar voice asked, "Did you
get sick?"

"Nope."

Still, he did not get up, but in a moment or two he
turned his head and looked into the First Sergeant's
impassive eyes. They stared at each other and the topkick turned slowly away to meander along the filthy
sinks. Just as slowly, Airman Mortensen rose and followed.

The First turned at the last sink and made a short
tour of the showers. He stopped in front of one and
stuck his head inside. Airman Mortensen lit a cigarette
and slouched carelessly against the wall. This act of
looseness did not go unnoticed and the First Sergeant
watched the latrine king through the thick part of his
bifocals for a full ten seconds.

Airman Mortensen's head was drooping. He was
aware of his boss but his fuck-it threshold had lowered
to nothing. He was absorbed in a study of the ribbons,
ribbons of cigarette smoke flowing upward from his
hand like streams of water. Something about the light
had turned them incredibly blue.

The First Sergeant dipped his head in and out of an-

other shower and made for the door. He placed a hand
on the metal pull bar and paused rather dramatically.
He tilted his head in Airman Mortensen's direction and
spoke in his flat, practiced tone. "I've got an airman
working the upstairs and another one down on the first
floor. When you finish up here you can knock off."

The door whooshed and the First Sergeant was gone.
His charitable pronouncement had done nothing to
lighten Airman Mortensen's mood. He slumped into a
squat at the base of the wall and said to himself, "I
guess that's s'posed to make me real fuckin' happy."

He got up and shuffled to an open window. The big
death birds, the B-52s, were parked out on the flight
line, their wings and fuselages painted for war in a gray
camouflage motif. They did look like birds—evil birds
full of evil eggs.

The landscape beyond the flight line flattened into
nothing but the day was clear enough to make out the
cinder-block speck that had been his workplace as a radio operator. Which was worse? This place or that? No
way to tell. No way to tell the difference between a pilot
or a cook, a sharpshooter or a pencil pusher. "It's all
like this," he said to himself. "It's all latrine duty."

Going over the hill. Everyone thought about that. He
did too. But almost no one went. The finality of military jail was too horrible to contemplate.

He knew a cook, a smart, handsome guy, who had
reported to work with one of his brogans painted Day-
Glo orange. Within a week they had discharged him as
unadaptable to military service. No jail time, just walking papers. He was walking somewhere at this moment.
A free man with an honorable discharge.

There was an air policeman—a tall, gawky, fast-
talking surfer from California. He had faked going nuts
by emptying a carbine into the belly of a KC-135, an
aircraft he was supposed to be guarding. But instead of

handing the surfer a discharge, they'd merely disarmed him. He was working his butt off at the base printing plant. And they were watching him.

There would be no Day-Glo boots or empty carbines for Airman Mortensen. That would mean jail. He flicked his Pall Mall through the window and watched its long, floating tumble to the sidewalk. The cigarette landed in a patch of dry grass and began to smolder. The smoke seemed to grow. Hell, even that could be jail.

☆ 26 ☆

The call came at mid-afternoon and as soon as he heard her voice he knew the plague of doubt that had hounded him the past twenty-four hours was unfounded. He felt like an idiot.

After a couple of innocuous sentences she blurted, "I love you," and started to cry.

The surge of emotion threw him. "Are you okay?" he asked.

"Yes . . . I just love you so much . . . I can't think of anything else."

Airman Mortensen's throat started to close but there was no way he was going to cry.

"If we're so happy, why are we like this?" he laughed.

"God, I don't know," she laughed back.

It took awhile to get his bearings after they hung up. He walked outside, lit a cigarette and walked back inside. He bought a Coke out of a machine but couldn't drink it. He walked upstairs and drifted into the day room with the aimlessness of an expectant father. For no good reason he sank into one of the pseudoleather easy chairs and fired up another cigarette.

Jethro Clampet was on the TV, throwing a childish tantrum as he tried to convince Jed of his sincerity in wanting to become a brain surgeon. Airman Mortensen was fond of Jethro and his moronic delusions but he realized that he was watching shadows. He was staring straight through the television and into the wall.

'She loves me.'

Everything was small again. Latrine duty and pork chops and court-martials and Bernie Testa—all these things were being reduced. The whole damned Air Force was nothing but a penny-ante irritation.

He saw, but didn't, see Jethro dashing through a major metropolitan hospital with a toy doctor's bag, eager to perform his first operation.

Words were beating in his heart, repeating themselves constantly, fresher with every hearing.

'She loves me. She really loves me. Claire Brill loves me!'

Lathering in the shower, another thought came to him as he daydreamed about this first date that was coming. The thought breezed through his head like a signpost flashing by on the highway.

'Man . . . there is gonna be a world of shit comin' down . . . a world of shit.'

Going, Going, Gone

☆ 1 ☆

The new lovers saw each other three times the following week but their encounters were so charged with romance that after each meeting they found it difficult to unravel what happened. At least Airman Mortensen found it difficult.

When he wasn't with Claire he was daydreaming about her. He knew the taste of her tongue now and the soft contours of her breasts but as the latrine king steered his buffer up and down the halls or sprinkled ajax on the sinks, his thoughts, even the purely carnal ones, were encased in the thick gloss of romantic love.

Her tennis shoes and lipstick and bell-bottom pants, the dirt under her fingernails, the stray hair hanging off her shoulder, the little lines of sweat along her neck— all these things had been elevated to a precious status.

The new light served Airman Mortensen well. His step was definitely brighter, his chest seemed to have expanded overnight and he detected a face that might actually be called handsome when he looked in the mirror.

He even had a new view of his cock, which was now rising with the innocent stimulations of her fingertips playing in his palm or a sweet intonation in her voice. In the past his cock was just his cock, something to be taken for granted most of the time. In times of loneliness or frustration he had regarded it as a nuisance. He had fantasized about cutting it off.

But now he viewed it as a kind of living miracle, an

extension of the sacred feeling in his heart. The latrine king hadn't just surrendered to his first, big love. He'd surrendered unconditionally. He'd gone over like a sawed tree.

There were moments when he had to smile and shake his head. Three fleeting meetings were all they'd had, three tiny, almost wordless reunions spent kissing and hugging as their minutes ran out. Not much to go on for such a big love.

They had so little time. Claire was still in high school and Airman Mortensen was still in the latrines. And the Brills, as might be expected, had a well-regulated family life. The girls' presence was required for the evening meal and a long-standing curfew of ten o'clock prevailed during weeknights. The curfew was stretched to midnight on Friday and Saturday. When homework, routine domestic chores and frequent family outings to official officers'-club functions were figured in, free time was at a premium.

Claire and Airman Mortensen were content to sit in silence for many minutes at a time, not daring to speak or move as they silently contemplated the extraordinary thrill of having found each other.

Airman Mortensen wished that these times of silence could be bottled or frozen, somehow halted and held so that the bliss of absolute togetherness could go on forever. Nothing could fracture the beauty of those moments. The low, whispered conversations that came before and after seemed to support the moments. And when she was physically gone and he was alone in the barracks, silence would bring her back. They were together in a way that defied any power to pull them apart.

Positive side effects of love were everywhere. The latrines didn't bother him much and Airman Mortensen's relationship with the First Sergeant took a pronounced turn for the better. The change in attitude was not lost on the topkick and at the end of the week, after inspecting the day's work, he announced that there would be no need for the usual report in on Saturday morning. Then he muttered, "Don't fuck up," and pressed a weekend pass into Airman Mortensen's hand. He was going to sneak off base that night anyway but the pass made his date with Claire sweeter still. He wouldn't have to look over his shoulder.

They were going to the dance at the Masonic Temple. The band was reported to be hot and the place would be jammed. They would be in public for the first time. Everyone would see how they were. They'd have a whole night together, a night of dancing and touching and talking and nuzzling and God only knows what.

The minutes crawled as Airman Mortensen watched set after set of headlights pull into the squadron lot. And as time dragged, his mind sped with thought.

"Her. Where is she? Her. Her."

At last he heard the high whine of a foreign engine. A small car downshifted and swung into the parking lot. It's radio blasting from afar, the VW pulled up to the curb and Claire hit the brakes so hard she killed the engine.

Airman Mortensen opened the door and contorted himself into the passenger seat. Claire was staring seriously at the red generator light. She twisted the ignition but the car was still in gear. It jumped forward and died again.

"What are you doing?" Airman Mortensen laughed.

"I don't know," she said tensely. She wiggled the shifter into neutral and tried the ignition again. Now it was cranking but it wouldn't turn over and suddenly her hand was off the key and she was collapsing against him.

"I just wanted to get here," she sputtered. "I just love you so much."

Her lips searched out his mouth and they kissed.

"What a relief," he mumbled.

"Oh God," she sighed and they kissed again.

"You know what?"

"What?" she answered. Her eyes were closed and in the dim light he could see the moisture of their kisses, still glistening on her parted lips.

"I gotta keep pinchin' myself."

"Why?" she whispered.

"I can't believe you're real," he whispered back.

"I can't believe you're real," she countered, her voice far away.

Airman Mortensen was already hard. He pulled her close. Claire tried to climb into his lap but only made it halfway because of the shifter. They kissed for a long time, opening their mouths as wide as possible. But it was still not enough. It could never be enough.

At last they broke apart, panting for breath. A pair of soldiers passing nearby couldn't resist a flurry of catcalls but Airman Mortensen paid them no mind.

He looked down at the face against his shoulder. The streetlight had turned her skin an exotic blue. He ran a fingertip over the lids of her still-closed eyes.

"You're so beautiful," he said sadly.

She cupped a hand over his ear and pulled his face gently to hers. They floated together in a minute of silence. Maybe two or three.

"You want me to drive?"

"Yes," she whispered.

Like people trying to get out of bed on a Sunday morning they pulled themselves out of the seats. When their paths crossed in front of the headlights they fell into each other's arms and might have stayed that way had the parking lot been empty. But there were too many cars and people.

He turned down the radio as they passed through the

main gate and left it there as they headed for town in one of their splendid silences. Claire's hand was in his but her body was slumped against the door, her pretty head jiggling lightly on the window glass. She seemed drained.

"Are you okay?" he asked quietly.

She moved her head slowly up and down as the VW zoomed past the line of pawnshops and down the long, dark approach to the first lights of Roswell.

"I told my mother," she said lowly. Her head was still resting on the window and her eyes were still closed.

"What did she say?"

"She wants to meet you."

The latrine king downshifted for the first traffic light.

"Did you tell your dad?"

"Not yet." Claire lifted her head and blinked at the lights coming up.

"Did you tell her I'm an airman?"

"Uhh, huh."

"What did she say about that?"

"Nothing."

"Did you tell her we were in love?"

Claire nodded.

"I haven't told anybody really," he said. "I keep thinking . . ."

"What?"

"I keep thinking it's all a dream or something."

Claire laughed. She dipped her head toward his shoulder and kissed it. "Well, it's not." She gave his shoulder a quick burst of kisses and settled her face against his neck.

Blue Cheer's version of "Summertime Blues" came on the radio. Airman Mortensen turned it up.

"God, I wanna dance," he said, his head bobbing up and down to the beat.

"Me too."

Claire turned the radio all the way up, so high that
the little speaker sounded like it was going to explode.

☆ **2** ☆

He'd been to dances at the Masonic Temple before.
It was like all the other teen dance halls—a big, style-
less fifties building made of brick. Outside there was
room for hundreds of cars on the big dirt lot. The hall
itself was nondescript except for the mysterious Masonic emblem plastered over the entrance.

Inside, the temple was barren, nothing more than a
large rectangle of empty space. Sometimes lines of
metal carts, loaded with folding chairs, hugged the plain
walls. Otherwise there was no furniture. Closed serving
windows hid the kitchens that handed out pancake
breakfasts on Sundays to aging men and women wearing strange hats. Stages were rare. Occasionally, a plywood platform appeared, giving the musicians some
elevation but, most often, the bands set up their stuff
on the floor.

The bands came from everywhere and they all played
the kind of music that every kid in every isolated town
wanted to hear. They wanted songs from the outside
world, the songs which came to them through radio
stations and record stores. They wanted to hear Top 40,
and if bands wanted to play they had to learn Top 40.

Looking at the parts, Friday and Saturday night
dances seemed small-time, even in 1966. But when the
parts were put together it was a different story. When

the dusty parking lot was full of cars and the temple was full of kids, when the band was on stage and when the first raunchy notes of "Dirty Water" were echoing off solid walls and low ceilings, it was a great gathering of the teenage tribe.

It was kicking out the jams and it made adult chaperones nervous because they became small, standing back in the shadows with cotton in their ears, powerless to stop the bonfire of adolescent passion burning in front of their eyes.

Claire and Airman Mortensen wove through clusters of kids hanging out near the front doors and plunged onto the dance floor where a hundred others were already careening around to the beat of a Paul Revere and the Raiders number called "Hungry."

It was a perfect entrance for the new couple. They were too intent on dancing to be affected by the notice of friends and strangers and, after a week of constant thinking and stolen moments, it was a great relief to be jumping around to the sound of music they loved.

The band played nonstop and they danced the same way, stomping through "Little Red Book" and "96 Tears" and "Pushin' Too Hard" and a great version of "I'm A Man" that went on for ten minutes.

In the space between songs the lovers leaned on each other and touched hands. But this was done with discretion. They were still too shy for anything more overt.

When the band took a break, however, they found themselves surrounded by friends and friends of friends. And in the eyes of all these people Airman Mortensen could see worlds of curiosity. Everybody knew something was up. It was exciting.

When Claire hurried off to the bathroom with a pair of giggling girlfriends, Airman Mortensen followed after the swarm of dancers headed outside. His shirt was drenched and he had started to sweat through his Levis.

These were the days before hand stamps and uni-
formed security and body checks. Teenagers ran in and
out of the temple all night long, some to get air, some
to gulp down alcohol stashed in cars.

As Airman Mortensen smoked a Pall Mall on the
curb outside the temple, he connected with two friends
who had such a stash. Van Whitehead was nineteen but
his height, glasses, and receding hairline let him pass
for thirty. He had long, bony fingers and a stupid laugh
that was sometimes irritating. Dick Ronn was eighteen
and looked like somebody's little brother. He was short
and innocent-eyed and had long, feminine hair that was
constantly being swept to one side of his baby face.

The two were always together and, though it was not
the case, they were frequently kidded about being
"queer for each other." Like Airman Mortensen, they
were learning guitar. Van nervously picked out lead
notes while Dick strummed sensitively on a twelve
string. Airman Mortensen liked them.

The three boys hustled across the parking lot and
hopped into Van's dad's Oldsmobile. In the dark safety
of the parked car they sipped at a pint bottle of vodka
and chased it down with icy cans of Burgermeister.

While they drank, the boys spit out a steady and
meaningless patter of male gossip. The Oldsmobile af-
forded a full view of the parking lot, now crowded with
groups of restless teenagers loitering next to their ve-
hicles, and each person had a story. This girl was
stacked, that one wasn't. This girl was reputed to go
down, that one was strictly first base.

Airman Mortensen enjoyed his friends and their talk
and their liquor. But he felt restless too. Being away
from Claire made him nervy. His hand kept fiddling
with the door latch. But that strange and wonderful bulletproof feeling was upon him again, so he stayed a

little longer. Plus, he liked those hits of vodka going down.

"Watch it!" Dick hissed and Airman Mortensen jerked his beer can down as a squad car crept past his window. The cops glanced at the boys in the Oldsmobile and kept on creeping.

"Shit, man . . . ," Van gasped.

"That was close," Dick whispered. He'd been sitting in the back. Now he was hanging over the front seat, between Van and Airman Mortensen. "It's lucky I saw those fuckers."

The boys watched the police cruise through the parking lot, then out.

"The fuckin' fuzz," Van grumbled.

Airman Mortensen lifted his beer can to the departing squad car. "Fuck the fuckin' fuzz," he said bravely.

"Yeah . . . fuck the fuzz," Dick chimed and they banged their Burgie cans together.

Some of Airman Mortensen's beer sloshed over the lip of the can and dribbled onto the seat. Van sprang at it, brushing furiously at the place where the beer had fallen.

"Hey, be careful . . . my dad'll shit."

Airman Mortensen stared down at the spot but it was too dark to see any damage.

"It's just a couple of drops of beer."

Van was still brushing furiously. "He'll have a kitten."

"I hate to tell you guys," Airman Mortensen insisted, "but beer doesn't stain."

"Yeah, but it stinks," Van shot back. Now he was dabbing at the spot with his shirttail.

"Your dad won't have a kitten," Dick laughed, "he'll have a fucking elephant."

"No shit, Sherlock," Van answered. The drops had

long ago sunk into the upholstery but he was still dabbing.

"For God's sake," Airman Mortensen shrugged. "It's nothing' . . . it ain't gonna stink for chrissakes."

"Yeah, right . . . easy for you to say," Van countered. Little bubbles of sweat had broken out along his receding hairline.

Airman Mortensen had never met Van's father but he remembered now that the tall, old-looking boy always stayed clear of his dad.

"Okay, okay," Airman Mortensen said, giving it up.

They sat in silence for a few seconds, waiting for Van's stress to subside. At last, he took a long swig from his Burgie can and licked his lips.

"Guitar player's pretty hot," he said.

"Yeah, he gets around the fretboard pretty good," Airman Mortensen put in.

"Yeah, he's good," Dick agreed, reaching for the vodka bottle.

"Watch it," Van warned, his eyes following the bottle as it traveled over the seat.

"I like those Gibson hollow bodies," Airman Mortensen continued.

"Yeah, they're cool." Van took the vodka bottle out of Dick's hand and tilted it high over his mouth for a long drink. Some of the alcohol backed up into his nasal passage and the tall boy fell into a brief coughing fit. Then there was silence again.

"Who's that girl?" Van asked. He was facing straight ahead but Airman Mortensen could see a leer coming from the corner of his eye.

"What?" the latrine king answered.

Dick gave Airman Mortensen's shoulder a shove. "The girl you came with, dork."

He wished that no one would ever ask. He wished everyone could just see and understand without detail.

But of course no one could. That would be too perfect. He shook the beer can to see how much was left and drank the remainder. Then he sighed.

"Claire."

A lurid grin flashed across Van's face. "Are you in luuuuve?" he giggled.

Airman Mortensen dragged a hand across one eye and shook his head.

"Boys . . . I believe I am."

Van and Dick shifted happily in their seats.

"You wouldn't shit me?" Van asked.

"Not my favorite turd," Airman Mortensen said smugly.

Dick was suddenly sober. "She's really fine," he said earnestly.

Airman Mortensen looked at his hands. Van and Dick dreamed of girls constantly and neither one had a steady. He was feeling lucky.

"Yeah, she is."

The first notes of the next set carried over the parking lot and into the Oldsmobile.

"In fact," Airman Mortensen continued, "I gotta go find her . . . right now."

"Hey, man, you gotta tell us about her," Van said, taking hold of Airman Mortensen's forearm.

"I will, I will . . ." He pulled away and slid out the door.

"She's a fox," Dick called after him.

Airman Mortensen strode through the temple entrance with a purpose that made him feel ten feet tall, his one and only mission in life to reunite with his girl. When he saw Claire's face he knew she felt the same.

Their arms went around each other's waists in that old familiar way. They didn't speak. They watched the band finish its first number. When the last chords fell away Claire looked up at him with a coy smile.

"Where were you?"

"I was outside," he teased, "with Van and Dick."

"Van Whitehead and his little friend?"

"Yeah."

"Where?" she asked.

"Just in the parking lot."

He felt her fingers entwine with his. The bass player was making everyone wait while he fiddled with his amp.

"Next time I want to go with you," she insisted.

"You were gabbing with your friends."

"I was not gabbing."

"Telling stories then . . . I don't know."

She leaned in against him, her mouth brushing his ear. "All I did was talk about you."

Airman Mortensen shrugged as if he didn't care. But of course he did. "What did you say?"

"None of your business." Sassy, she pulled away. "But next time, I want to go with you."

"You will."

"Promise?"

"Promise."

"Cross your heart and hope to die?" she laughed.

Airman Mortensen made the sign on his chest. "Cross my heart and hope to croak."

She nodded her head like a little girl. The latrine king dipped his face close to hers.

"Hey."

She looked so sad. He thought he could hear the sound of his own heart breaking.

"I love you," he said, making the words sound like the last he might ever speak.

She fell against him and they kissed, right there on the Masonic Temple dance floor, right in front of everyone. The kiss went on, the mouths gradually open-

ing as they hung together. It might have gone on for a
very long time had it not been for the band.

The next song was "Liar, Liar (Pants On Fire)." A
big roar went up at the first notes and the lovers were
jostled by dancers flooding onto the floor. As they
pulled slowly away and started to dance Airman Mortensen saw smiling faces everywhere he looked. The
smiles were shy, just flashes, but they were encourag-
ing. You had to be brave to kiss like that.

Airman Mortensen looked at his partner. She was
stomping around with her eyes on the floor, too embarrassed or too lost in the music to look up. The latrine
king glanced once more at the many eyes trailing him.
'You've got something to look at,' he said to them silently. 'Fuckin' A you do.'

He was pacing himself now but otherwise the pattern
remained the same. Dance, dance, dance. Halfway
through the set the band played a slow song and, because he was soaked, Airman Mortensen tried to beg
off. But Claire smiled dreamily and ran her arms around
his neck. She pressed herself against him and they began to move in an easy clinch, barely shuffling their
feet. A gum wrapper could not have been wedged between them.

At the break another gang of school chums monop-
olized Claire's time, finally talking her into another
bathroom conference. With little gestures of helpless-
ness she let herself be dragged away.

Airman Mortensen passed his time with Van and
Dick, both of whom had been lurking on the fringes of
the dance floor all night. The trio of friends hung out
in the vicinity of the flimsy, plywood stage, admiring
and criticizing the band's equipment.

After a minute or two of quibbling, it was agreed that
the lead guitar player's Silvertone amp was a miracle of
cheap engineering and anybody playing lead in a band

should consider using one. For something that could be
found in any Sears and Roebuck music department it
had a lot of punch.

Though he liked a straight guitar sound, Airman
Mortensen had to admit that the Farfisa Mini-Organ was
a versatile instrument. Tons of bands were using them.
And you could buy one on time without much trouble.

All three agreed that the bass player's brand-new tuck-
and-roll Kustom cabinet looked and sounded sharp.

And on they went. Like everybody else who lived for
music the three friends dreamed of making the big
move, of starting a band. For some reason they didn't
do it. They regularly talked their way to the edge but
they never jumped.

On this night Airman Mortensen was only half absorbed in the future. It was impossible to keep from
thinking of Claire and, as they stood around in front of
the stage, he thought himself incredibly lucky to have
any kind of girl, not to speak of this particular girl.
While Van droned on about the differences between
first- and second-rate tuning pegs it occurred to Airman
Mortensen that to have come this far in life without
Claire Brill was hard to believe.

Every time he saw her it was like a dream come true
and a trivial event like her return from the girls' bathroom was just as dreamy as any other. The band was
still nowhere in sight and, wanting nothing but the company of each other, they stood around, idly visiting with
friends.

During a lull in the conversation Airman Mortensen
bent close to her ear and whispered, ''You are so beautiful.''

Someone distracted her with a question but Claire
leaned closer and talked to him with her hand. It ran
under his shirtsleeve and began to stroke his arm in a
steady, methodical way.

Airman Mortensen caught a glimpse of someone's wristwatch and was seized with a craving to go someplace where they could be alone.

He bent to her ear again but found her neck instead. He had to put his lips there and, as he did, Airman Mortensen felt the neck harden against his mouth. He felt her hip rub against his thigh.

"It's after eleven," he whispered.

She turned her face to his, placed a hand on each of his shoulders and rose to the tips of her toes as she whispered back.

"Let's go."

"Yeah," he answered, "let's go."

☆ **3** ☆

But there really wasn't anywhere to go. The Brill house was out. The barracks was out. With so little time left before curfew a drive to a secluded country road was out. The squadron parking lot was the only spot that made sense and it was no place at all.

Another silence, this one was tense and gloomy, fell over the VW on the drive back to the base. They talked in lifeless snippets, never gathering enough momentum for a full-blown conversation. They were silent most of the way back.

By the time Claire pulled into the lot they weren't talking at all. She flicked off the ignition and punched the lights with the heel of her hand. Still they didn't speak.

Accompanied only by the sounds of the cooling en-

gine, Airman Mortensen stared tight-faced through the
windshield. How could it be that in a few moments he
would have to go home. It seemed so unfair. 'Goddamn
the fucking Air Force,' he thought. 'Goddamn the fucking Air Force and everybody in it. Dead halls, dead
rooms, dead hard-ons. Dead. In a minute I'm gonna
have to leave the only person I love and go back to that
fucking place.'

The latrine king glanced at Claire. Her eyes were in
her lap. She peeked at him.

"What's wrong?" she whispered.

She looked hurt. He touched her hand and it closed
around his.

"I can't believe I gotta go back in there."

She nodded, pulling his hand deeper into her lap. She
covered it with both of hers and stared down at the three
hands as if she was in possession of something price-
less.

Airman Mortensen knew she was working up to
something. Minutes seemed to pass. All the while she
stared at the tangle of fingers in her lap. The side of his
hand was resting against the special place. He could
feel the heat of it through her jeans.

Then, in a voice barely above a whisper, she said,
"I want to sleep with you."

Airman Mortensen looked at her.

"I want to make love with you," she added.

Airman Mortensen searched her eyes and saw only
resolve.

"Me too," he answered somberly.

"You want to sleep with you?" she said seriously.

"No . . . I . . ."

Then she flashed her beautiful smile and he knew
he'd been tricked at the most delicate moment. She was
cracking up and he grabbed playfully at her shoulder.
She fought him off, her hand going around his wrist

and a moment later they were entwined again, unable to come fully together because of the stupid shifter.

They kissed, long and hard.

"I love you," she moaned, "I love you, I love you."

He knew the time had come to tell her. But he didn't know how this could be done, so his eyes went back to the windshield, staring through it as he tried to think. The barracks filled his view. There was no way to say it.

"What?" she asked worriedly.

Airman Mortensen sighed. He felt his jaws tighten. He couldn't look at her.

"It's so stupid," he said, shaking his head.

Still he wouldn't look at her. Claire twisted around in the seat and thrust her face in front of his.

"What is it?" she demanded.

"I've never done it."

He waited for this bombshell to sink in but it didn't. Her face remained a blank.

"You've got yourself a virgin," he said flatly.

Claire's face remained blank for several more seconds. At last she pulled away. She put a hand over her mouth and Airman Mortensen was astonished to hear a giggle escape her fingers.

"What?" the latrine king asked.

She dropped her hand. The smile was still on her face. Her eyes looked weirdly electric.

"I am too," she said.

☆ 4 ☆

They met the virgin dilemma head-on. Claire knew just what she wanted and, after weighing it for only a few seconds, Airman Mortensen agreed that the plan was good. Besides, he had no plan of his own.

She wasn't taking the pill, didn't know how to get it and was afraid of side effects. Plus, she didn't know how long it would take for the pill to kick in even if she did have it and now that the cat was out of the bag she didn't want to wait any longer than was absolutely necessary.

Of course, neither did Airman Mortensen. The frequency of his hard-ons seemed to be increasing. Erections were so constant that he had begun to wonder if something abnormal might be going on.

They didn't want to use a rubber, especially since this would be the first time. Not knowing what to expect was bound to carry a certain degree of stress. Adding any kind of device would only muddy the waters.

They decided to do it naturally. But this approach would require some research, some looking into cycles in order to figure it all out. The scene of operations would be the base library, there to peruse up-to-the-minute information on the vagaries and absolutes of the female reproductive system.

It seemed an excellent way to proceed and, once she was gone, Airman Mortensen didn't think much more about it. This stuff about eggs floating down tubes and

146

all the rest was pretty much Claire's show and he was content to follow her leads.

He did think about the flesh. He lay in bed that night, his cock board stiff as he listened to Bernie snore, and thought about the parts he knew so far: the small hands, the downy arms, the smooth shoulders, the rounded knees, the wet tongue, the well-nippled breasts, the moist V in her levis. He only knew them by touch. Soon he would know them by sight as well. It was exciting.

He slipped a hand under the covers and grasped his cock. But, instead of feeling a tactile rush, he marveled at how something so small could get so big. He thought about his time and how, after all these years, it had finally come.

"What a life." He smiled to himself in the darkness. "It's impossible to figure out what's going to happen."

When Claire's face appeared, turning slowly in front of his, jacking off seemed about as appropriate as sleeping in a dress uniform. Still holding it, he gave his cock a few lifeless strokes and shook his head. It wasn't for him anymore. It was for her.

Sighing, he twisted onto his stomach and began to dream about their morning rendezvous at the base library. In seconds he fell into a deep, happy sleep.

Sadly, there is nothing more fragile than a plan and by nine o'clock the next morning Claire was on the phone with disappointing news.

She'd forgotten all about Uncle Troy and Aunt Verna and their three kids, all of whom were descending on the Brill residence within the hour. There was no time to talk. She'd just started polishing a tea service and had to finish before the relatives got there. They might still be able to see each other and she would try to call again but it didn't look good. A big dinner at the club was scheduled for tonight and on Sunday both families were caravanning to Ruidoso for a day in the mountains.

The two lovers whispered "I love you" back and forth a half dozen times and hung up.

Airman Mortensen sat in the GQ's office and stared at the phone, wondering why he didn't feel crushed. Maybe it was the desperate, dispirited sound of her voice. That seemed genuine. He didn't know her all that well but she wasn't the giddy type. Claire was sensible. And sensible girls stuck to their commitments. Maybe he was subconsciously sweating out the virginity thing and was glad to have it postponed. Maybe, for some completely unknown reason, he just didn't give a shit.

The latrine king shook his head as he stared at the phone. "Fuck, I don't know," he said listlessly.

"Don't know what?"

Bernie was standing in the office doorway, grinning like a Cheshire cat.

Airman Mortensen laughed. "I don't know how you can breathe with your pants up around your neck."

Bernie looked down at his dull, woolen trousers. They weren't around his neck.

"Whatd'ya mean?"

"You got any money?" Airman Mortensen asked.

"Yeah."

"Wanna take in a movie or something . . . go downtown?"

"Sure."

"I got a pass."

"Yeah?"

"Yeah."

As they walked up the stairs Airman Mortensen noticed that Bernie was preoccupied with his waistline. When they reached the second floor landing he stopped and began to tug downward on his belt loops.

"You think I wear 'em too high," he said. His face was twitching with worry. "I've always worn 'em this way."

"Well . . . ," Airman Mortensen started, suddenly wishing he'd never brought it up. "Yeah . . . they usually seem kinda high . . . but if it's comfortable for you . . ."

"It doesn't look stupid, does it?"

Bernie had worked the trousers down to a natural position just over his hips. They looked much better.

"That looks good," Airman Mortensen remarked quickly, stepping back to admire the new fit.

"Yeah?"

"Yeah, really. How do they feel?"

Bernie walked around in a circle.

"Pretty good . . . pretty good."

The new look didn't last long. In the time it took them to walk from the barracks to the shuttle stop, Bernie's pants had returned to their old location.

☆ **5** ☆

To Airman Mortensen a movie theatre was like no other place on earth. There was an anonymous security about the dark and there was all that entertainment on the screen. The enormity of the view had a tendency to keep him focused; even when the movie was lousy the focus blotted out everything that was going on in his life. Just being in the theatre was great. A half-decent film was a bonus.

He and Bernie hit the concession stand hard, loading

up on buttered popcorn, large Cokes and family-sized boxes of Milk Duds and Dots. Bernie bought a Black Cow to hold in reserve.

The Tower Theatre had been built in the thirties and, though not close to the scale of a palace, it was a true movie house. The two airmen spent a pleasant afternoon watching a few tight-lipped Englishmen in tight uniforms slaughter untold thousands of black African warriors in a picture called *Zulu*. The film was supposed to be the true story of a battle which took place in 1879. Airman Mortensen found the one-sided victory hard to believe but he enjoyed the film.

What he enjoyed most of all was the African setting. He would gladly have traded his current circumstances (Claire notwithstanding) for all that open, free and totally wild country. Even the bloody fighting with the scary Zulus seemed a bargain compared to a life of urinals, deodorant cakes and birdbrained, chickenshit regulations.

Following the decimation of the Zulus, they strolled up the main drag, working off some of the crap they'd eaten. Airman Mortensen window shopped. Bernie stared shamelessly at every girl who came within range, his head swiveling like a toy. The gawking finally got on the latrine king's nerves.

"Jesus, Bernie."

"What?"

"Did you grow up on Devil's Island or something? You'd think you'd never seen a fucking girl in your whole life."

"I'm just lookin'."

"I feel like I'm walkin' around with an orphaned puppy or somethin'."

"What's that supposed to mean?"

"Aw, forget it . . . Jesus."

"I'm just lookin' . . . a girl looks nice, you wanna give her a look."

"You're not lookin', you're x-rayin'."

"Get out."

"You are, I swear to God."

They stopped in at Radcliffe's Music and Airman Mortensen's heart broke as he thumbed through the record bins. There were at least half a dozen new releases he needed but could not have. Payday was Monday and, like ninety-five percent of the other airmen, he'd been broke for a week.

Airman Mortensen was not a thief but the idea of stealing the records crossed his mind. They represented so much more than diversion or entertainment. The music hidden in the rings of vinyl was the closest thing he had to religion. It absorbed his grief, fired his joy and kept hope alive like nothing else could. At the darkest of times it steadied him, fixed him with a beam of light in the way a beacon comforts the lost. He often thought he would have no life at all were it not for the music. The spirit of freedom announced its existence on every cover; it was alive on every disc. To walk out of Radcliffe's and leave it all behind was hell.

As always, he chickened out, telling himself that the big square albums would be too hard to conceal and that, while stealing from the companies might be acceptable, taking money from the artists was not.

At the end of the business district they stopped at Chew Den. Of all the eateries in Roswell, Chew Den was the most popular, its five-page menu uniting ranchers, teenagers, businessmen and base personnel at all hours of the day and night.

Sitting with Bernie in a corner booth, Airman Mortensen scanned the limitless, delicious food items on the Chew Den menu and felt his last shreds of optimism slip away. These things too were beyond his reach. The loose change in his pocket was all he had left, maybe enough for a cup of coffee.

He got a kick out of Bernie. The little Italian was running his eyes over the menu in the lust-driven way a stockbroker studies his portfolio. He finally looked up at Airman Mortensen.

"What?"

"Nothin', Bernie."

"C'mon . . . what, goddammit."

"I was just thinkin' . . . you know how guys think through their pricks?"

"Yeah . . ."

"You think through your stomach."

"I think through both of 'em." Bernie grinned. "They're interchangeable."

"Now that's no shit."

Bernie's eyes returned briefly to the menu.

"What're you gonna have?" he said absently.

"Nothin' . . . coffee."

"Aren'cha gonna eat?"

"I'm tapped out."

"I'll get'cha somethin'."

"I don't want you to do that," Airman Mortensen said, shaking his head halfheartedly.

"C'mon, ya gotta eat," Bernie pressed.

"Well . . . you can stake me to some rings if you want."

The onion rings at Chew Den were a legendary bargain. They came huge and fresh and deep-fried, a great tower of them served on a steak platter for the price of one dollar.

Bernie ordered a gigantic meal of sweet-and-sour pork and when it arrived all table talk ceased. Once the little Italian lowered his face to the plate it rarely came back up.

Airman Mortensen crunched in silence on his onion

dinner. Many of the golden rings had to be folded just
to get them into his mouth. As usual they tasted good
but on this day they were strangely unsatisfying. Airman Mortensen was thinking and the more he thought
the more glum he became. At last he said to himself,
'What am I eating these stupid things for?' and shoved
the platter toward his roommate.

It was one of those times when the idea of freedom
could not be forced from his mind. How could he have
joined the military? There were plenty of excuses—a
dollar twenty-five a day hotel room a thousand miles
from home—the upcoming draft—no job, no money, no
prospects—that thing about getting the commitment out
of the way. But none of the excuses washed. No ration-
ale could excuse the supreme stupidity of what he had
done.

He lit a cigarette and, as his grief deepened, he noticed that five boys had appeared in the restaurant's
foyer. While they stood around waiting to be seated,
every diner stirred to get a look at them.

The boys stood out. A couple of them were wearing
old-fashioned, double-breasted suits. The others wore
what could probably be called ''show clothes'': ruffled
shirts, bell-bottoms, wide belts with cast-iron buckles
and black, pointed Beatle boots.

What really had the restaurant's attention was the hair.
Three of the boys had hair which was growing close to
their shoulders. It was outrageous.

The boys tried to act casual, talking and joking
amongst themselves, but they could feel the scrutiny. It
was the same kind of scrutiny black people were getting
at lunch counters in Georgia.

These boys would have no trouble receiving seats,
however, and the fact that they would soon be led to a
table, offered chairs, handed menus and have their orders taken, heightened the tension in the restaurant.

You could chase out a redskin or a greaser or a nigger but these boys were white and that made things awkward for the restaurant's patrons, many of whom felt they were being invaded by aliens.

Adults squirmed uncomfortably in their seats, averting their eyes. Their children, already trained to reject anything outside the mainstream, giggled openly. Some of the kids pointed brazenly in the direction of the foyer and had to be shushed by their parents. Working men peered sullenly from under their cap bills, fantasizing about dragging these queers behind tractors. Even the restaurant staff skipped a beat.

Bernie looked up, his cheeks bulging with pork. "You want some?" he asked. "It's fucking great."

Airman Mortensen waved him off and was relieved to see Bernie go back to his dinner. True to form, he hadn't noticed the boys standing in the foyer and it was just as well. Airman Mortensen didn't want to be disturbed in his watching.

He knew they were in a band and, as the boys followed a waitress to their table, the restaurant vibrated with their passing. He admired the spirit of these boys. They courageously ignored the turning heads.

'They must be playing somewhere tonight,' he thought. 'So strong, standing up to all this shit. They're onto something. They're affected by the gawkers but in the end they don't care. They've got something to hold onto, even if just the parts of a song. G . . . L . . . O . . . R . . I . . A . . .'

The band members disappeared behind one of the restaurant's accordion partitions and Airman Mortensen solemnly plucked another onion ring off the platter. He held it in front of his face for a moment, then flipped it back on the plate.

He looked once more at the people in the restaurant and suddenly he knew exactly what would satisfy him.

Growing his hair to his knees would satisfy him. Wearing anything he wanted would satisfy him. Being with whomever he pleased would be satisfactory. Saying whatever he pleased would be satisfactory. Doing whatever he pleased would be satisfactory. Nothing else would do. It had to be all-out, full-tilt, undiluted freedom. Freedom was the ultimate goal.

They paid the bill and left. It shocked him now to watch Bernie. Bernie was purely oblivious.

They stood at the GI bus stop a block from Chew Den and waited twenty minutes for the blue Air Force shuttle to pick them up.

It carried them back to the base.

In the barracks Airman Mortensen got into a card game. He was lucky. The loose change he started with grew to more than ten dollars. But he didn't care.

There was whiskey at the table and he drank a lot of it.

Sometime in the morning he staggered down to his cubicle, pulled off his clothes and fell into the little, metal-frame bed where he spent a third of his life.

But he'd drunk too much. The white room was spinning.

He got up and stumbled into one of the latrines. He paced up and down in front of the sinks, trying to walk it off. But the spinning wouldn't stop.

He stepped into a dry shower stall and curled up in a corner. He laid his face on the cool tile and counted to a hundred.

Finally the spinning seemed to slow and he fumbled his way back to the cubicle. Number 209. His home.

Lying in bed again, he focused on a fingernail moon poking through the window. Seeing the moon gave him a good feeling about freedom. Seeing the moon made it seem more possible.

He thought of Claire. She was with him in all this. She was unconscious in her bed but she was with him.

It was one of those nights he couldn't remember going to sleep.

☆ **6** ☆

Somewhere in the fog there was banging on the door.

Airman Mortensen rolled over and blinked. It was early morning, too early to be awake after last night's whiskey. Bernie was sitting straight up in bed, trying to figure out whether the barracks was on fire or what.

The insistent knocking came again and the door opened. MGT stuck his head inside. His big lips were pulled back in a pained smile.

"Y'all bitter git yo' asses outta them racks . . . there's a goddamn major downstairs . . . he goin' thru all da rooms . . . 'sprise inspekshun."

"Inspection?" Airman Mortensen growled. "On fuckin' Sunday mornin'?"

"Don' look at me," MGT warned. His eyes took in the room. "Y'all bitter git dis shit picked up."

His face disappeared and a moment later Airman Mortensen could hear knocking on the next door down as MGT spread the alarm.

Bernie was already out of bed. Though his area was always in order he began fussing with his stuff as if a girl was on her way up.

Airman Mortensen lay back on his bunk and heaved a gloomy sigh. He picked up his cigarette pack and yawned deeply as he shook out a Pall Mall.

Bernie continued his preoccupation with light house-keeping and it wasn't until the Pall Mall was smoked halfway down that he noticed Airman Mortensen was still sprawled in bed. Instantly, he stopped spacing the clothes in his wall locker and stared incredulously at the latrine king.

"Hey . . . what're you doin'?"

"What's it look like I'm doin'?" Airman Mortensen replied languidly. "I'm smokin' a goddamn cigarette."

"Yeah, but . . . Jesus . . . look at that mess."

Airman Mortensen didn't want to look. The whiskey had fuzzed his brain linings. The room jiggled when he moved. But in deference to Bernie he turned on his side and pushed up on an elbow.

It was a pretty good mess alright. A week's worth of dirty laundry, little islands of it, was piled along the floor and in the corners on his half of the room. Long, tubelike dust formations hung around the dirty clothes and hugged the baseboards. He didn't look under the bed but he knew there was a quite a buildup down there.

The wall locker didn't have much in it. Most every-thing, civilian and military shoes, sweaty socks and a few books, had been dumped in the bottom. Only a winter overcoat and a dress blue uniform in need of cleaning were on hangers.

The stereo standing on the gray desk at the foot of the bed, was surrounded by his entire collection of rec-ords. They looked like discards on a poker table. More books were stacked on the desk and sitting proudly on top of the haphazard stacks were three or four half-filled ashtrays.

It made Airman Mortensen sicker when he looked at all this crap. He swung his head slowly back. His eyes were too sore to open all the way and he had to squint across the room. When he was able to focus he could see that Bernie's jaw was protruding. He was silently demanding an answer.

"It's not the worst," Airman Mortensen yawned.

"What?" Bernie hissed. His eyes were popping out of their sockets. They had begun to take on an oval shape.

"It looks lived in . . . it's okay for a Sunday morning." Airman Mortensen's fingers pounded the Pall Mall into an overflowing ashtray perched on the sill just above his head.

Bernie lurched forward mechanically, his arms outstretched like a ham actor.

"You gotta do somethin'," he blubbered.

"It's not like a white glove inspection . . ."

Both of Bernie's fists rose even with his chest. "We don't know that."

"How could it be?" Airman Mortensen countered. "It's dawn on Sunday morning. They're lookin' for stolen stuff or something . . . God, I feel like hammered shit."

"But we have to . . ."

"Besides . . . ," Airman Mortensen interrupted, "I could care less."

"Well, I care," Bernie hollered. One hand was clutching the crucifix and the grip was turning his knuckles white. "You gotta clean this up. We can't have an officer come in here with this . . ."

The latrine king's covers flew up. "Okay, Bernie, O fucking K!" Angrily, he pulled a chair away from the desk, slid it across the floor and parked it in front of the wall locker. With a little stagger he climbed onto the chair and ripped open the doors to a small storage area located just above the locker. It was the one space which all airmen could call private, a space that was immune from inspection. At least, that was the unspoken rule.

Standing in the center of the room, Airman Mortensen threw his shoes in first, pitching them through the
open doors one at a time. The big combat boots hit the
metal hard, making a loud banging noise and Bernie
flinched at each impact.

The latrine king scooped up his ashtrays and threw
them in. One of them shattered as it hit the back wall
of the storage area but he paid it no mind.

He crow-hopped around the room, bending unstead-
ily at each pile of dirty laundry. Gathering all of it in
his arms, Airman Mortensen climbed onto the chair
once again and stuffed the clothes into what little room
was left. Then he dove into the bottom of his wall locker
and snatched up a few miscellaneous items, including
a couple of stray boots.

He had to hold the bulging contents with one hand
while he struggled to shut the twin doors with the other.
Finally, the latch clicked into place.

Airman Mortensen hopped down and brushed the
work from his hands.

"Well, I'm ready," he announced combatively.

The Italian stood motionless, his head hanging sadly.

Airman Mortensen picked up his shaving kit, grabbed
a towel off the bedpost and marched triumphantly for
the showers. He wasn't going to let the Air Force harass
him with a stupid inspection on Sunday morning. They
could fuck with anybody they wanted but they weren't
going to fuck with him. He was going to take his sweet
time and if they didn't like it they could lump it.

Instead of speeding through the morning cleanup as
usual, he let the hot water beat against him for five full
minutes on each side. He dried off slowly and shaved
with the care of a groom on his wedding day.

At last, he wrapped the towel around his waist,
stepped into the hall and noticed immediately that
something was up. Too many airmen were hanging

around the doorways to their rooms. And they were all
in uniform. Then, as he stood barefooted in the hall,
he saw the officers. There were two of them and they
were both in dress blues. One held a clipboard as they
swept out of one room and into another.

"Oh God," he said to himself, "it's a real inspection . . . I don't believe it."

A little tremor of panic passed through him but by
the time Airman Mortensen got back to his cubicle he'd
decided to continue the resistance. It wasn't fair and he
wasn't going along with it. That's what he told himself
over and over.

Dressed in fresh khaki, Bernie was bent over a dust-
pan, sweeping up a thin line of dirt. He stood up, dust-
pan in one hand, broom in the other and glared at the
towel around Airman Mortensen's hips. Sticking his
nose in the air, he turned away and dumped the dirt in
a small trash can next to the communal desk.

Airman Mortensen noted that Bernie had tidied the
records and books that stood on the desk. It made him
mad.

"You're pissed at me, aren'cha?"

Bernie said nothing. He squatted next to his bed and
arranged three pairs of shining shoes which were already in perfect alignment.

"What is this," Airman Mortensen challenged, "the
silent treatment or something?"

Bernie kept fiddling with the shoes. "I got nothing
to say to you."

The little Italian moved back to the desk and self-
consciously straightened a box of Kleenex. At last he
turned and faced his roommate.

"Aren'cha gonna get dressed?" he pleaded.

Airman Mortensen waved at his wall locker. "What
d'ya want me to wear? . . . my fucking overcoat?"

Bernie stared at him contemptuously. Airman Mortensen stared back. Finally, the Italian turned his back once more.

"Don't be such a baby," Airman Mortensen scolded. "What the hell is wrong with you?"

Bernie whirled, his huge jaw aimed like a spear.

"What the fuck is wrong with you?"

"Nothin'," Airman Mortensen hollered, "nothin' except the goddamn Air Force!"

"Well, you're in it, aren'cha?" Bernie's eyes were suddenly fiery, redder than the latrine king had ever seen them.

"Yeah, well I don't have to like it," Airman Mortensen grumbled.

"I don't like it either!" Bernie screamed. He stabbed an index finger against his chest. "But that doesn't mean I gotta bitch and moan and run everything down all the time. What makes you so special? Huh? Huh? Why don'cha just shut up for once? You're in with all of us guys. Why don't you shut up?"

There was silence.

Bernie stood trembling in the center of the room.

Airman Mortensen sat wearily on his bunk and automatically reached for a cigarette. Bernie had something alright. He did gripe constantly, too much probably. He hated the military and he let everyone within earshot hear about it. What was he trying to prove? That he was miserable? Suddenly the latrine king felt shitty about himself. Suddenly he felt stupid and worthless. And lonely.

"Okay, man," he said lowly, "I've got a problem. It's my problem and I'm sorry if you feel like you're gettin' sucked into it. I'm sorry. Okay?"

Bernie sighed. "I'm sorry too. I shouldn'ta yelled at ya like that."

"That's okay. You got a right to yell. But I can't help it. I get so pissed at these idiots."

Bernie sat on his own bed. He saw a crease in the blanket and smoothed it out with the flat of his hand. "There's nothin' we can do about it though. Just stick together is all."

The two friends thought in silence for a few seconds.

"You better put somethin' on," Bernie said blankly.

"Naw," Airman Mortensen said, shaking his head. "It's too late." He heard footsteps in the room next to theirs. "See?"

Bernie got off his bed and smoothed the blanket again. Airman Mortensen thought about smoothing his own but decided it wouldn't make that much difference. He came to his feet, tightened the towel at his waist and made ready to come to attention.

Junior-grade officers had a touchiness that was universally feared. Youth and inexperience placed them on the lowest rung of an elite, military ladder. These young and inexperienced men were expected to perform mistake-free work and exhibit blind obedience at all times, a combination that kept most of them on the verge of nervous breakdowns. They caught shit from every conceivable angle. They were manipulated cleverly by old-timers in the enlisted ranks and routinely dumped on by field-grade officers. First and second lieutenants were regularly eaten by the larger fish which surrounded them. Airman Mortensen would have pitied the boys with the single bars except that, in his eyes, they deserved every ounce of the abuse which was heaped on them. With few exceptions, they lived up to the description someone had given them in basic training—"a pure race of assholes."

The grades above first lieutenant weren't much better. Poised as they were for the long climb to the top, captains were known as a vicious breed. Most lieutenant colonels stalled out at that rank and weren't too much trouble unless an airman locked horns with one (as the latrine king had with Tollefson). The main trait of full colonels was intense neurosis but contact with them was rare. Rarer yet were the generals. However, the members of this highest rank were used to having everything their own way and the great nightmare of all airmen was somehow being noticed by one. Generals were like toddlers with unlimited power and anyone who bungled into one of their tantrums was a goner.

Airman Mortensen's favorite rank was major. These men had enormously good dispositions. They were fatherly in many ways and the latrine king theorized that their positions in the military hierarchy were more secure than any other. They didn't walk the halls of power. At the same time they were free to pass tricky administrative dilemmas down to the captains and lieutenants. Most of them smoked pipes and were dangerous only when cornered. A few, known to be insane, were carefully avoided.

Bernie stood rigidly at attention and Airman Mortensen threw out his bare chest as the two officers walked through the open door. The first one in was a pie-faced, middle-aged major. Sure enough, there was a pipe in his hand. Following behind, clipboard in hand, was a skinny second lieutenant with a huge Adam's apple.

"Good morning, men," said the major, stepping to the center of the room. "At ease."

Bernie's shoulders fell about a half inch but he remained tense. Airman Mortensen, who had never really come to attention, didn't move. The major smiled thinly at the airman in the towel. He seemed mildly amused but didn't say anything. Airman Mortensen returned the glance and spied the name tag pinned on the officer's breast pocket. The name tag read Work.

Bernie's area was closest to the door and the inspection started there. Major Work didn't seem very intent. The half smile was still on his face and, while one hand clutched the pipe, his other nestled casually in a pants pocket. In the same way a tourist browses in front of a museum case, he gave Bernie's wall locker the once-over.

Airman Mortensen noticed that the second lieutenant was writing stuff down on the clipboard but couldn't imagine why. 'How can we be at the mercy of two dorks we don't even know, who could care less about us and our shit?' he thought.

Now the major discovered that Bernie was still at attention and said kindly, "At ease, son."

Bernie moved his feet slightly and acknowledged the major's gentle request with a bright and proper "Yes, sir."

Airman Mortensen's eyes rolled under his lids. 'I've got a West Point Cadet for a roommate,' he thought.

"Where you from, son?" the major asked.

Bernie swelled with pride. Then he grinned and, to Airman Mortensen's astonishment, the Italian began to blush. He was actually turning red.

"I'm from Connecticut, sir . . . Bridgeport, sir."

Airman Mortensen's eyes rolled again. 'Jesus H. Christ, Bernie . . . what's next? . . . a picture of the pet hamster you left behind?'

Major Work looked baffled by Bernie's zeal. When the airman from Bridgeport bashfully dropped his eyes, the major saw his chance for escape and turned away. He stepped up to Airman Mortensen's locker.

It was obvious to everyone that Major Work was momentarily puzzled. He twisted his head and checked on the lieutenant but the assistant didn't know what was wrong. He lifted the pencil above the clipboard, poised to write.

Not knowing what else to do, the major stuck his head all the way into the locker as if he might have overlooked a secret panel. Then he turned to Airman Mortensen.

"Where are your uniforms, airman?"

The latrine king said the first thing that came into his mind. It sounded rational.

"At the cleaners, sir."

"All of them?"

"Pretty much, sir."

"What are you planning to wear to work in the morning?"

"I'm off tomorrow, sir," he lied.

Major Work's eyes shifted back and forth as he thought this over. He looked in the locker again. Then his gaze traveled along the floor under Airman Mortensen's bed.

"Where are your shoes?"

"Shoes, sir?"

"Shoes, yes . . . for your feet."

"They're out, sir."

The major stared at him. "Out where?"

Airman Mortensen didn't mind lying to officers. Once you got started it was like any high-stakes contest, dangerous but fun. Airman Mortensen was particularly good at it.

"They're getting shined, sir."

"Shined by whom?"

"Another airman, sir . . . he's broke. He owes me money so he's working off what he owes."

Major Work nodded. "I see . . ."

He turned his back and, tilting his head slightly upward, swept the entire room. His gaze came to rest on the storage area above the empty wall locker. Airman Mortensen's scalp began to tingle.

In a leisurely motion, the major reached out and pulled a chair across the floor. He positioned it directly in front of the locker.

Airman Mortensen wanted so badly to say "Stop!" but if he opened his mouth now the game would be up for sure. He stood helplessly as Major Work climbed onto the chair.

'My ass is grass,' he said to himself.

Major Work's hands began to fiddle with the latch and a moment later everything in Airman Mortensen's view shifted into the curious slow motion he seemed to experience in times of trauma.

The twin doors swung slowly open and out poured Airman Mortensen's belongings. Instinctively, the major tried to duck. He jackknifed on the chair, his head bent into his upraised arms as ashtrays, bundles of letters, belts, dirty clothes, flight caps and miscellaneous junk rained down on him.

At the height of the avalanche a stray combat boot, riding the crest of a rolled-up uniform, flew out of the locker and conked the major square on the head, knocking his service cap to the floor.

When time resumed its normal speed, the stunned officer was still standing on the chair, staring in disbelief at the mess which lay all about him.

"What the hell is this?"

Though he knew it was hopeless, Airman Mortensen tried to sound serene. "Just some stuff I had stored, sir."

"You store things like this?" the major questioned. He was climbing down from the chair now.

Airman Mortensen didn't answer immediately. While Major Work retrieved his hat the latrine king glanced at Bernie. The Italian was perfectly still and very pale.

"I was unprepared, sir," he said at last, giving up the game.

Major Work looked once more at the debris scattered on the floor. Then he took a step toward Airman Mortensen.

"Who's your First Sergeant?"

"Senior Master Sergeant Pomeroy, sir."

The major surveyed the mess again. Then he said, "I'd get this in order if I were you," and walked slowly out of the room, the second lieutenant trailing after him.

There was a moment or two of pronounced silence. As Airman Mortensen's heartbeat slowed, Bernie gradually came to his senses. The Italian sank onto his bunk and covered his face with both hands.

"Oh God . . ." he moaned.

Airman Mortensen lit a cigarette.

"Oh God what?"

"We're fucked."

"We're not fucked, I'm fucked. You're in the clear, you're from fucking Connecticut."

"Aww, shut up," Bernie whined. He dropped his hands and the two roommates stared each other down.

"Okay," Airman Mortensen said, 'I'll shut up."

He squatted next to the dirty clothes and grabbed a pair of fatigue pants from the pile. While he pulled them on a leg at a time, Bernie stared gloomily at the stuff on the floor.

He started to shake his head and, as Airman Mortensen watched, a crazy-looking smile appeared on the Italian's face. Then it was a full grin, far away and goofy, as if he was recalling some pleasant childhood memory.

"What?" Airman Mortensen asked sourly.

Bernie looked up, his eyes shining merrily. He wouldn't stop shaking his head.

"What?" Airman Mortensen repeated.

"I . . . I can't believe . . ."

Bernie couldn't get the rest out because he had begun to do something unusual. He had begun to giggle. It started like a leak, swelled into a stream and, as Bernie fell backward on his bed, it became an insane, unbridled flood of laughter.

Airman Mortensen began to chuckle.

"What? . . . for chrissakes, Bernie?"

It was only with great difficulty that the Italian answered. He had to work hard at squeezing the words through the seams of his laughter. He was literally gasping for breath.

"I can't believe . . . I can't believe . . . that boot . . . that boot hit him . . . hit him right in the head." He rolled onto his side, holding his ribs with both hands.

"Yeah . . . it was a perfect shot. Did you see that . . . ?" Airman Mortensen was giggling now too. "It damn near knocked him off the fucking chair!"

"Yeah!" Bernie squealed.

"We're lucky it didn't knock him off the fucking chair," Airman Mortensen blurted. "The fall probably would've killed him."

Bernie tumbled onto the floor and flopped around like a fish. His face color went from red to blue. The veins on his neck were popping. He tried to speak several times but each attempt was smothered by another wave of spasmodic giggling.

Airman Mortensen was out of control too. He dropped to his hands and knees and crawled over to Bernie.

"What?"

Bernie managed to get out the word "Dead . . ." but again he could not continue.

"Dead major . . . dead major in 209."

Airman Mortensen saw it all—Major Work dead on the floor, the brogan boot a few feet from his head, investigators milling around, two airmen being led away in chains, massive news coverage. He saw the news angle in a bold, banner headline—"Fatal Inspection!"

The two friends lay side by side on the floor, their bodies contorted hysterically, their faces awash with tears. Just when Airman Mortensen thought he was coming to composure, Bernie would go off again and vice versa.

They laughed straight through their respective thresholds of pain. They laughed until they were sure they would die.

☆ **7** ☆

As routine and boring as military life might have been, it was not wise to make book on any specific event. Soldiers might bet on ball games or poker hands or even the number of flies that might be found in a particular room at a particular time. But betting on the base theatre's marquee living up to its billing or a three-day pass on the word of an officer or a long-promised "guaranteed" promotion was strictly taboo. Nobody could figure out how the system worked and anyone who put faith in it was considered brain-dead.

This point was dramatically illustrated when, late on Monday morning, a runner stuck his head in the latrine and told Airman Mortensen that the First wanted to see him "on the double."

It hadn't been a good morning for the latrine king. With payday so close most guys, too broke to go anywhere else, hung around the barracks all weekend and the latrines were trashed.

Claire hadn't called—not Saturday, not Sunday, not this morning. He kept reminding himself to keep the faith but couldn't resist the idea that kept creeping into his mind. "If she's so in love with me why doesn't she call?'' And now he was being ordered down to face another distasteful development.

Major Work's report must have reached the First Sergeant.

Thinking about punishments, he descended the stairs slowly, one methodical step at a time. Perhaps it wasn't a report; perhaps the major was really mad. Perhaps he had phoned the First. They probably talked for awhile, running down the multitude of available torture options. They might have him stand inspection every day for a week. Or a month. All shoes spit-shined, all uniforms spotless, a bed made so tight you could drop a quarter and see it bounce back up. They would probably cook up some simulation of basic training, that was the obvious choice. But, of course, it could be anything.

Coincidentally, the First was on the phone. While he waited outside, the suspense doubling with each passing minute, it occurred to Airman Mortensen that the storage area affair might end with him being kicked out of the service. It wasn't that farfetched; guys had been kicked out for less, and he let his mind run with the idea. A week ago he would have prayed for this to happen. He would have crossed his fingers, hoping against hope that he would be discharged. But now it was the worst thing that could happen. A discharge would mean no more Claire. Maybe they could work something out if he did get discharged but his mind shuddered at the complexities. No more Claire. Not that. Anything but that.

His armpits were clammy and his palms were slick with sweat. When the First Sergeant hung up the phone and beckoned him in with an ominous crook of a finger, Airman Mortensen thought his legs might go.

He halted submissively in front of the topkick's desk. Words of atonement were hurriedly forming into sentences.

"Sit down," the First said softly.

Still trying to piece together a speech, Airman Mortensen started for a chair against the wall.

"No," the First commanded quietly, "sit here." He tapped a chair sitting flush against the desk.

Airman Mortensen obediently took his seat. The latrine king joined his hands and twiddled his thumbs. He leaned forward in the manner of a confessor.

"Sir," he began contritely, "I don't know what Major Work had to say . . . I only know that I . . ."

"Who's Major Work?"

Airman Mortensen looked up quickly. The First's expression was genuine. He didn't know.

"Me and my big mouth . . . goddammit."

The First Sergeant sighed.

"I don't think I want to know." He didn't say anything else and neither did Airman Mortensen.

He was hoping that they could just start over and the First Sergeant acknowledged his wish. He picked a sheet of paper off the stack on his desk and laid it in front of Airman Mortensen.

"Look at this," he said.

It was a military form, a printout memo originating from Base Personnel. Airman Mortensen read some of the words but he was too addled to put them together.

"What does this mean?" he asked feebly.

A scowl started on the First's face. "Now, I know and you know you're not stupid; don't play games with me."

"No, Sarge . . . can you just tell me? I just see all this jargon and . . ."

"Alright."

The First Sergeant picked up the form and held it in front of his face. He pushed the bifocals toward the tip of his nose.

"This came in this morning . . . it's from Personnel."

"I got that."

"Don't interrupt."

"Okay . . . sorry."

"What this says is that you are no longer a radio operator."

"I'm not?"

"You're not. The Strategic Air Command had decided to phase out ground-to-ground radio operators."

"All of them?"

"The whole career field."

Airman Mortensen thought for a moment.

"Well, what does that make me?"

The First Sergeant smiled tightly, too tightly for his teeth to be seen.

"Right now that makes you nothing. However," here he slid the form under Airman Mortensen's nose again, ". . . the directive says that all ground-to-ground radio operators are to be cross-trained immediately into one of these seven fields—these seven, right here."

The topkick ran his freckled finger down the list and, mesmerized like a chicken on a piece of scratch, Airman Mortensen followed it. Fuels specialist, food services tech, air police, information specialist . . .

Airman Mortensen gasped audibly. Information specialist! The two words got big in his eyes, so big they were the only words on the paper. He held his breath.

"Wait a minute, Sarge . . . you mean I can cross-train into one of these career fields?"

"If there's an opening."

It was a dream, a crazy dream he'd had since basic training. It was the field he'd wanted all along. It was a job he could do, a contribution he could make. He'd discussed it with the First several times. Now the dream was staring him in the face. He held his breath again.

"How do I find out if there's an opening?"

The strange, toothless smile was still on the topkick's face.

"You know," he began offhandedly, "I called up there this morning. I've got a buddy up there . . . Master Sergeant Shoemaker . . ." He looked into Airman Mortensen's eyes. "He wants to see you right after lunch, at one o'clock."

Airman Mortensen did not reply. He was gazing at the form beneath his fingertips. It was too much to absorb, to think that his long exile in the latrines might end. He needed to be pinched.

Finally he looked up at the First Sergeant. "Is this a joke, Sarge? I can't believe this."

"I spoke up for you, so don't you fuck up. If you do, you'll make me look bad. We can't have that."

"I won't fuck up, no way."

"Maybe Sergeant Shoemaker will want to put you on, maybe he won't. But if he does . . . and if you fuck up . . . your ass is back on latrine duty that fast."

Airman Mortensen sat still. He was numb.

"Better move your butt," the First Sergeant suggested, his face dropping down to the mound of paperwork in front of him.

Airman Mortensen came slowly off the chair. He remembered something important.

"What about Lieutenant Colonel Tollefson?"

The First looked up.

"What about him?"

"Well . . . uhh . . . I don't know."

"Tollefson has nothing to do with this. This came down from SAC Omaha. He can't say shit."

"But this court-martial thing."

"They know about that at PIO."

"And they still want to see me?"

"What did I say?"

"You said, uhh . . ."

"I said you were supposed to see Master Sergeant Shoemaker at one o'clock." The topkick lowered his eyes to the paperwork again. "Get moving."

"Thanks, Sarge. Thanks a lot."

The First Sergeant said nothing. He placed a hand over his brow as he continued to eye the paperwork.

Airman Mortensen wanted to say something. He wanted to say something that came straight from his heart. In the end he just got out of the chair and left.

☆ **8** ☆

The next three weeks couldn't have gone much better for Airman Mortensen.

He got the information specialist job. Though it didn't become official for several days, he sensed the deal was going to go down ten minutes into his interview with Sergeant Shoemaker.

Shoemaker was the perfect picture of an upper-level lifer: perfect uniform and shoes, perfect haircut, perfect bearing and perfect devotion to duty.

He was also a perfect crackpot. His close-set eyes were encased in heavy hornrims, the lenses of which gave him a distinctly cross-eyed look. His shoes weren't just shined, they were patent leather. His bearing, effected by chronic lower back problems, was ridiculously erect. The sides and back of his head were mostly scalp and the hair that grew on top looked like a bed of nails. He had the metabolism of a hummingbird and was so high-strung that, at the sign of the most trifling crisis, a trembling started all over his body.

Master Sergeant Shoemaker was also a decent man and on the day of their initial interview he treated Airman Mortensen with courtesy and respect. The trembling affliction made the encounter seem a little weird but the latrine king found it refreshing just to be treated like a human being.

Sergeant Shoemaker knew about the trouble in the Comm Squad and the impending court-martial. It didn't seem to bother him and he went so far as to imply that if Airman Mortensen went to work in the PIO and did well, they would try to help him out. He also implied that the office was understaffed and that the recommendation from the First Sergeant counted heavily in Airman Mortensen's favor.

After a cram course in the Air Force style of journalism, Sergeant Shoemaker guided the potential newshound into a partitioned cubicle, empty except for a desk, chair and typewriter. Telling him to relax and take his time, Sergeant Shoemaker temporarily departed the scene, leaving the would-be journalist to bone up on his writing skills.

It was a test of sorts. He had three tasks: caption an eight-by-ten picture of an awards ceremony, correct the errors in a standard news story and write a short press release on an airman's promotion.

The work was easy and it was fun to use his brain for a change. He finished quickly but, not wanting to look like an eager beaver, he remained behind the partition, reviewing the work he had completed and dreaming about the possibilities of life as an Air Force journalist.

"Pssst."

The face of a strange-looking airman was craning around the partition. Now he was sliding into the cubicle, glancing over a shoulder as if worried about a tail.

He parked his rear on the edge of the desk. His eyes were darting all around, touching on everything but Airman Mortensen.

"Got a cigarette?"

"Sure." The latrine king shook one out.

The strange airman took the Pall Mall and patted the breast pockets of his uniform.

"Light?" he smiled.

Airman Mortensen struck a match and held it to the cigarette. The strange airman sucked at the flame several times. This sucking caused the paper match to flare wildly and, as Airman Mortensen snuffed it with a quick flick of his wrist, cigarette smoke billowed upward in great clouds. The strange airman closed his eyes, raised them to the ceiling and continued to puff, his mouth working like a bellows. Then he stopped and brought the cigarette close to his face, contemplating it ecstatically.

"So, whatd'ya think of Shoemaker?" he asked, looking the other way.

"He seems like a nice guy."

The strange airman began to twirl the head of his cigarette around the lip of an ashtray.

"He's a nervous Nellie . . . nervous as a cat." Saliva sprayed from the strange airman's lips and he quickly tidied the corners of his mouth with the back of his hand.

"Yeah, he does seem kinda edgy," Airman Mortensen concurred.

"He's scared to death of the brass but I think his lunches have somethin' to do with it too."

"How come?"

"Aw, he eats fish and shit all the time. He's married

to some Korean babe and she's always puttin' squid and seaweed in his lunchbox . . . shit like that.''

"Does he eat it?''

"Oh yeah, he woofs the shit right down. Says it's fuckin' brain food.''

"It's supposed to be ball food.''

"I don't think that's the case with Shoemaker. What's he got you doin'?''

Without waiting for a reply, the strange airman snatched up the practice work and began to scrutinize it.

"Just routine stuff, I guess,'' Airman Mortensen replied. But the strange airman wasn't listening. Squinting through the smoke of his overheated cigarette, the fast, smart eyes were racing over the lines Airman Mortensen had written.

"This is pretty good,'' he said. "You had experience?''

"A little.''

The strange airman's head bobbed up and down as he stared at the picture caption. His short, stubby body squirmed on the desk top. Airman Mortensen thought of cartoons. Pudgy arms, pudgy chest, pudgy thighs, all bulging against his uniform like wads of dough stuffed in a sausage skin. A small mouth, full of crooked, smiling teeth. Dark hair, thick as lawn grass, a great hunk of it hanging over his left eye.

'Cartoon,' Airman Mortensen thought again. 'This guy is a cartoon.'

Sergeant Shoemaker suddenly stepped around the partition. He seemed shocked to see the strange airman lounging on the desk.

"What are you doing?''

The strange airman gave Sergeant Shoemaker an insultingly brief look and returned to his study of Airman Mortensen's work.

''Nothin'.''

Sergeant Shoemaker's face flushed. He reached out and trapped the paperwork between his fingers. He gave the pages a light pull but they didn't give. The strange airman was ignoring Sergeant Shoemaker's tug.

Airman Mortensen couldn't believe what he was seeing.

Sergeant Shoemaker pulled at the paperwork again and this time the strange airman looked up.

''What?'' he said sourly.

Sergeant Shoemaker's face turned pink as he indicated the paperwork.

''I don't think that's any of your business,'' he said, beginning to tremble.

''I'm just lookin','' the strange airman whined.

''Give it to me . . .''

''Just a second.''

''Tom!'' Sergeant Shoemaker tugged violently at the worthless sheets. ''Give it to me.''

''Okay, okay . . . geez . . . I was just checkin' it out.''

''Go check something else.''

Tom didn't move. He sat sulking, swinging his legs back and forth like a kid.

''If he's comin' here, are you gonna put him on the newspaper?''

''We'll discuss that later.''

''I need help,'' Tom cried, saliva spraying six inches out of his mouth. ''I've been doin' it practically by myself.''

''We'll discuss it later. Now go.''

''I'm gonna be really pissed if I don't get . . .''

''Tom!'' Sergeant Shoemaker had spread his legs in the style of a gladiator. One hand had gone to his hip. The other, Airman Mortensen's work displayed prominently between the trembling fingers, was pointing out of the cubicle.

"Go!"

Reluctantly, Tom slid off the desk.

"Alright, alright, don't get bent out of shape." He swung his smiling face in Airman Mortensen's direction. "Got another butt?" he asked cheerfully.

"Get out!" Sergeant Shoemaker yelled.

Tom shrugged his shoulders as if it was no big deal. "Geez," he sighed, "a guy can't even bum a cigarette around here." Shoving his hands into his pockets he made a slow, shuffling exit.

Like a harried grade-school teacher who disciplines one child in order to attend to another, Sergeant Shoemaker bent to the desk.

"Alright," he said to the still-seated latrine king, "let's take a few minutes and go over this."

Sergeant Shoemaker made tiny, fevered corrections as he delivered a running commentary on various rules of official Air Force style. But Airman Mortensen only half watched and listened. He couldn't stop replaying the confrontation between Sergeant Shoemaker and the strange airman.

It was so weird—a geek (Sergeant Shoemaker) and a spoiled brat (Tom) waging infantile combat over a few meaningless pieces of paper.

They were grown men in uniform, their country's first line of defense. It was ludicrous, and the more Airman Mortensen thought about it, the more he came to realize that the conflict he'd just witnessed had a distinct quality of the routine.

'Oh God,' he thought, 'they must fight like this all the time.'

He watched Sergeant Shoemaker's jaw. It was moving rapidly up and down as he spewed out words Airman Mortensen was not hearing. He was fascinated by

the moving jaw and its dense, blue forest of stiff folli-
cles, hiding in the pores, waiting only to grow and be
cut. Over and over. No wonder razor blade companies
were huge and rich.

Sergeant Shoemaker's jaw was so close now that he
could smell the residue of this morning's Aqua Velva
splashing. It made him faintly nauseous.

'What am I doing here?' he thought suddenly.

And just as suddenly Airman Mortensen knew that
his stroke of good fortune was in no way consistent
with his cool dream of respectability and pride as an
Air Force journalist. Working in this office would carry
with it the same madness that infected every level of
military life. It wouldn't be as bleak and boring as the
latrines but, like dog shit unwittingly tracked into a dinner party, the lunacy would follow wherever he went.

☆ **9** ☆

Airman Mortensen didn't know how he felt. It just
wasn't possible to click his heels but things were turning out too well to be depressed. Colorful new energies
were swirling about inside of him but they couldn't get
out. Maybe it was the stinking, ugly uniform that, except for hands and face, covered all of his skin.

The latrine king diverted his uncertainty into the old
crocodile game as he walked back to the barracks.
Every seam in the sidewalk was a boiling pit of snap-
ping, thrashing crocodiles. He kept his head down,
guiding the black toes of his low-cut service shoes away
from the cracks as he walked.

While he concentrated on the crocodile game, little thoughts, like minnows flashing in the shallows, swam between his ears.

Sergeant Shoemaker walking him to the door. ''Be ready to go to work,'' he said. Sergeant Shoemaker introducing him to the cool, correct and ambitious Captain Hart. ''Airman Mortensen here knows how to put a sentence together.'' Captain Hart's steady, brown eyes hardly moving at all. ''Very good.''

That stupid court-martial. It was a splinter that no set of tweezers could reach. It oozed a little pus every time he thought about it. How could anybody be so stupid as to get into a mess like this? Well, he was.

Where the fuck was Claire? Why didn't she call? How was he supposed to feel about her? How could he feel anything about a mirage?

How was he supposed to feel at all? In San Francisco people were enjoying—no, they were celebrating— absolute freedom. And he was watching pictures of it on the TV in dusty dayrooms on a low-profile military base in an isolated part of New Mexico.

Airman Mortensen became so addled with all this thinking that, less than a hundred yards from the barracks, he stepped on a crack. He wanted to cry. Then he wanted to laugh. In the end he just stood there, a mental patient fixated on his foot during a stroll around the grounds.

'Everything that is given can be taken away,' he thought. 'For every June wedding there is a nasty, drawn-out divorce. For every life bawling in a delivery room there's someone being lowered down into the cool dirt. For every whiff of honeysuckle on a summer night there's something dead in a storm drain at the edge of the street.'

He was still standing in the hot sun, staring down at the dumb crack, when a low voice called behind him.

''Mortensen.''

Carl was walking up slowly, working out the knot in his tie. As usual he looked fresh and handsome but in the shade under the brim of his service cap Airman Mortensen thought he looked a little pale.

''What're you doin'?'' Carl asked, looking down at the seam in the sidewalk. ''Step on a crack, break your back?''

''Pit of crocodiles.''

''Oh . . . ,'' Carl smiled sickly. ''Too bad.''

''What're you doin'?'' Airman Mortensen questioned.

Carl squinted at the heat waves dancing along the sidewalk. ''I told 'em I couldn't make it. I took off early. I'm fuckin' hung over,'' he laughed.

They started to walk.

''With that gang you run with I'm surprised you're not hung over every day,'' Airman Mortensen observed. ''I don't know how you do it.''

''I'm okay if I don't mix stuff,'' Carl explained. ''If I stick to one thing I'm fine.'' He tipped his hat back and placed a hand gently on his forehead. ''It's that fuckin' Newt and his crazy mixed drinks. When I start on that shit I go right over the falls.''

The two friends suddenly froze at the sight of something rare, so rare that neither had ever seen it before. A girl had come out of the barracks' ground floor. The girl turned in their direction. A fantastic, spontaneous smile blossomed on her face. It was Claire.

The big, beautiful smile came straightaway to where the two airmen were standing. It propelled her arms around his neck. He could feel it shining on the face that was pressed against his own.

''God,'' Claire gasped, ''where were you?''

''I was here.''

''I tried to call you all weekend.''

"I never got a message . . . not one." Airman Mortensen made a quick mental note to murder whoever had handled phones over the weekend.

"Oh, I couldn't stand it," Claire cried, hugging him again. "It was like prison."

"What?" Airman Mortensen asked. He tried to look concerned but, in truth, he had no idea what she was talking about.

"Being away from you . . . it was like being in prison."

"Oh, yeah."

She sniffled as she clung to him. She was trembling a little and Airman Mortensen could feel wetness against his face. Over his shoulder he could see random groups of soldiers stopping to gawk. From the corner of his eye he could see Carl standing by awkwardly.

"Wait a second, Claire." He pulled away from her softly. "I want you to meet my friend, Carl."

Claire brushed at her tears. "Excuse me," she laughed. Then she shook Carl's hand. They exchanged hellos. Airman Mortensen said a few words about Carl and what he did in the Air Force but had only gotten through two or three sentences before he became distracted by the dreamy look on Claire's face. Carl broke in.

"I'm . . . uhh . . . gonna get going. Nice to meet you, Claire. See you later, Mortensen, you dog."

Airman Mortensen blushed as the lovers fell into another embrace on the sidewalk.

"Oh Jesus," Claire started, breaking off the clinch. She looked down at her wrist with a childish wonder that made it seem she had just learned to tell time. Airman Mortensen's groin had begun to ache.

"I've only got twenty minutes," she announced.

"Oh, noooo."

"Let's go somewhere," she said, taking him by the hand.

"Yeah, let's do that."

They hopped in the Volkswagen and searched frantically for a place where there would be no people. After ten tense minutes they settled on a little grove of trees next to the chapel. The chapel was the loneliest spot on base.

For ten more minutes they hung out under the trees, making out furiously, each trying to climb into the body of the other. In a delirium they lay down for the last minute or two of Claire's time. They rolled and squirmed and humped like a pair of eels until Claire, by force of will alone, threw herself away, climbed to her feet and stood panting, her forehead resting against the smooth trunk of a tree.

Airman Mortensen stood up behind her, straightening his twisted pants. The dull pain in his groin was now creeping toward his stomach.

"We better do it pretty soon," he said flatly.

Claire had a hand on either side of the tree trunk. Her head was still bowed and Airman Mortensen could see the breathless heave of her shoulders. Her head was bobbing slowly up and down, nodding affirmatively.

☆ 10 ☆

In succeeding days Airman Mortensen sat in his cubicle up at headquarters, working hard and fast to make a good impression in his first week as an Air Force journalist. The stress of this break-in period was aggravated greatly by the behavior of the strange airman, Tom Pittman.

Tom waged a relentless and highly irritating campaign to have the "fresh meat" assigned to the base newspaper. He pestered the sergeants every five minutes with a new angle and was finally granted a private audience with Captain Hart. The meeting started calmly enough but Tom had a problem with self control and, as his time wound down, the strange airman rose to his feet and paced back and forth in front of the captain's desk, spraying saliva randomly as he brayed out his final, impassioned arguments.

By the end of the week Tom was in a state of near collapse. Everyone else in the office was exhausted too. A decision had to come soon. Perhaps it was because they saw the wisdom of his argument, or perhaps they just wanted him off their backs but in the end Tom got his wish. Airman Mortensen was permanently assigned to the base newspaper and the gang of one became the gang of two.

It was a load for two airmen. Each edition of the newspaper fluctuated between sixteen and twenty blank pages which had to be filled with reams of official drivel in just five working days. The sergeants kicked in feature articles and "sensitive" press releases. Captain Hart occasionally wrote some hokum about the mission of the Public Information Office. There were guest columns from various commanders. But most of the writing and editing was left to Airman Pittman and Airman Mortensen.

And they only had three days to write and edit. A full day and a half of each week was spent downtown putting the paper together: setting the type, writing headlines, cutting in pictures, scrambling for filler, making corrections, etcetera.

They got to wear civvies, eat real food and flirt with

the print shop's pretty, middle-aged bookkeeper. Sometimes they jangled each other's nerves; sometimes the
deadlines were hell and superiors were constantly looking over their shoulders, giving them shit for one thing
or another. Captain Hart was particularly troublesome
because he knew nothing about putting out a newspaper
and suffered from the delusion that he did.

The gang of two fought back on every front with the
only ammo available to them. They laughed. They made
jokes out of everything and they laughed their asses off.

Sergeant Shoemaker was ripe fruit. Everything from
his haircut to his weird, Korean lunches ("What's that
there, Sarge, baked dog?") was exploited for laughs.
Probing his low anxiety threshold, they frequently wrote
phony press releases about prominent officers getting
busted with underaged girls and slipped them into
Shoemaker's "in" basket ("Oh, ha, ha, ha, someone
is very, very funny . . . so funny I forgot to laugh. You
guys quit screwing around in there and get some work
done.")

Military personnel of every stripe visited the office
in a steady stream, all of them lobbying for something
they needed to get into print. Depending on exactly
what they wanted, these people were either scorned or
ridiculed. Officers expecting special treatment were
scorned. Enlisted types suggesting feature ideas were
ridiculed.

When the day was particularly dull and they were in
sync intestinally the two airmen would sit in their respective cubicles and hold farting contests, loudness
being the yardstick for success. The winner was the first
one who farted loud enough to catch the attention of
someone in the outer office.

Perhaps once a week some insane little event led the
two newspaper editors to prolonged hysterics. When this
happened they would excuse themselves from the office

and stagger up the hall to the nearest latrine. Here they would smoke and talk in adjacent stalls until they were sober enough to return to work.

Through it all they tried hard to wedge a little laughter into the base newspaper. They came up with all kinds of cornball headlines which gave Second Coming status to the blandest news items. The *Stars and Stripes* sent features and filler to every base in the world and there were several pinups in each weekly batch. Zealously, the boys rewrote the pinup captions, trying for lurid, double meanings ("Loretta lists pork and cucumbers as her favorite foods"). Combing through the endless photo proof sheets, they tried to select awards ceremony pictures which portrayed the participants gazing down at a plaque or proclamation or trophy as freaks.

Only a tenth of the stuff they concocted got past the paranoid eyes of superiors but it took these tiny victories to keep them going from week to week.

When the paper came back from the printer every Friday, Airman Mortensen (like everyone else) would sequester himself in his cubicle, throw his feet on the desk and spend half an hour looking over what he and Tom had wrought. If he had an article running there would be a fleeting thrill at seeing his name in boldface under the headline. But most of his attention was directed at how the paper looked and at the subversive items that might have made it through.

He fought for innovative layout ideas but much of the time they didn't look as good as he thought they would. Sometimes they did.

At first glance, the tricks he and Tom got away with pleased him. They were like messages in a bottle thrown overboard and there was always a chance that someone out there would pick up on the disrespectful parodies they had intended.

But invariably, as he sat sucking on a Pall Mall, an inescapable malaise would overtake Airman Mortensen. The story with his name on it, squeezed and bleached of all vital semblance, wasn't about anything. The look of the paper? Well—the look is academic. This is shit. No matter what it looks like, it's still shit. And the jokes—they were like radio signals beamed to deep space. Nobody answered. Nobody ever said diddly squat about the dumb stuff because it was in the paper. And everybody hated the stupid paper.

Tom's attitude was better. He always came into Airman Mortensen's cubicle spraying saliva as he cracked up about the jokes that made it through. But a certain irony didn't escape Tom either and sooner or later he suffered a letdown on the day the paper made its appearance.

The irony was simple. They worked like slaves but all their work made them sick when they saw it. Airman Mortensen had a theory about it. Anything that was done in the military was ultimately not worth doing. The newspaper he and Tom edited was only one example of thousands.

By night Airman Mortensen either dreamt about Claire or talked to her on the phone or saw her at the base library.

They called each other several times a day now. And they met two nights a week at the library. Once, during the day, she had performed the innocent act of coming to the PIO office and asking for him in person. In the process she gave her full name to Sergeant Shoemaker and the little visit became the stuff of legend.

Everyone's mind was blown, especially Tom's. For several days the strange airman remained uncharacteristically subdued, poleaxed by the incredible achievement of his pal and co-worker Airman Mortensen.

''Brill's daughter! You're goin' with Brill's daughter!

I don't believe it, man, I can't believe it. But it's fucking true, isn't it? You're a goddamn slick-sleeve, dogface nobody and you're goin' with the base commander's daughter? How the fuck does that happen? Why don'cha let us all in on the secret? Huh? Huh?''

"I don't really know how it happened," Airman Mortensen would reply. "It just did."

Of course that answer wasn't satisfactory, not only to Tom but to the uncounted multitudes who pondered the same questions as news of the impossible romance went basewide.

People he hardly knew were looking at him funny and guys that had always rubbed him the wrong way (and vice versa) were now making serious attempts to become his friend. Even Bernie wouldn't let him alone. If he came back to the barracks late Bernie would automatically rouse himself and yawn, "Were you out with Claire?"

Newt had a strange reaction to the new celebrity. Every time they passed in the hall or ended up side by side in the latrine Newt would grin and shake his head and say, "You dum, gray, muthafucka . . . you in sum deep shit now."

By saying as little as he could Airman Mortensen only fueled the hunger for detail. But still he kept his mouth shut, confiding only in the little Italian. He had to confide in someone so he told Bernie about the romantic side of the liaison, going into real depth at times. Bernie listened, fully absorbed, as Airman Mortensen explained the nuances of a silence between lovers, but eventually it all came down to one, penultimate question.

"Did anything, uhh, happen yet?"

"Bernie, nothin's happening."

"But you're gaa-gaa for each other, aren'cha?"

"Yeah, but . . ."

"But what then?"

At this point Airman Mortensen would consider telling Bernie about the plan he and Claire had contrived, how they were waiting for just the right moment, just the right night. But he couldn't.

"I don't know what the fuck's gonna happen. I don't have any fuckin' idea."

"But you're gonna make love with the girl, aren'cha?"

"That's what it looks like, yeah. I promise I'll tell you."

"You promise?"

"I promise. You just have to stay tuned. That's all I'm doin' . . . stayin' tuned."

"Yeah," Bernie sighed, laying his great jaw on a set of knuckles. "Wow, man . . . do I envy you. I'm green with it."

"Yeah, well, before you get too green check this out," Airman Mortensen confessed. "I'm a virgin."

Bernie was a virgin too but had never admitted it. Blushing a little, he smiled up at Airman Mortensen. "Are ya really?"

"So is she."

"Oh, my God," Bernie gasped, a hand going quickly to the crucifix. "Holy shit."

"Yeah, see, it's more complicated than you might think."

But Bernie was already thinking, his eyes going filmy as his brain shot off in a hundred different directions at once.

"Complicated is what it is," Airman Mortensen repeated.

☆ **11** ☆

Well it was and it wasn't.

Sometimes, if he was sitting across the table from her in the library, if he had enough distance to gauge her with one ounce of objectivity, it did seem rather complicated.

When her face was buried in a book and he had a chance to just watch her, Claire seemed like another person, a young, pretty, anonymous girl studying in the library, the kind of girl he would like to have for a girlfriend. When he tried to link this wholesome high schooler who actually was his girlfriend with the girl/woman who, in only a few days, would be surrendering all of herself to him, complications set in for Airman Mortensen. He would begin a process that was poison to romance. He would begin to think.

All kinds of ideas and speculations jumped onto the stage in his brain shouting, 'What about this . . . ,' 'Consider the possibility . . . ,' 'What if . . . ?' There were far too many of these thoughts. And none of the speculations ended with solutions. It was just junk in his head, junk Airman Mortensen didn't want to think about. But he couldn't help it. Sometimes he wanted to chop his head off.

Fortunately, Claire never let him think too long. After a couple of minutes she would lift her head and stare at him with those green eyes, so clear and mysterious and the useless thoughts in Airman Mortensen's mind would evaporate.

"What're you thinking about?"

"Oh, nothing," Airman Mortensen would lie.

"Aren't you thinking about me?" she would ask sincerely.

"Of course."

"Don't you want to sit next to me?"

Airman Mortensen would smile and shake his head.

"You're too much," he would say.

Then, with no thought at all save a wonderful, driving urge to feel her, he would scoot back his chair, sweep around the big oak table and pull out the chair next to her. A second or two later his chair would be flush against hers and his hand would be knifing gently between her thighs. Her legs would squeeze his hand and Airman Mortensen's cock would start to tingle.

"I thought you wanted to study . . . that's why I was sitting across the table."

"I couldn't stand having you that far away from me."

He would have to kiss her when she said stuff like that. And Claire would come right to him because that was the only thing she wanted in the whole world. To be kissed by him.

If there were other people around they would have to stop. But if the coast was clear, the charge of the first kiss would drive them back into the stacks where they could stand pressed together in the seclusion of some seldom-used section. Here, they would try to devour each other with kisses and breath-flattening embraces.

It went like this with each passing day and night, the desire for each other doubling, tripling, quadrupling. There were times when Airman Mortensen thought his fingertips would blow off and all of him would run out of the holes. At these times nothing was complicated.

Airman Mortensen met Colonel Brill. As might be expected it was a weird meeting, made all the weirder by the fact that absolutely nothing of note happened.

The colonel opened the door one night when Airman Mortensen arrived at the house to "pick up" Claire. The man and the would-be man stared at each other for a few, long, surprised seconds.

Colonel Brill looked completely different out of uniform. His dark complexion tended to heighten the glow of his well-formed teeth and there was a strong hint of the tropics in his creamy slacks and colorful floral shirt. He looked like a rich importer, not an Air Force lifer. Airman Mortensen was stunned.

The colonel introduced himself and, smiling confidently, jumped to the conclusion that Airman Mortensen was Airman Mortensen. Then he invited the latrine king inside and they sat alone in the living room for a few minutes, waiting for Claire to "get ready."

As he sat on the couch, answering innocuous questions about where he was from and what his dad did, Airman Mortensen suddenly realized that it was all a setup.

The colonel didn't need to know any of this crap. He already knew the stuff that mattered. Undoubtedly his wife had told him that Claire was really stuck on the airman, undoubtedly he had checked up and found out that Mortensen was a lousy soldier, undoubtedly it had crossed his mind that Claire would be in danger of losing her cherry.

'What a sharp cookie,' Airman Mortensen thought as Colonel Brill asked him about the fishing off the coast of California. He didn't let on that he knew anything and in ten minutes of casual questioning the colonel didn't come close to any kind of power tripping. He didn't mention the military, nor did he mention his daughter, except to ask Airman Mortensen how long he had known her.

He gave no advice, nor did he make any pronouncements. In no way did the colonel try to exert any control over the situation and, much later, it occurred to Airman Mortensen that Colonel Brill knew better than anyone else that there was no need to exert control. He had all the control he wanted and the only possible way he could lose it would be to alienate his daughter. Colonel Brill was far too smart for that. You had to be cunning to make rank the way he did. You had to be smarter than everyone. And he was.

On that night, however, Airman Mortensen was struck mainly by physical things, like Colonel Brill's eyes. They were just like the eyes he'd seen in the spooky family portrait. They didn't laugh and they didn't cry. But they were always on a person. And they knew what they wanted.

Claire appeared in perfect time. Airman Mortensen shook hands with Colonel Brill and the lovers departed for a dance off base at the Eagle Lodge. Airman Mortensen put Colonel Brill out of his mind. He didn't give a shit about Colonel Brill. Or anyone else for that matter. He had Claire and what anyone else thought or did was of no consequence. He had Claire.

Airman Mortensen did not know that the uneventful ten minutes which had just passed was the longest one-on-one meeting he would ever have with Colonel Brill. He would see him again of course but only in the fleeting exchange of pleasantries, a minute or two at a time.

The unfathomable Colonel Brill had known before he ever set eyes on Airman Mortensen that a GI would not do. No boy would do. Claire was too young for a serious relationship. But wisely the colonel did not panic. He had decided (again the decision was made before he met Airman Mortensen) that his best course of action lay in doing nothing.

In his cold, calculating and murderously efficient way the colonel had decided to take a seat in the stands and watch the action unfold on the field. There was no reason to get caught up in the drama of his daughter and the soldier. He was already certain of the outcome.

☆ **12** ☆

The morning of the day of the big night passed easily.

The latrine king looked at the clock a couple of times and each time it was clipping right along. Noon chow was on him before he knew it.

The afternoon was another matter.

There seemed to be something wrong with the clock. When he was sure an hour had passed he'd look up to find that the hands had moved only ten minutes or so. Once they only moved five minutes. The clock with a mind of its own became a recurring hallucination.

It was a Friday and the paper was out. Friday was usually a day for everyone to backslide a little, so time had a tendency to pass slowly, but this particular Friday was the all-time slowest in memory.

The officers were off attending a mandatory leadership conference. Sergeant Shoemaker was darting around the base, sweating out his afternoon assignment as aide and guide to a visiting general.

Only the genial Sergeant Henderson and the two airmen newshounds remained behind in the silent office tomb. Henderson had found contentment with a thick book of crossword puzzles while Tom, suffering the effects of an enormous beer bust at the enlisted men's club the night before, alternately napped in his office and shuffled back and forth to Sergeant Henderson's

desk, complaining about being sick and begging to be
let go for the day.

By mid-afternoon even the unflappable Sergeant Henderson was becoming irritated with Tom's bellyaching.
For the fiftieth time he told Tom to amuse himself in
any way he wanted. Just don't leave the office. Someone
has to be here for appearances.

"Appearances!" Tom sprayed. "Look at me, Sarge . . .
I'm sick . . . I look like shit."

"Well go sit down then, rest yourself."

"I don't need to sit down, I need to lie down." For
added emphasis Tom latched onto his stomach with a
claw grip and grimaced, "Arrrrgggg."

But Sergeant Henderson merely looked at him se-
renely and said, "Well, clear off your desk and lie on
that."

"Oh God," Tom whined, "let Mortensen stay for
appearances. You don't need both of us . . . for chrissakes, Sarge, I'm fuckin' whipped . . ."

"That's enough, Tom, subject closed."

"But, Sarge . . ."

"Subject closed." Sergeant Henderson picked up his
book of puzzles, making it clear that he didn't want any
further disturbances.

His head hung in defeat, Tom clomped morosely back
to his cubicle and, making much more noise than was
called for, began to clear off his untidy desk.

Airman Mortensen had been sitting all the while in
his own smoke-filled cubicle, trying to involve himself
in a news magazine. The lack of movement on the clock
had become so horrifying that he no longer dared to
look at it. Concentration on the news magazine (he had
no interest in it) was hard enough but Tom's crashing
and banging in the next cubicle made it impossible.

Airman Mortensen laid his face on the gray desk top

and prayed for Tom to stop thrashing around so he wouldn't have to get in trouble for killing him.

Twice, Sergeant Henderson had called out "tone it down" but Tom's pout was a lulu and the ridiculous noises continued. Henderson finally had to get out of his chair. Airman Mortensen tried but failed to shut out the conversation floating over the partition.

"What are you doing?"

"I'm trying to make a bed out of this crazy desk."

"Well?"

"Well, my feet hang over. I'm trying to get this chair to hold still but it won't. It keeps moving around. It's on rollers."

"Get something without rollers then."

"Well actually, Sarge, the way this office is, I figure I might step in some kind of shit if I drag a chair in from somewhere else without getting permission."

"You have my permission," Sergeant Henderson said.

"Yeah?"

"Yes, you do."

Airman Mortensen listened as another chair was found and brought into Tom's cubicle. There was a little more scuffling and then silence.

"How's that?" he heard Sergeant Henderson ask.

"It'll do, I guess." Tom's tone was markedly softer now. "I'm not feeling well. I hope I can sleep."

"Do you want me to turn off these lights?"

"Yeah, that might help. Thanks, Sarge."

"No problem."

Airman Mortensen's face was still pressed against his desk. His eyes were wide open. He too wished for sleep but he knew there wasn't going to be any.

Sergeant Henderson's typewriter started to click clack and he heard Tom flop around a few times in his crib. There was a brief silence. Then there was snoring. It was loud, obnoxious snoring, filled with gasping and gagging.

Sure that Tom was faking, Airman Mortensen got on tiptoe and peeked over the divider. Tom's doughy form was stretched out on the desk. His heels were perched on a chair back. His face had that happy, town-drunk look. He was dead to the world.

The latrine king got off his toes, returned to his seat, threw his feet on the desk top, shook out another Pall Mall and had himself a serious think.

After a few minutes' calculation he tabulated a total of five hundred and eighty-three days.

He gazed out at the half-filled headquarters parking lot, shining in the sun. All the neat little slots for the neat little cars.

He looked at the flat-roofed buildings that lay beyond the parking lot. They looked like the hotel buildings in a Monopoly set. They didn't look real at all.

He heard clanking on the flagpole and looked at the big American flag flying proudly against the blue sky. There was a smaller New Mexico flag underneath. They were flapping in patriotic unison, like some insert from a propaganda movie.

For a few minutes he didn't think of Claire.

Five hundred and eighty-three more days.

No way was he going to make it.

✰ 13 ✰

Sergeant Henderson let Tom go about four o'clock. Airman Mortensen had gone to the can to kill some time and when he came back Sergeant Henderson said he could go too.

It was all anticlimax now. He'd wanted the day to end for so long that, like a kid anticipating Christmas, he'd worn himself out before the big event arrived. Maybe the sun would still go down. Maybe they would be together on this specially planned night. Maybe it would finally happen. Maybe nothing would happen. Maybe a B-52 would hit the barracks while he was in the shower. Who the fuck knew?

He was shifting listlessly through his desk drawers in the office to see if there was anything he should take back for the weekend when the phone rang in the outer room. Airman Mortensen was suddenly holding his breath. 'Please, c'mon, please.'

Sergeant Henderson's amiable voice carried into his cubicle.

"Mortensen, telephone."

He lifted the receiver, heard Henderson click off and spoke in a hush.

"This better be you."

"You're crazy," she laughed.

"I'm gonna be if I don't see you pretty soon."

She giggled again and the line between them lapsed into silence.

"I love you," she said soberly.

Airman Mortensen didn't say anything.

"All I want is to be with you," she whispered.

"I want you to come right now," Airman Mortensen groaned. "I want to hug you right now."

Claire sucked in her breath.

"I can't till six."

"Okay," he sighed, "I'm gonna get off the phone. I'll see you in the parking lot at six . . . right?"

"I love you."

"I'm hanging up now. Six o'clock?"

"I love you."

"I love you," he answered as he pressed the disconnect button. Then he replaced the receiver and watched the phone as if she was in there. His legs were weak.

Airman Mortensen prayed as he walked back to the barracks. He prayed that Bernie would not be there. The longshot prayer was answered and as Airman Mortensen thanked God, he embraced the idea that perhaps something really mystical was about to happen.

He showered quickly and hopped back into the precious solitude of his home cubicle. Then he sat by the open window, a thin white towel spread in his lap, listening over and over to "Mr. Tambourine Man," "The Gates of Eden," "It's Alright Ma, I'm Only Bleedin' " and "It's All Over Now Baby Blue." He didn't actually listen to the music so much as he allowed it to cover him. All the while he smoked his Pall Malls and watched the zigzag traffic of soldiers on the walkways below.

Merciful shadows were beginning to collapse across the concourse. It had been another hot day and Airman Mortensen thought about the enormity of change that took place in the few hours that marked the shift from day to night, night to day. Whole miracles of change. He felt right in step with momentous change. What was about to happen, uncertain as it might be, was bound to thrust him onto a new stage of experience. It was hard to believe.

He wanted to stay calm and sitting naked on the chair seemed to work. Just before six he threw on some clean clothes and walked down the stairs.

There was resistance as he pushed through the doors to the outside. A chilly, little breeze had come up. 'Strange to have a breeze like this on a lazy summer evening,' he thought.

The latrine king had barely reached his customary spot on the curb when the tan VW rolled into the parking lot. Claire's face was smiling through the windshield.

They kissed for a few minutes in the idling car. Then Claire's head dropped against his neck and a little sigh came out of her.

"Are you nervous?" Airman Mortensen asked.

"A little," she said calmly. "Are you?"

"I don't think so . . . not that I can tell."

They rode to town in one of their splendid silences. Airman Mortensen watched Claire as she concentrated on the road. She was unbelievably pretty. There was no one else he wanted. No one else existed.

"Are you staring at me?"

"Yup."

"How come?" she smiled.

Airman Mortensen leaned over the emergency brake and put his mouth on her cheek.

" 'Cause you're so goddamn, fucking beautiful."

Claire sighed and slid a hand between his legs.

They stopped at the Chew Den. Food didn't appeal to either of them and they left the cherry Cokes they ordered half full. A restaurant, with all its distractions, wasn't the right place to waste time. They wandered down main street, arms around each other's waists, glancing halfhearted in the store windows. The funny, little breeze was blowing strong enough to kick the trash around and Airman Mortensen figured it would be a relief when sundown finally came and the wind died. Claire didn't say anything about the breeze. She seemed kind of dazed.

Toward sundown they got back in the car and killed the last minutes of daylight cruising the main teenage hangouts. Greer's was mostly empty and they pulled in at the far end, waving off the girl who came out for curb service. Claire was talking aimlessly about school and studies and Airman Mortensen was watching the slow, spectacular sunset light up the long western horizon.

At last, Greer's outside lights clicked on. Airman Mortensen took her hand in his and lowered his eyes.

"Wanna go for a drive?" he asked, peeking up at her.

"Uhh, huh."

It was fully dark and the road was completely deserted when the car's headlights flashed on a black-and-white sign peppered with gunshots. It read "Bottomless Lakes State Park, 6 Miles." An arrow pointed east. The VW turned that way and, bouncing off the main highway, started down a level, hard-packed dirt track.

The lovers looked at each other.

"I'm so glad it's you," Claire said sweetly.

"Me too," said Airman Mortensen and they both laughed.

A late-rising moon had started into the cloudy sky and Airman Mortensen noted the speed with which the clouds were being carried across the face of the moon. He didn't like it. Neither did he like the tufts of grass which were zipping by along the side of the road. They were bent to one side, vibrating with the wind. It seemed to be getting stronger by the moment.

"God, the wind is really blowing," he said sourly.

Claire looked at him impishly.

"You want to go back?"

Airman Mortensen continued watching the tufts of grass as he shook his head.

"Nope."

He didn't let on but the latrine king's thoughts had begun to give him some trouble. Just having thoughts was a main part of the trouble. Instead of concentrating on sex he was trying to figure out how to be. He didn't have any idea how he should feel, how he should behave, what the tone of his voice should be, how his touch should come off. Soft, hard, gentle, strong, easy, intense, light, sober? There was no end to it.

He kept reminding himself that since he had never experienced sex it was impossible to know how to be. But this reasonable logic was eclipsed by a pressure-filled, heart-stopping desire that the thing be pulled off right. It had to be pulled off right. If it didn't go well it might never go again. And if it didn't keep going . . .

He couldn't think of that. He loved her, this Claire Brill. He would never make it without Claire Brill. No way.

Airman Mortensen wondered what she must be thinking at this moment. She always seemed so steady but she had to be feeling the pressure too.

It was a little shocking to glance over and find a placid, half-smiling expression in the dash light. Aware of his eyes, she turned her head. She looked drugged.

"We should stop pretty soon," she said blankly.

Airman Mortensen's heart was starting to pound.

"Yeah."

A few minutes later they found a wide turnaround with a picnic table and some trees. The land out here was flat and, though he couldn't see any headlights now, Airman Mortensen knew that approaching cars could be seen from very far away. He also knew that the funny, little breeze was a big wind now. The trees overhead were being bent by it. When Claire turned off the engine he heard the wind's wail, bleeding through the seams in the windows.

They sat in the dark, listening and watching. Every few seconds a gust would shake the VW.

Airman Mortensen found her hand and held it quietly. He didn't feel the least bit sexy. As the seconds stretched into minutes he felt even less sexy. The sexless feeling built and built until the feeling burst and vanished as if it were something imagined.

In a twinkling Airman Mortensen didn't give a shit. Fucking, scoring, losing his virginity, screwing, turned on, being a man, pussy, going all the way—it didn't matter.

What mattered was this wonderful person, the girl sitting there in the dark, the girl with her hand in his. He could see the outline of her pretty head behind the steering wheel. He thought he could feel the pulse of her blood in the hand he was holding.

Airman Mortensen, now fully and miraculously relaxed, threw his head back and laughed.

"What?"

Airman Mortensen bent close to her face and kissed it suavely.

"Nothing my darlin'. I was just thinking . . . ," and here he had to chuckle once more, ". . . it just seems like we've come so far so fast . . . it's amazing."

The hand he was holding lost its tension. Her lips peeled back in a grin and he could see her small teeth in the dash light.

"It really is amazing, isn't it?"

"Yuuuuuupppp." With a self-satisfied sign Airman Mortensen settled back into the seat. "Not the kind of thing you could explain to anyone."

"Nobody would believe it," she put in.

"I still don't know if I do," Airman Mortensen laughed.

"That's not funny."

"It's not?"

"No," she said emphatically. Her face dipped toward his and he could see that she was wearing her playful, mock pout. "You're supposed to believe that I love you more than anything."

Her lips brushed against his as she spoke and when Airman Mortensen felt the moist breath of her mouth he wanted to stop talking.

"Do you?" she demanded.

"Do I what?"

"Do you believe I love you more than anything?"

"I believe anything you want me to."

"No you don't, you . . ."

Then they were kissing. It was a long, slow, beautiful kiss. It was something like a first kiss. But familiarity made it something delicious, something to be tasted and then devoured. Their hugs and squeezes and kisses escalated until they were having sex with their mouths.

Tonight they were going further but the car impeded their progress. The front seat was particularly bad, being encumbered with the steering wheel, shifter and emergency brake.

When they broke for the fourth or fifth time Claire panted, "Oh God, let's get outside."

"Yeah."

A blast of air hit him as he pushed out of the door. It was icy, the kind that goes to the bone. He couldn't believe it was June.

"Back seat," he called to Claire and they dove back into the Volkswagen. It wasn't much roomier than the front seat and now the car was cold, so cold that Airman Mortensen put his hands between his knees and shivered.

"Shit," he chattered.

Claire had already begun to dig through the junk in a cubbyhole behind the back seat. "Let me find the blanket."

Airman Mortensen's boner was gone. While Claire fumbled for the blanket, he started a cigarette. And then, for some unknown reason, he thought about the smell of Volkswagens. He'd been in a bunch of Volkswagens and they all had the same, distinct smell. Though he knew it was silly, Airman Mortensen theorized that perhaps Germany smelled like that, the inside of a VW. If it did, he would probably like Germany. Airman Mortensen put great stock in the way things smelled, as much as the way they looked or tasted.

Claire had a smell that sent him. She was draping the blanket around them and her smell was billowing through the car. He pressed his nose against her hair and inhaled. She smelled great. There didn't seem to be any way to get enough of her smell.

The car was warming up and he could smell her skin again. Her skin smelled . . . it was impossible to describe the quality. It was potent. Just the smell of her skin made him hard.

She nestled against him without saying anything. Airman Mortensen ground out his cigarette and touched her. She murmured something and pulled his shirt a little apart and kissed him on the chest.

He hugged her closer and discovered that she'd somehow slipped off her bra without him noticing. His hand snaked over her shoulder and down the front of her sweater. But it couldn't get far enough to fully grasp the naked breasts. Claire suddenly twisted away, lay back slightly against the seat and pulled his free hand under her sweater, arching a little to offer her breasts. He put his mouth on hers and began to knead one of her nipples.

He'd felt naked breasts before but there had always been some kind of struggle involved. There was no struggle with Claire. She wanted to be touched. He felt her pull up the sweater and press one of her breasts against the flesh of his chest. He kissed her deeper as he massaged one breast and ground his chest against the other. Claire began to moan and Airman Mortensen thought if his dick got even a tiny bit harder it was going right through his Levis.

She twisted again and when his hand dropped to the front of her pants, Claire's did too. Then there were two hands working together on the buttons. Then it was just his hand, moving beneath her underwear, sneaking through the stiff hair and into that mysterious, incredible place. It was wet and his fingers moved easily.

Claire moaned harder and suddenly she was brushing his finger out of there as she went for the buttons on his pants. Airman Mortensen helped her rip them open and pushed his Levis past his knees.

Claire was trying to squirm out of her jeans but they were tight and she needed help. Airman Mortensen pulled the legs off one at a time and she struggled to get under him, kicking her legs violently at the wall of the car.

At that moment Airman Mortensen experienced the subtlest of revelations. It was so subtle that Airman Mortensen was not able to articulate it in his own mind.

He felt something, something in the way Claire's legs squirmed under him. It was something he hadn't known in her before, something not teenaged. It was something older than that. It was strong. It said, "Come on, just come on." Airman Mortensen wanted to. But he couldn't. Neither could Claire.

The car was too small.

After an exhausting series of contortions and gyrations Airman Mortensen whispered breathlessly:

"Outside."

Claire whispered back:

"Yes."

Dragging the blanket with them, the lovers tumbled out of the little car and into the icy, howling night.

Airman Mortensen had a difficult time trying to spread the blanket on the bare ground next to the car. The gale was blowing so hard that every time he shook it out the blanket tangled in midair.

"Don't you want it over you?" Claire yelled above the wind.

"No . . . I want it under you."

Airman Mortensen had resorted to kneeling on one end of the blanket while he held the other end with both hands.

"Get on it," he yelled.

Claire sat on the blanket. The latrine king pulled her into his arms and at last they went down. Claire's pants were in the car and Airman Mortensen's were hanging around his ankles. She spread her legs and he let himself come against her. What a pleasure to move without hitting something. What pleasure to feel her completely naked body touching his.

But it was hard to find the opening of a place he'd never seen. After a kiss or two and some heavy grinding he had to talk into her ear.

"You have to help me."

"Okay."

"You have to help me get in."

"Okay."

She took hold of him then and the sensation of her hand, coupled with the cold and the wind, made it extra hard to concentrate. Airman Mortensen didn't know where he was. Suddenly, she moved her hand away.

"There?" he asked.

"Yes."

She tilted her head back. It looked like she was holding her breath. Airman Mortensen pushed and Claire made a little jerk. He looked at the outline of her face. Her head was still tilted back. Her eyes were closed. It made him feel odd. It made him feel like a stranger.

He pushed again, harder this time. And again. And again. And each time Claire jerked.

He was just getting the hang of it when his cock fell out.

"Oh God," he gasped.

"Put it back."

"Yeah."

She didn't help him this time. She waited. But Airman Mortensen was too cautious. He couldn't find the spot and finally Claire had to guide him in again.

Now he pushed with shorter, harder strokes. A sharp intake of pain sounded in Claire's throat. On the next stroke she shrieked.

"Are you okay?"

"Yes."

"If I'm hurting you we can stop."

"No, no . . . go."

Still not knowing where he was exactly, Airman Mortensen kept going. Claire was crying out with every stroke. The wind was stinging his bare bottom. He was arched over her and the cold was cutting across his chest too. He could see Claire's face wincing at every stroke. Her little cries turned into a long, low wail.

"I hate hurting you," he yelled.

"No."

"I'm gonna stop."

"No," she yelled, "no, go on, go on."

Airman Mortensen, slick-sleeve latrine king, looked down at the clenched face of Claire Brill, base commander's daughter, and thought, 'This isn't the way it's supposed to be.' But he bent close to her anyway, close enough to put his mouth against her ear.

"Okay," he whispered and pushed harder than ever. Claire jumped under him but he held her fast and, only able to imagine that he might be inside her, he kept pushing.

The unique feeling, the feeling of not turning back, came over him and moments later Airman Mortensen was jerking as his sperm flowed. Claire was still shrieking and only began to quiet down when Airman Mortensen's strokes slowed and then stopped.

"Am I all the way in you?"

"I think so," she answered. Then she let out a long, satisfied sigh and mouthed words as she kissed him.

"I love you . . . I love you."

Airman Mortensen lay blinking in the dark. His ass was cold and his crotch was clammy but he was only mildly aware. The latrine king was dumbstruck by the mystery of what had happened. This was it? The whole deal? How could that be? This is it? Really?

Claire shifted uneasily under him. "I'm freezing, aren't you?"

✪ **14** ✪

It didn't take long for the VW's powerful heater to toast the car.

'Trial by ice,' thought Airman Mortensen. 'Usually, it's trial by fire . . . trial by ice . . . huh.' He was sure he'd messed things up. It hadn't turned out. The whole fucking thing had been a bust. 'Not the kind of item she's gonna cut out and paste in her scrapbook. Our whole thing could be finished right now.'

He was afraid to look but when he finally did Airman Mortensen was surprised to see a face full of sweet dreams. Before he could look away her eyes caught his and the smile that seemed to be Claire's personal invention lit on her face.

She worked her hand into his.

"We did it," she said warmly.

"Yeah, I guess we did."

"We did it and I love you."

"God knows I love you . . . maybe too much."

She only smiled and trained her eyes on the road again. She pulled his hand over the emergency brake and tucked it in the special spot as if she were fluffing up a pillow.

Maybe things weren't so bad after all. Airman Mortensen felt himself relax as they drove along in silence. He shut his eyes and concentrated on his hand and the special spot. God, that was nice. He dreamed about his fingers being in her again. The more he visualized it the more he wanted it and when Claire downshifted to pass through the main gate his cock was hard again.

They kissed languidly in the barracks parking lot and when Claire realized he was stiff again she murmured in an amused way and whispered through her smile that there would be plenty of opportunities for more. She wanted more too, she said.

At last there was nothing more to be done but part. Claire was already past curfew and the parking lot as always was too public. They kissed romantically for a few more minutes and then Airman Mortensen was alone with the parked cars, watching until the tan VW was out of sight. Then he listened until he could no longer hear its engine. Then he was just standing, drained and dazed and alone.

Finally he turned and faced the barracks. For once he was forgiving with his thoughts. All those poor guys, none so lucky as him, the slick sleeve. He noticed now that the night had gone perfectly still. The wind was gone. The clouds were hanging motionless, like glued cotton, in front of the moon.

Airman Mortensen stared at the sky in disbelief. He stared at the barracks in disbelief. He stared deliberately in the direction of her house and thought he could see Claire getting into bed. He saw her turn onto her stomach and spread her legs. He heard a long and satisfied sigh fill up her room.

When she was asleep he walked slowly into the barracks.

By the infinite grace of God Bernie was unconscious and the devirginized latrine king was able to sit in silence by the open window and smoke. His normal mind seemed to have shut down. His senses alone were drifting pleasantly: inspecting the splashes of moonlight on the concourse below, listening to Bernie's breathing, watching the Pall Mall smoke surge through the window screen. Sandwiched among these visions were pornographic images of Claire, underneath him, on the ground.

"It happened," he said to himself. "After eighteen years it happened . . . and it's gonna happen again!" Airman Mortensen was so happy that he shook his head. Dirt fell past his eyes. Curious, he ran a hand through his hair. It was coated with the dust of Bottomless Lakes State Park. The nonvirgin pulled off his pants in the dark, wrapped a towel around his waist and padded dreamily to the latrine for a late-night shower.

He looked at his face in the big mirror. It was unchanged but it was smiling. Watching himself in the mirror, Airman Mortensen danced an odd little foot-to-foot jig and thrust a triumphant fist overhead. In the midst of all this he ripped off his towel and his mirth stopped as surely as if a switch had been thrown.

There were streaks on his cock. There were streaks on the inside of each thigh, streaks reaching halfway to his knees. He looked down on his cock and saw it caked here and there in his pubic hair. He rubbed some of it between his fingers and watched the dried particles fall away to the floor.

Airman Mortensen looked at the latrine entrance and listened. No one was coming. Spellbound, he looked again at the spectacle of his body spread before him in the mirror. All that blood. Claire's blood.

He stepped into the protection of the shower but turned around to face the mirror again. He couldn't stop watching. And when he finally washed the blood away, he did it slowly and deliberately.

☆ **15** ☆

Claire was a bright, industrious student. She was well liked and got good grades. She also wanted to get out of high school and into a "good college." In a bid to graduate as quickly as possible, she enrolled full time in the summer session that year.

Although he tried hard not to show it, Airman Mortensen was deeply disappointed. He had looked forward to her being out of school. There would be more time to be together, more time for adventures in love, more time to be free.

This conflict led to their first argument which, unfortunately, took place on the phone.

"I'm not mad, I just . . ."

"Just what?" she said flatly.

"I just . . . I was looking forward to being together."

"We will be together."

"I know."

"Well, what's the matter then?"

"Nothing's the matter really."

"Then why are we talking like this?"

"I don't know," he laughed. But it was a nervous laugh.

"Well, I don't like it."

"Me neither, let's just forget it. When am I gonna see you?"

"Not tonight."

"You don't have to say it like that," Airman Mortensen snapped.

"I didn't say anything 'like that' . . . I just said not tonight."

There was silence on Airman Mortensen's end of the line. Then he said:

"I think we should hang up and try this again later."

"Alright," she said.

Again there was silence. Airman Mortensen sighed audibly.

"Well, goodnight."

Claire's voice got very small. "Goodnight," she said softly.

They hung up and, as he so often did, Airman Mortensen stared at the dead phone for awhile. Did this argument mean that something was wrong with them? Was it a normal thing? It was impossible to tell which. The argument was confusing. They were so close. How could they get so far apart? A strange panic settled on him and Airman Mortensen was seized with a frantic need to hear her voice.

He reached for the phone and it went off in his hand. It was Claire. She was scared too. The first thing they did was reswear allegiance to one another.

Then Claire said, "I want to see you."

"God yes."

"I'm coming over . . ."

"I'll be outside."

A few minutes later she careened into the parking lot and leapt out of the car. They hugged and kissed desperately at the curb. Then they got into the car and drove to the darkest part of the parking lot, where he ended up sucking her breasts while one of her hands rubbed at the front of his Levis.

Without really knowing how it happened his stiff cock came out of the pants and Claire's hand went around it. She pulled at it and Airman Mortensen shifted to give her a better angle.

"Go ahead," he said into her ear.

Claire dropped her head and watched her hand pull on his cock. She made her hand move faster and harder until he was moaning and jerking with each stroke. Then there was warm sperm shooting onto her arm, some of it collecting around the lip of her hand.

She said nothing.

Neither did Airman Mortensen.

He thought he'd died and gone to heaven.

☆ 16 ☆

In the next week they saw little of each other and when they did there was no time to be alone. Airman Mortensen didn't like it but he kept his lip buttoned and tried to veil the doubt on his face. It wasn't easy.

When the guys in the barracks saw him hanging around three or four nights in a row they started questioning their hero. They kept asking why wasn't he out with Brill's daughter and Airman Mortensen could only answer lamely that she was studying.

To the boys in the barracks this was cause for concern. The latrine king's romance was a shining symbol of faith. They wanted him to be getting laid every night.

"Studying?" they all said sourly. Even Vic was suspicious.

It was during this difficult period that Bernie's friendship came to the fore. Airman Mortensen had to confide in someone and the role of father confessor suited the little Italian to a T. He listened bug-eyed and quiet, fingering the big crucifix, as Airman Mortensen gradually revealed more and more inside information. Though he sidestepped most of the more graphic descriptions, he did tell Bernie about the blood on his legs.

And he told about the doubts. "I don't know what to think . . . I know she loves me but shit, man, there's always somethin'; there's always some fucking obstacle to us being together. Sometimes I don't know what to think. But if I have these doubts it's just gonna fuck it up worse. See what I mean?''

Hearing this, Bernie would drop his huge jaw into the cradle of a hand. "Yeah," he would say, "I see what you mean . . . like a vicious cycle.''

"A vicious circle, that's what it's like.''

"Geez . . .'' Bernie would purse his lips and shake his head sympathetically. "That's tough . . . that'd be tough for anybody.''

With this kind of pressure building inside him, Airman Mortensen was secretly relieved when the entire Brill family evacuated to a family reunion in Kansas City. For four whole days he wouldn't have to mask his doubt.

At the same time he harbored the secret hope that Claire would miss him to the point of pain, that she would return teary-eyed and submissive, wanting nothing more than to be held by him.

Airman Mortensen entertained these desperate and foolish hopes to the exclusion of all else during Claire's absence. In fact, it could be said that while she was gone the latrine king did little else besides wait for her to come back. He felt like an idiot for being so weak and dependent. But he couldn't help it. Claire was the one bright spot in his whole life. He didn't dare think what he might do without her.

Saturday night found him moping in his room instead of going to the movies with Bernie. He couldn't stop wondering what Claire might be doing in Kansas and he wanted to be alone while he wondered. Out of boredom he fell asleep early and woke early. He lay blinking on his bunk in the quiet of Sunday, trying to decide what activity might hurry along the last day of their separation.

Thinking he would resolve the question with a hot shower, he wandered down the deserted hall to the latrine and was surprised to find Michael G. Taylor standing alone in the can. He was still dressed in Saturday-night clothes. His head was bent over a sink. There was a towel hanging off his shoulder. Using his big, black hands as a cup, he was splashing water on his face.

MGT raised his head and stared queerly at Airman Mortensen. His lips were unmoving and unsmiling. His eyes looked swollen. Water dripped off his face as he stared.

"What's the matter, Michael?"

"Oh, man . . . ," MGT's voice cracked pathetically and he turned away, brushing at his face with the towel.

"What's the matter?" Airman Mortensen insisted.

"Oh, man," he said again. Then the big hands went to his face. MGT started to weep.

"Michael, what is it?"

"Carl's dead."

"Carl?"

"He dead man."

MGT's head fell toward the sink. He grasped its edges and sobbed so hard it looked like he was going to throw up.

In a comforting way Airman Mortensen moved to the black boy's side and dropped a hand on his shoulder. For a few seconds MGT cried even harder and Airman Mortensen listened to his friend's sobs echo off the latrine wall.

MGT straightened up. He wiped at his eyes with the backs of his hands and looked at Airman Mortensen's stunned face reflected in the long mirror. He shook his head sorrowfully.

"Dead on the muthafuckin' street . . . Carl, man."

"What happened?"

"Muthafucka cave 'is head in wid a baseball bat. Poor Carl, man . . . I seen 'im onna street, twitchin'

and shakin' like a dog hit by a car. The whole backa
'is head was caved in, man.''

Michael stooped to pick up the towel which had fallen
off his shoulder and ran more water, splashing the last
wave of tears from his face.

"Why?" Airman Mortensen asked hollowly.

"Why what?"

"Why did this happen?"

MGT toweled his face. "We were inna cafe an dis
dufus starts thinkin' Carl is hittin' on his ho'. We all
said no but this mothafucka don' leave it alone. Him
and Lee start talkin' shit and we all get our asses outta
there. We jus' walkin' down the mothafuckin' street
man . . . dis dude come runnin' up behind wiffa bat
. . . whack! Damn.''

"Did the cops get him?"

"Oh yeah, they got his wurfless black ass in de jail
right now.''

"Where's Lee?"

"I don't know . . . inna room I guess.''

Lee DeHart was in but he wasn't moving. He was
sitting at the gray government desk, staring through his
clasped hands.

Newt was folded in a corner on the floor, his faint,
high-pitched wail sounding like a distant siren.

Airman Mortensen stood in the open doorway.

"I'm sorry, Lee.''

Lee DeHart didn't blink. His round, brown eyes continued to gaze blankly at his hands as he spoke.

"Carl was my best friend, man.''

"I know, man, I'm sorry.''

"He was my best friend.''

When he told her about Carl's murder Claire said,
"God, that's horrible.'' But a couple of moments later
she was asking him when he wanted to go out. Airman
Mortensen was still shook up and wasn't sure he liked

her attitude. When he reminded her of the meeting with Carl that hot day on the sidewalk she made some other exclamation and changed the subject.

Maybe it wasn't fair to expect any other response but the latrine king wanted to talk about it. If the subject hadn't been sloughed off he could have told her how Newt had said he couldn't "dee wid da' manny whi' peepa" and had declined to go. He wanted to tell her how touching it was when Lee DeHart asked MGT and MGT accepted. And how they took Carl's body home on the train to Wisconsin. And how he, Airman Mortensen, thought it was very cool that these two black men were taking their white buddy's body home.

But he didn't get to any of this because he knew Claire wasn't interested. And he didn't want to push it so he stifled the things he wanted to share and they made a date to "watch TV" later in the week.

Airman Mortensen hung up the phone and found his thinking confused again. Her attitude rankled him somehow and yet he couldn't blame her for not being interested in a stranger's murder. She didn't seem to have missed him all that much either. But was that just his imagination? He knew it was foolish to have expectations and yet he had them. He wished it was all clear. He wished he knew how to be. He climbed the stairs to his cubicle with a head full of tangled thoughts.

☆ **17** ☆

On the day of his date "to watch TV" Airman Mortensen and Airman Pittman were working downtown on a ticklish problem.

They had been ordered to run a story brought in by Colonel Overton's pushy, social wife. She was one of several people who considered the base newspaper a part of their personal property. In another world Colonel Overton's wife would have been told to go fuck herself. Unfortunately, saying such a thing here would infuriate Colonel Overton. He would shit on Captain Hart. Captain Hart would then shit on Sergeant Shoemaker and on down the chain of command.

No one wanted trouble but on this particular afternoon the so-called feature story and its batch of amateur photographs was, in the opinion of the boy editors, too ridiculous to print under any circumstances.

A group of officers' wives had organized and conducted a sickening event, supposedly for the benefit of the enlisted men's wives. Colonel Overton's wife, along with a committee of the like-minded, had scoured the base for human dregs and had succeeded in producing five of the earth's most wretched women. They were married to lifer fuck-ups who knocked them up, then knocked them around; guys who drank their paychecks and whacked their kids when they didn't behave.

The five poor creatures whose lives were a living hell had been convinced or tricked into entering a competition that could only be called grotesque.

221

Each wretch was to testify at a mass gathering held in the officers' club banquet room. A panel of leading officers' wives would listen carefully. The woman with the most hopeless, sordid story would be the winner and get prizes. It was ghastly.

"We can't run this," Airman Mortensen said as he proofread the dumb story. "This is sick."

"You think the story's sick," Tom giggled. He offered his friend an eight-by-ten photo. "Get a load of this."

Airman Mortensen gazed with disbelief at the "official" Queen For A Day photo. The woman was perhaps thirty-five but she looked sixty. Her hollow eyes were partially crossed and looking away from the camera. An ill-fitting crown tilted over one sorrowful eye. A scruffy fur cloak was hanging off her bony shoulders. A dozen roses lay unattended in her lap while her long, pale fingers clutched a scepter wrapped with tinfoil. She looked like a mental patient.

In stark contrast to all this was a covey of smartly dressed officers' wives, Colonel Overton's spouse included, who were flanking the "winner" of the bizarre contest. The winner was the only one not smiling.

"Tom," Airman Mortensen began, fixing the co-editor with his most serious look, "we can't do this."

Airman Pittman glanced at the phone. "Hey, be my guest."

Airman Mortensen considered for a moment. Then he picked up the phone and called Sergeant Shoemaker back at the office. He made a sincere and reasoned complaint. He said the story was too far below standards. He read most of it over the phone. Sergeant Shoemaker agreed that it was pretty bad. He had Airman Mortensen hold the line while he checked with Captain Hart. After a long wait, Shoemaker's voice broke over the phone again.

"No, you gotta run it. He says you can spruce up the copy if you want but the story and the photo have to run."

Airman Mortensen slammed down the receiver and turned to Tom.

"Can you believe that?"

"We gotta run it?"

"Yeah."

They both looked at the winner's picture again. It was horrible to contemplate.

"Let's run the fucker big," Tom whispered.

"Fuckin' full page," Airman Mortensen hissed.

"No, no, full page and they put us in the fucking brig. But shit, man, let's scale this puppy . . . like four-column by whatever."

Airman Mortensen looked again at the hideous picture. "Five-column," he sneered.

Tom hesitated a second. "Okay, five-column. I don't give a fuck."

"Me neither, man."

When Airman Mortensen saw Colonel Brill that night he wondered if there might be serious trouble over the picture. They had sent the entire paper to the printer that afternoon, the Queen For A Day picture included. It was five columns wide by fourteen inches deep, enormous by any standard. It was by far the biggest picture ever to appear in the base newspaper.

Seeing Colonel Brill, all decked out in his sumptuous dress uniform, did little to reassure the latrine king. And Betty was the perfect Air Force wife, enveloped in some exotic scent that seemed to be wafting up from the bodice of her fancy gown. The minute he saw them Airman Mortensen knew that neither would find the picture amusing. And, if the base's leading officer didn't find the picture amusing, no one else would either.

But as the well-dressed couple left for some officers'

club function, Airman Mortensen's fears about the picture went with them.

He and Claire were alone in the house. Jancy was spending the night at a friend's and the latrine king had detected a particular look in Claire's eye when she answered the door. It was a weird look which he could not quite fathom. But he could make out the message. He was remembering it as he followed her into the den. The look said something good was bound to happen.

For a few minutes they halfheartedly tried to hold back. They pulled some wine out of the liquor cabinet and Claire spun the channel selector, trying to find something worth watching. Moments later she gave it up. She settled next to Airman Mortensen and mouthed at his ear.

"I want you so much," she whispered.

The two teenagers flung their clothes into every corner of the den and, in what seemed like only seconds, he was in her again. This time in the colonel's house.

The second attempt was more assured than the one at Bottomless Lakes. He was more confident. He was also excited and came very fast but all in all it felt better.

Naked in the blue glow of the TV, they were toying with the idea of doing it again when both heard the quick and muffled, one-two slam of car doors. The sound seemed to come from the Brill's garage.

Airman Mortensen never saw Claire's reaction. He dove on his clothes like a spider, grabbing up everything in sight. He couldn't find one of his sandals but there was no time left. As he raced nude down the hall to Claire's bedroom, his arms filled with clothes and cigarettes and keys and a bottle of wine, he could hear the colonel and Mrs. Brill's voices at the other end of the house.

He flew through the bedroom doorway and let Claire's

hand guide him into her small closet. Airman Mortensen squatted on the floor as she shut the door. He crouched breathlessly in the dark, teetering on a bed of girl's shoes, his heart pounding ferociously enough to make his whole body a drum.

He was still blinking in the dark, trying to make out anything at all when he heard a tapping at Claire's bedroom door. Then the voice of Colonel Brill.

"Honey?"

"I'm in bed, Daddy."

"So early?"

"I was tired."

There was a fleeting silence on the colonel's side of the door.

"Well, your mother's not feeling well so we came home early."

"Nothing serious?"

"No, just an upset stomach . . . if you're not too sleepy, I'd like to talk to you for a few minutes."

This time there was a momentary silence from Claire's side of the door.

"Alright," she said, "just a minute."

"No hurry," came the easy reply.

Airman Mortensen heard the colonel's soft footsteps fall away from the door and a moment later a crack of sharp light cut the darkness of his hiding place. One of Claire's eyes moved into the crack.

"Are you alright?"

"Yes."

"I have to talk to my father for a few minutes."

"How am I gonna get out of here?"

"I don't know."

"These shoes are killing me!"

"What shoes?"

"There's shoes all over the floor."

"Well, wait, I won't be long."

"Don't leave me in here all night."

"I won't."

The seam of light went with the closing door and Airman Mortensen was left naked in the dark again. Now he realized that some of the wine had dribbled onto his clothes. Since there was nothing he could do and since his hand was already around the bottle's neck, he decided to chance a drink.

With nightmare visions of somehow losing his grip and letting the bottle clatter onto the floor, he lifted the jug to his mouth and took a pull.

The red wine was wet and warm and sharp. It ran softly into the bottom of his stomach. The burgundy had a calming effect and, after several more solid belts, Airman Mortensen was flushed with enough bravado to risk an attempt to sit.

He let his butt go the last inch or two and the sound of it hitting the closet floor seemed deafening. But no one came and, much more comfortable now, he coaxed a little more wine out of the bottle. He was just beginning to think that there were lots worse situations than this when Claire came back. Her father had wanted to talk about school.

Airman Mortensen's whisper floated out of the dark hole of a closet. "What school?"

"Just college in general."

"You're not even out of high school till January."

"We're just talking about it."

"Oh . . . yeah."

The chat with her dad had given Claire time to concoct a flimsy story about how she suddenly wasn't sleepy anymore and needed to run out to see Pat the German girl. Her parents bought this, thereby opening the way for an escape.

The plan was simply to sneak through the house and into the VW parked on the street outside. The first part

was the scariest. It was absolutely quiet in the house
and, terrified of making the smallest noise, Airman
Mortensen decided against putting on his clothes.

The door to the Brill bedroom faced Claire's, the two
rooms being separated by a twenty-foot length of hall.
Claire passed out of her room, crossed the hall and
stood a few feet inside the living room. She held up a
hand, silently telling Airman Mortensen to wait a moment.

As he waited for her signal the latrine king heard the
rustle of newspaper, heard it as clearly as if the paper
had been in his own hand.

The next thing he knew she was motioning him forward. Clutching the clothes and cigarettes and wine to
his bare chest Airman Mortensen stepped into the hallway. To his horror he found himself staring down the
carpeted hallway and into the Brill bedroom. The door
was open and from where he stood Airman Mortensen
could see about half of the base commander's bed. He
could see Colonel Brill, propped up on some pillow,
his brown hands grasping the edges of a newspaper
which he was holding in front of his face.

Airman Mortensen stood inexplicably frozen in the
hall and for a second or two he was sure the paper was
coming down. For a second or two more he was cap-
tivated by a mad desire to be seen by the colonel. By
his wife too.

But Claire was tugging on his arm and, once across
the hall, they tiptoed successfully through the house and
out a side door. Airman Mortensen wriggled into his
jeans, they dashed for the car and, seconds later, the
VW zoomed off into the night.

In many ways it had been a typical night for the two
lovers. They reviewed the excitement on the way back
to the barracks, sharing a few laughs over their close
call. As always they had to part but on this night, for

the first time, their parting was difficult in a different way.

Airman Mortensen couldn't put his finger on it but as he hugged and kissed her goodnight in the parking lot he felt an odd kind of chill. The constant leaving made him shudder. They were always leaving each other for some reason. Because she had school and he had the paper. Because she and he were young. A portent of doom leapt up in Airman Mortensen's head. They would always be parting. Always.

He looked at his girl. She seemed her cheerful self. She was cheerful to see him, to love him and, yes—it was unmistakable here in the darkened parking lot—she was cheerful at their leaving. Didn't mind at all. Happy. Happy?

Airman Mortensen felt dreadful. He was nervous. For the first time he felt deep doubt. As usual he watched her drive off before going in. But much later he was still awake, lying back on the bunk with his eyes wide open, trying to divine a future that could not be predicted.

☆ 18 ☆

It was all slipping away from him and it gained momentum as that long-ago summer in New Mexico flew past.

Airman Mortensen had no idea he was losing her. Until the very end he was only baffled. He could not imagine what was destroying her affection. In the space of only a few weeks it dropped to practically nothing

and stayed there. By the end it would have to be said
that Claire had become cold.

The magical silences they once enjoyed turned into
nerve-wracking voids in which nothing could be said.
The silences were no longer dreamy, they were awkward.

The phoning slowed and then stopped. And the in-
frequent calls they did share were usually to settle some
scheduling question. Toward the last of it, Claire never
called at all and Airman Mortensen got very shy. He
was worried that his calls were intrusive. They were
making things worse so he too stopped phoning. He
couldn't imagine what had happened.

The Queen For A Day thing was a bust. To both
airmen's surprise no one paid it any attention. No phone
calls. No comments. No nothing. Only Claire, who
never took the slightest interest in the paper, bothered
to register her displeasure. She told him at a drive-in
movie that she found the article and picture in "poor
taste" and assumed that he found the picture "funny".
Airman Mortensen launched into a long explanation of
how the thing came about but that only seemed to make
Claire madder. The more he defended himself, the
madder she got. They watched the second feature
mostly in silence. Another night was added to a long,
consecutive string without sex.

Sex had become rare in what Airman Mortensen
thought was a very short time. All at once everything
was complicated. Every potential lovemaking setup was
defeated by a never-ending parade of hidden obstacles.
They were just getting started when everything stopped.

And it seemed to happen overnight. Only yesterday
he was playing catcher for the squadron team and Claire
was coming to the games. Colonel Brill even stopped
by once to watch a couple of innings. It made him so

proud to have his girl sitting in the bleachers, made him feel like he was really playing for something.

Now she didn't come at all. He didn't know what to say when Vic asked where she was.

Airman Mortensen began to function in a perpetually stunned state. He shuffled from place to place and spent most of his time staring into space, always trying to answer the same unanswerable question. 'What is happening?'

For a time he thought it was something he must have done and, like someone who has misplaced the car keys, he searched desperately for what the something might be. Maybe she was tired of him. Maybe there was someone else. Maybe the Queen For A Day story. Or something he said about the Air Force or her father. Maybe it was his clothes or his face or the sound of his voice. There was no way to know.

At length, Airman Mortensen's fear began to show and after a couple more agonizing weeks he spoke to her the words that are the death of romance.

"Is something wrong?"

"No," she said, half smiling, "why do you say that?"

"I don't know," he sighed, embarrassed by the Pall Mall smoke belching out of his mouth. "It just kinda seems like something's changed."

"Like what?"

"I don't know . . . we're not going to bed hardly at all."

She wouldn't look at him then. He could see her jaw ripple as she ground her teeth in silence.

"Well, doesn't it seem that way?" Airman Mortensen would continue, digging his grave deeper.

"What are we supposed to do? . . . have sex every hour?"

"No," he stammered, "you know I don't mean that."

"What do you mean then?"

"I don't know . . . it just seems like we're drifting apart."

"Oh God . . ." Claire would roll her eyeballs. "When are we going to stop having this conversation? You keep asking, 'Is something wrong?' and I keep telling you everything's okay, but you keep wanting to know if anything's wrong. Something will be wrong if you don't stop bringing it up. This is boring and awful. It really is."

After these sad exchanges they would do their best to make up. But they could never generate any real feeling, not like the kind they'd been feasting on only a few weeks before.

She was right about it being the same conversation over and over. Airman Mortensen felt possessed by a sickness that doomed him to repeat the same awful question. "Is something wrong?" He kicked himself every time he said it but no matter how often he punished himself, the latrine king found himself facing the same question. It was killing him.

At last it all came to a head on a double date. They were on their way home, sitting in the lovers' sanctity of the back seat. Airman Mortensen tried to take her hand, and for the first time she refused him. She pulled her hand away without explanation and picked up some chatter with the couple in the front seat.

Airman Mortensen was so hurt and angry that he slid a few inches away from her.

'You don't wanna touch, I don't wanna touch,' he stewed.

He sat in silence all the way home, crushed and heartbroken. He couldn't fully admit it yet but when Claire pulled her hand away that night in the car he knew that the last cord of what held them together had been severed.

☆ **19** ☆

A rumor concerning Colonel Brill had been circulating for several weeks, starting about the time Claire and Airman Mortensen began their downward slide. It was being widely whispered that preparatory to getting his general's star the old man would be transferred to a larger, more important base.

When Airman Mortensen found this out he suspected that if the rumor were true it could be the source of all the trouble. Maybe Claire knew she was leaving. Maybe she couldn't bear the idea of leaving him. Maybe she had gone mildly insane. Maybe she loved him more than he knew. He constantly ran the new angles through his head. But he couldn't be sure.

These new theories were merely straws in the wind. For almost ten days after the fateful double date, the lovers did not lay eyes on each other. Scheduling itself had become a huge barrier, so huge that Airman Mortensen finally had to conclude that she might be lying about all the stuff she had to do. Even so he clung to his foolish hopes and, after a protracted negotiation, they had agreed on a Friday night date. No time had been set and Airman Mortensen would phone toward evening on Friday. Then he would find out what time he should arrive at the Brill home.

He was edgy at work and was still bubbling with anxiety when he got back to the barracks. Without

knowing exactly why, he worried a lot about the phone
call. In his old way he sat by the open window in his
room and stared out at nothing while he practiced what
he would say on the phone. When he tired of dreaming
up things to say he dreamed about having sex with her.
It was warm outside. And the air was slow. Evening
would be incredibly sensual. Yes, they might have sex
tonight. Everything was possible.

Instead of talking in the GQ's office he went to one
of the pay phones in the lobby and dialed the colonel's
number.

Claire answered.

Airman Mortensen tried to sound casual and bright
at the same time.

"Hi, it's me."

Her voice was heavy with disappointment.

"Oh . . . hi . . ."

There was a long silence during which Airman Mortensen felt his heart disintegrating. He knew she didn't
want to talk to him but still he could not accept the
unacceptable. He went blindly on.

"Well, uhhh, what time should I come by?"

Again there was a long silence. When Claire spoke,
her voice was final.

"I don't want to see you."

Airman Mortensen slowly closed and opened his
eyes. He felt like he was drowning.

"Why?"

"Because I don't love you anymore."

It took a second or two to find his tongue.

"What do you mean?" he asked.

"I don't love you anymore and I don't want to see
you."

"Wait a minute, Claire, you can't just say that. You
have to give me a reason."

"No, I don't," she said flatly.

"But what am I supposed to do . . . ?"

He let the words die away. Claire stayed on the line but made no response.

"How can this be," he said unhappily. "You do love me, I know you do."

"I don't."

"But what about all that's happened? I mean a lot's happened. Is it just gone?"

Claire did not answer.

"Aren't you going to say something?" Airman Mortensen pleaded.

"I've got to go."

"Wait a minute. Claire, please . . ."

"I have to go."

"We have to talk."

"There's nothing to talk about. I have to go."

The phone clicked off. A dial tone started in his ear. It was a big sound, hollow and final as the slamming of a door. Airman Mortensen couldn't put the phone down. He listened to the tone for several minutes. His life had been devoured by the tone in his ear. It was all that was left to him. But how could that be? It couldn't be. It was a horrible nightmare from which he would have to awaken.

When he finally put up the phone Airman Mortensen sleepwalked into the GQ's office and sat down. He picked up a magazine and pretended to read it as he smoked. He waited for more than an hour. He was sure she would call. She would say it was an awful mistake. They would be in love again. Nothing would stop them from being in love.

It was Friday night and the phone rang a lot. But none of the calls were for Airman Mortensen.

When he could not rationalize waiting any longer the latrine king went up to his room. He sat by the window and smoked a half a pack of Pall Malls, one after another.

☆ 20 ☆

At first he careened through life and work in a state of disbelief. Still convinced there had to be a mistake, he phoned the Brill home several times. But he was never able to talk to Claire. He talked to her mother twice but Betty Brill wisely disqualified herself, saying that he and Claire would have to work out their own problems. On each occasion Airman Mortensen ended the conversation by asking her to please have Claire call him. She never did.

He didn't want to call anymore but he couldn't help himself and, after a week of hell trying to decide, he dialed the Brill number for what he told himself would be the last time. This time Jancy answered.

"Jancy . . . hi."

"Hi," she said in her deep voice. "What's up?"

"Well, I guess you know what's going on with me and Claire."

"Not really."

"She says she doesn't love me anymore."

Jancy was silent.

"But she won't say anything about why," Airman Mortensen continued.

"She doesn't have to say anything."

"Well, no, but God . . . I can't believe it went away just like that . . ."

"What?" Jancy asked.

"Her feelings."

"I can't talk about Claire's feelings."

"No, but see, I have to know something about why. I'm cracking up."

Jancy sighed. "I don't know what to tell you," she said.

"I just want Claire to tell me something."

"She doesn't want to talk to you."

There was a long silence as Airman Mortensen tried to think of a new tack.

"Are you guys leaving?" he blurted.

"I guess so," Jancy said without interest.

"When?"

"I don't really know."

"Do you think Claire could possibly let me see her before you go?"

"Oh, man, I don't know . . . I gotta go."

"No . . . please . . . wait a minute."

"I gotta go . . . really. Goodbye."

"Goodbye," Airman Mortensen said defeatedly.

He never talked to Betty or Jancy or Claire again. He never saw them either. A couple of times he glimpsed Colonel Brill sweeping briskly down the headquarters hallway or sliding into the back seat of his blue staff car. But he never talked to him either.

Even people who didn't know what spiritual collapse meant could see that Airman Mortensen was in one. The boys in the barracks knew he'd been kissed off but no one dared question him. From the way the latrine king looked it was like he'd lost his whole family in a fire or something. No one wanted to talk to him. No one but the Negroes. And Bernie.

Newt and Lee DeHart stopped him in the hall when they found out. They both knew about things that hurt the heart. They were in pain from some kind of heartache every day of their lives. They were longtime veterans of spiritual collapse. They knew how to handle it with a few words to live by.

"Cannot truss the bitches," Lee said somberly. He lifted his reading glasses for further emphasis. "Dey will fuck you mind."

Newt bobbed as he talked, his hands deep in a pocket, fondling his knife. "You lissn ta 'im, lil' gray brudda, dat's de trufe . . . dey will fuck yo' mine . . . heh, heh, heh."

Michael G. Taylor came by Airman Mortensen's room one Sunday morning after church. He told the latrine king that prayers had been said for him. MGT also said he was sorry Airman Mortensen had lost his girl and that if there was any way he could be a better friend, all Airman Mortensen had to do was ask.

There might have been one or two others who expressed sentiments similar to MGT's. Airman Mortensen was grateful but the kind words were gone as soon as he heard them. He was sick in his mind. In a short time he came to think of himself as a dead person. He worked on the paper, he watched TV with the guys in the dayroom, he helped get the floors and latrines ready for inspections. On the surface he looked alive as anyone else but deep inside his light was very low.

It's possible that Airman Mortensen might have ended up all the way dead. The thought was never too far from his mind when things were really bad. And it might have been.

But he fought hard to keep the idea of his own dignity alive. In service to his own dignity he refused to call again after he had talked to Jancy. He didn't make any morbid walkbys of the Brill house. He didn't stand outside Claire's window at midnight. He wanted to see her face and hear her voice and kiss her lips to the exclusion of all else. But he was steadfast in his discipline. He refused to indulge his grief. It helped him keep his feet while the broken heart locked inside his chest tried to heal.

One night he let Bernie see the breakage. The little Italian had shown great patience. All through Airman Mortensen's ordeal the loyal roommate had waited with great patience, waited for his friend to choose the time and place to tell what happened. They sat in the cubicle all of one night as Airman Mortensen performed the postmortem.

By the time he got to the end the latrine king was crying and Bernie was shaking his head, saying "Goddamn" over and over.

☆ **21** ☆

There was still a bottom to get to and, if Airman Mortensen felt dead in his heart, it was greater hell the day the Brill family moved to the greener pastures of a huge base in California. It was like being lowered into a grave.

The devastation showed on his face like a blinking sign. People that didn't know him avoided the latrine king. Those closest to him felt terrible pity. There was nothing anyone could do for him. Even his co-workers stayed mum on the subject of the base commander's daughter.

Except for Tom Pittman. One afternoon when there was nothing to do he swiveled in his chair and asked, "Geez, are they gonna get on with the court-martial now that Brill's gone or what?"

Airman Mortensen stared disgustedly at Tom. The

strange airman was grinning nervously. The latrine king stared at him until the grin was gone. Then he said, "How the fuck should I know?"

Ironically, it was only a couple of days after this exchange that Sergeant Shoemaker broke the bad news to Airman Mortensen. Sure enough, the matter of the court-martial had been revived. A firm date had been set for early September. He would then meet a board of officers who would rubber-stamp him guilty.

Sergeant Shoemaker, along with the entire staff at PIO, was sorry about this. They didn't want to lose such a talented information specialist and would keep doing all they could to have the charges dropped. Some of them might even give character testimony on his behalf.

Airman Mortensen said "uhh, huh" because he barely cared. Inwardly, he actually chuckled. How could they punish someone who was already dead? It was too funny.

Of course no one knew, least of all Airman Mortensen, but the reappearance of the court-martial was a turning point of sorts. There are times when one irony begets another and that was exactly what happened to the latrine king.

Toward the end of August word was flashed from Strategic Air Command headquarters in Omaha, Nebraska. Airman Mortensen and Airman Pittman were to share in a great honor. They had been chosen co-editors of the quarter, singled out as the best Air Force editors in the world for the three months just passed.

A general flew down from Omaha to shake their hands and give them each a plaque. Airman Mortensen appeared for the ceremony in an unpressed uniform and scuffed shoes but no one seemed to mind. *Stars and Stripes* sent a special photographer to take pictures of the boy editors, which would appear all over the globe.

Airman Mortensen wondered if Claire would see the picture and try to get in touch with him. The commandant who replaced Colonel Brill gave them certificates of merit. They got gift coupons for the enlisted men's club and a day off with pay.

As a result of all this attention Airman Mortensen's court-martial became a nonevent. It was never heard of again.

None of it mattered to the grief-stricken latrine king. All through September he continued to make only the motions of living. He visited with other GIs in their rooms, hung out at work, occasionally had a beer or two at the enlisted men's club. Most of the time he sat by the open window in his cubicle, listening to his precious music and smoking his Pall Malls.

Most of the music had belonged to them. Byrds, Animals, Dylan—especially Dylan. The songs filled his head with thoughts of her. She had been his reason for being and he wanted the memory of that to stay alive. In a way he thought it was the only chance he had for recovery.

The memories hurt him too. The sense of loss and the pain that went with the songs lurked in every line of the music. No matter how hard he tried he could not understand how something so wonderful could be taken away so quickly.

He checked his box every day and every day her letter didn't come. He wondered at every phone call. But it was never her. It was hopeless but he kept hoping. He still could not believe that she didn't love him. He couldn't believe that she would not return to him somehow. He sat by the window and listened to the Byrds and tried to dream her back.

☆ **22** ☆

On the last day of October a little tremor passed through Airman Mortensen. He didn't know it at the moment but the stirring he felt that day was the first sign that he might be getting better.

The tremor came in the form of an urge. He was seized with an urge to dance.

Since Claire left he had only gone downtown a handful of times, usually for a movie. Duck in the theater, watch a movie, duck out, return to base. He hadn't shown his face in the old haunts for months. He hadn't seen any of his old friends. Mostly he'd sat by the open window.

But it was now Halloween Saturday. A great band out of Oklahoma City was playing a big dance at the armory out on Six Mile Hill Road.

Why couldn't he dance? He'd suffered enough to have a dance. What the fuck? It wouldn't kill him to go out there.

The more he thought about his coming out, the more excited he got. 'I oughta have a drink on this,' he thought. Then, after more thought, he said to himself, "I ought to get really fucked up."

He bought a fifth of rum and sat at the open window all afternoon. He listened to all his records and smoked a million cigarettes and let the rum soak into him. After five or six hours of steady sipping, the bottle was gone.

Airman Mortensen nearly fell down when he stood up. He staggered down to the latrine and took a long,

cold shower. That made him feel fresher but he was
still bombed as he pulled on his going-out clothes.

After searching the barracks for a long time he finally
found a lonely airman with a car and nothing to do. He
bribed the lonely airman to take him out to the armory.

No one was there. It was too early. The sun wasn't
even down yet. Through his alcohol fog Airman Mortensen heard music coming through the armory's big
glass doors. Stepping carefully he tottered up and tried
one of the doors. It opened and he went inside.

The band from Oklahoma City was doing a sound
check. A security guard was watching from one side of
the platform stage. Otherwise, the big hall was empty.

Airman Mortensen strode brazenly to the front of the
stage and lit a cigarette. He scowled at the security
guard and the security guard smiled.

Maybe it was one cigarette too many on top of all
the rum. Whatever it was, Airman Mortensen suddenly
began to feel ill. The rum was coming up. He had to
lie down before he fell down. Stepping on the cigarette,
he about-faced and got himself outside just in time.

Reeling crazily, he made his way along the front of
the building until he hit chain link. Then he followed
the fence a few yards and found a little juniper tree. He
dropped to his knees and threw up until his stomach
was empty. Exhausted, he rocked on all fours for a few
minutes. Then he rolled under the juniper tree and fell
asleep.

It was dark when he woke up.

Lights were shining in his face. They were headlights. Cars were pouring into the parking lot. Airman
Mortensen stared back groggily at the lamps. He was
too wrecked to get up.

He must have passed out again because the next thing
he knew the lights were gone. The distant pump of rock

'n' roll was drifting out of the armory and the cars in the parking lot were quiet.

The latrine king was thirsty but he craved sleep even more. Going a knee at a time, he gained his feet and wobbled into the parking lot. There he groped blindly at the handles of car doors until he found one that yielded. Then he tumbled into the back seat and fell asleep again.

Some time later there was light in his face, an interior light. His cheek was pressed against the rich leather of a Lincoln Continental. He rose up to find out where the light was coming from and saw two middle-aged men. They were hanging over the front seat of the Lincoln, watching him curiously.

"You okay, bub?" one of the men asked.

Airman Mortensen rubbed his face as he sat up. "Yeah . . . I got sleepy."

The other man smiled at him. "There's a real good dance goin' on," he said pleasantly. "You ought to go in there and have ya some fun."

"Yeah," Airman Mortensen replied, sliding out of the back seat.

He tucked in his shirt, ran a hand through his hair, paid his money and went into the hall. The place was packed with dancers. Everyone was in motion. The music sounded primeval. Considering all the rum and throwing up and sleeping, he felt pretty good. In fact, he felt great. He wanted to dance. Dance all night.

A face from the crowd floated up to his. It was the face of a girl who had been friends with Claire. She wanted to know where he had been hiding. Airman Mortensen didn't answer. He asked her if she wanted to dance.

She was bright and wholesome and a good dancer. Not the kind of girl he could fall for but what did it matter. The latrine king didn't care about that.

He was dancing—wild and free and fierce, chewing up the hardwood floor with steps that pounded the ground like a warrior.

The girl could see how free he was and she liked it. Bouncing close to him she caught his eye and shouted: "What makes you dance like that?"

Airman Mortensen grinned. Then he shouted over the music:

"I believe in love!"

The girl's eyes widened. She hadn't expected that kind of answer. She was only making talk.

"Oh yeah?" she yelled self-consciously.

Airman Mortensen dipped his face close to hers and the word came out of his mouth in a long, triumphant wail.

"Yeahhhhh!"

About the Author

Michael Blake began writing professionally during his enlistment in the United States Air Force from 1964 to 1968.

Twenty years later he realized his first success with the paperback publication of an obscure novel titled *Dances With Wolves*. The novel resurfaced two years later with the release of the popular film of the same name and is now being read in more than twenty languages around the world.

Airman Mortensen, the author's second novel, was released in hardcover on October 25, 1991, by Seven Wolves Publishing. Early in 1992, Columbia Pictures acquired movie rights to the book. Michael Blake is writing the screenplay.

While Mr. Blake continues to write novels and stories and is preparing other new films, he is also devoted to public service. In addition to numerous awards for writing, the author's work on behalf of literacy, libraries, and animals has also been acknowledged.

In 1991 he was honored as a *Library Hero* by the American Library Association. In the same year he received the *Eleanor Roosevelt Award* for dedication to minorities, animals, and the environment.

He is the 1992 winner of the Performing Animal Welfare Society's *Amanda Award*, the Wolf Recovery Foundation's *Alpha Award* and is the Animal Protection Institute's *Humanitarian of the Year* for his efforts on behalf of America's Wild Horses. Cancervive has named him winner of *The Victory Award*, and he is the 1992 recipient of the United States Air Force Sergeants Association's *Americanism Award*.

The author makes his home at Wolf House in Arizona. He lives there with two dogs (Bear and Pal), a cat (Psycho), five horses (Twelve, Sammantha, Project, Quanah, and Reno) and his college sweetheart (Linda).

Also available in paperback
by

✪ **Michael Blake** ✪

The *New York Times*
bestseller
DANCES WITH WOLVES
Look for it in your
local bookstore.